JUSTICE
in the
SWAMP

By STEPHEN R. KOONS

JUSTICE IN THE SWAMP

1405 SW 6th Avenue • Ocala, Florida 34471 • Phone 352-622-1825 • Fax 352-622-1875
Website: www.atlantic-pub.com • Email: sales@atlantic-pub.com
SAN Number: 268-1250

Library of Congress Control Number: 2019010123

Printed in the United States

PROJECT MANAGER: Kassandra White
INTERIOR LAYOUT AND JACKET DESIGN: Nicole Sturk

Table of Contents

Dedication

This book is dedicated to those who advance the rights of the public in pursuit of legitimate claims against insurance companies.

It's also dedicated to those same insurance companies and their dedicated employees and staff, most of whom fairly evaluate, process, and resolve claims promptly. Unfortunately, not all claims are handled with the integrity that the law requires.

The evaluation process is a process borne of necessity adversarial, but the most distressing aspect of this process is the emergence of the scorched-earth mentality when the dispute gets into the court system.

The "win at all costs" strategy has raised its ugly head in various forms, from "gotcha" motions, hidden witnesses, and concealed evidence to dissemblance, lying, and "expert" witnesses whose testimony is bought and paid for—and, sometimes, even worse.

This is a story about such a case.

Author Biography

Stephen R. Koons is a 47 year member of the Florida Bar and has been a member of the Colorado Bar for 27 years. Mr. Koons is a former Assistant State Attorney for the Fifteenth Judicial Circuit, in and for Palm Beach County, Florida, and a former Assistant Attorney General of Florida. Mr. Koons is also a former Insurance Defense Lawyer.

Mr. Koons has been in the private practice of law in both Palm Beach and Brevard Counties, as a Board Certified Civil Trial Lawyer for 30 years.

From 2013 to 2019, Mr. Koons served as a County and Circuit Judge in the 18th Judicial Circuit in Brevard and Seminole Counties, before retiring from the bench in 2019.

Mr. Koons currently continues to practice law as "Of Counsel" to the firm of Crutchfield and Pyles, located in Rockledge, Florida, and is an active Supreme Court Certified Circuit Civil Mediator, with offices in Florida and Colorado.

Cast Of Characters

In Order Of Appearance

Inmate, unnamed. TBD.

Marvella Jones, mother of Marvin Jackson.

James Jackson, Marvin's father.

Keith Meisel, Partner in Law Firm of Shook and Meisel.

Travonte and Tyrel, friends of Marvin's.

Harrison Davis, CEO at major Florida HMO and drunk driver of Audi Quattro.

Dennis and Dave, Oeste Palma bartenders.

Naomi Goldstein, driver of 1976 Ford Granada, accident witness.

Marcus Smith, Fed Ex Driver at accident scene.

Deputy Billy Wilson, Brevard County Deputy Sheriff.

Trooper Odalys Roso-Martinez, rookie FHP Officer.

Sgt. Billy Thomas, FHP Officer.

Gretchen Davis, Harrison Davis's wife.

Howard Donohue, Davis's insurance company adjuster.

Mary Jo Stalinski, Claims Superintendent.

Jack Russell Shook, lead plaintiff's lawyer and partner in Law Firm of Shook and Meisel.

Harry Ranson, insurance company reconstruction expert.

Douglass Dragenleader, aka Dragman, chief investigator of Shook and Meisel.

Julio, Mary Jo's boyfriend.

Henry Horatio Hillman, professional engineer.

Jack Turner, owner of Jack's Towing.

Ben Baxter, criminal lawyer.

Erika, lawyer/investigator.

Greg Crutchfield, Rockledge, lawyer for Tyrel and Trevonte.

Mike Kahn, Palm Beach lawyer.

Ken Wheeler, Shook's investigator

Jerry Fox, Gretchen Davis's trainer.

Clovis, Marvin Jackson's grandmother.

Ed Baldwin, insurance defense lawyer.

Lucas McQuaid, insurance defense lawyer.

Melvin Fucerino, insurance company operative.

Calvin Fucerino, brother to Melvin Fucerino.

Harry Bennett, beverage director at Oeste Palma.

Tiffany Tredstone, Jack Shook's legal assistant.

Ralph Willis, Broward County detective.

Paco Sanchez, Mexican inmate.

Willie James, Mexican inmate.

Yovanda Ruiz, social friend of Jack Shook.

Judge Murphy, presiding judge.

Joe Caruso, Cocoa lawyer.

Brandon Dinkus, insurance investigator.

James Henry, insurance investigator.

Teresa Leonard, private investigator.

Walter Rosen, divorce lawyer.

Joe Murray, Oesta Palma Club head valet.

Henry Scruggs, mediator

Howard Dorfman, divorce lawyer.

Jim Rogers, insurance company VP.

Este Ramirez, Ken Wheeler's chauffer.

Sgt. Joe Datchko, Broward County Sheriff's office.

Attorney Dinkmeyer, Calvin's lawyer.

Terry Glocker, Melvin's cellmate.

Manuel Diego Gutierrez Sanchez, aka El Diablo Royo, Mexican drug
    lord.

Jose Morales, Mexican drug lord.

Paco Sanchez, Mexican drug lord, aka Juan Diego Rodriguez.

Fred Case, messenger lawyer.

Cleetus James, FDLE agent.

Thomas J. Brown, Broward Assistant State Attorney.

Brynn Brito, Broward Assistant State Attorney

Kory Pyles, Deputy U.S. Marshall.

Lorraine Thomas, Billy Thomas's ex-wife.

Mike Brady, Billy Thomas's alias.

Nathan B. Forester, Nazi.

Joe Bob Barfield, Nazi.

Stan Cooper, orthopedic surgeon.

Mike Rothstein, criminal lawyer.

Hung Ho, cab driver.

Phat Dat Ho, Thai police commander.

Shirley King, international court reporter.

I'm an inmate in the Florida Correctional system. My inmate number is 037672. If you know my number or my name, you can find out all you need to know about me if you visit the Florida Department of Corrections website, but the most important fact for me is my release date. It is scheduled for October 23, 2021. My release date represents 85 percent of my 20-year sentence. I will be 69 years old. Looking at it now, it seems foolish to me. No one in my family has lived past the age of 84. I don't know why, but, for some inexplicable reason, I know I'm going to walk out of here, free from my surroundings.

Here is the South Bay Correctional Center in South Bay, Florida. I don't mean to be unkind, but South Bay is a place where there is literally next to nothing. Why anyone would voluntarily reside here totally escapes my understanding.

No, the only reason this place seems to exist is that it is a suitable place for a prison—out of sight, out of mind, so to speak.

So, what happened? Why am I here? It's a long story. Let me share it with you, if you have a few moments.

I was born on April 23, 1959, in Hiawatha, Iowa. My parents were initially schoolteachers. We went to church every Sunday. I was a Scout. I never gave my teachers a bit of trouble, worked hard and got good grades. I graduated high in my class and went to college. I ended up in Florida as a child because my father had a major career change. I went to college. I graduated with honors. My chosen career was professional. I did well. I enjoyed great success, both financially and professionally.

But, somehow, someway, I ended up here.

What happened? Looking back on it, it all becomes clear. I had all the ability in the world, but I lacked a fundamental sense of good judgment; I lost it somewhere along the way. I also trusted the wrong people and had a sense of arrogance that I could not control. I also allowed things to occur around me, and I made no effort to stop them, even when I knew that they were wrong. I lost my moral compass and allowed myself to be seduced by money, power, and the circumstances of my life.

If I could boil it all down, I could reduce it to either winning or losing. Winning was the obvious path, and it held all of the rewards. Losing was ignominious. It was disgusting. It was depressing. If you were labeled a loser, you suffered in life. No one ever wanted to be around you. It was like a disease. People ran from you.

Winning was the only option. Therefore, you did all that you needed to do to win. Nothing was out of bounds. Rules meant nothing, except to give lip service. To me, they were there to bend or break, whichever was the most advantageous in achieving my current goal.

Sooner or later, you cross the Rubicon. First, it's the little things. You bend the rules, and then you cover your tracks. That was easy, so now the bad things you do get bigger. It's an insidious process. What started out as little "white lies," are now full-blown bad things, but you're still covering your tracks and nobody seems the wiser—until, one day, you look in the mirror, and you realize the person looking back at you is totally corrupt.

Some famous actor, I won't mention here, once said, "We are all part of the same hypocrisy." But this is just an excuse and a hollow rationalization for corrupt behavior. There comes a day of reckoning for those of us who don't reel in ourselves and control this impulse to always win at any cost.

My day of reckoning came, and my fall was complete. Looking back on it, I don't know how I survived it, but human beings are amazingly able to adapt to their surroundings. I have adapted.

It all started simply enough: a young, promising athlete unfortunately set in motion a series of events that led him, his family, and his representatives into a saga that left many victims in the dust.

I know the story. I was in it, and now I am here. See if you can make sense of it. In the end, you will know who I am and how I got here.

Automotive Event—Data Recorders

Contained within your car's electronic control module system is an event data recorder system, a "little black box." In the late '90s, this little black box was only present in luxury vehicles, but, within 15 years, it was a standard component of all vehicles. The devices record information that can be downloaded after a crash, including data about the performance of the vehicle. This development has revolutionized the accident reconstruction industry.

While humans can lie or be mistaken about events leading to a collision, especially if money is involved, the little black box has no motive to lie—no money in the game; it does not care. In the past few years, locking devices have been developed that prevent the information from being downloaded. Some states now regulate the circumstances regarding the retrieval and use of the information contained in the box.

This story is set back in 2001; it didn't have such limitations. The race for the data retrieval was on, and a lot of people were going to get hurt.

Chapter 1

Marvin focused, and every nerve in his body was firing as he was crouched low and ready.

The count was full, and I'm cheating to the left, because he's a lefty who can pull one down the line.

It's going to be a fast ball, and the batter knows it.

"Crack," *it's coming left, gotta move, got it, and flipped it back to second, got the runner coming to second, and it was flipped to first for a double play.*

"Nice play baby!"

Marvin could hear his mother's voice. He looked to her in the stands and smiled.

Marvella smiles back and yelled, "nice play Marvin."

Watching your child successfully do anything in life is a treat, but watching your child excel is a moving experience.

This was just such an occasion for Marvella. There she sat, quietly restrained, watching her only child, Marvin, yet again completely dominate the baseball game, going three for four, including one home run, and turning six double plays from his position at second base.

Marvella's heart swelled with pride as she watched. She could see others in the bleachers look her way at each succeeding point, smile, and nod. She smiled and nodded back. She usually was very quiet but would occasionally shout encouragement to Marvin loud enough for him to hear his mother's voice, which was comforting to him and motivated him to respond with another great shot.

Talent is obvious, even to the most untrained eye, and Marvin had it in buckets. Marvin was quick and possessed great dexterity. This was obvious even as a toddler. He was physically gifted beyond his years. He was a born and bred "Baller." His talent was ever-present, but he was also coachable and improved every year. His father, James Jackson, played college ball for Marquette and the Utah Jazz. He came out of Chicago's south side, as did his mother, Marvella.

As a graduate of Northwestern, class of '80, with a degree in linguistics, Marvella knew her degree held very little immediate value in the real world, except for the teaching profession. Her true gift, though, wasn't teaching; it was her beautiful mind and smile. She also was drop-dead gorgeous and had caught James' eye at a fundraiser for local kids with baseball aspirations in the winter of '85. One year later, Marvin was born at Holmes Regional Medical Center in Melbourne, Florida.

James was a talented NBA player, but not a superstar. He was a role player whose specialty was a longrange jump shot, which was "streaky" at best. Some nights, he would go 1 for 15—sometimes 10 for 15. His shot average was 40 percent. At forward, he stood 6'5" tall and weighed in at a slim 230. He was a handsome dude. His roots could be traced back to his Bahamian Conch grandmother, Jewel, whose side of the family had settled in what is now Riviera Beach in Palm Beach County.

Marvella and James continued the relationship for a few years, but James had many other relationships that had resulted in four other children, who could be found in Texas, Illinois, and Utah. James was a "Rolling Stone," and, as the song goes, wherever he laid his head was his home. When he died, all he had left was his name and his children.

James spent very little time with his children but did spend time with Marvin whenever he was in town. Marvella had been smart enough to secure a support order and received a monthly check directly from that as a result of her income deduction order, from James' employer, Utah Jazz. The other baby mamas also had secured such orders, which resulted in a significant monthly deduction in his salary. However, Marvella had been fortunate enough to be referred to the Space Coast law firm of Shook and Meisel and had secured the services of Keith Meisel, who had represented the mothers of children of other professional athletes in the past.

The order was a blessing at $10,000 a month, which provided a fairly comfortable lifestyle for Marvella and her son, but the total amount was not always available due to fluctuations in James' income and contract negotiations.

This lifestyle continued right up until James' untimely death in 1998. A single car crash in Houston, Texas. It seems that, one night in November, at three in the morning, as James was driving back to his condo, his black Lexus SUV had somehow left the roadway at a high rate of speed and smashed headon into a concrete pylon. James died on impact. The autopsy revealed THC, cocaine, and alcohol in his system.

This tragedy, of course, left Marvella without income. The NBA had a standard life insurance policy of $1 million, but Marvella was one of multiple claimants, which meant her share for her son, after two years of litigation, was $200,000. Apparently, James had married a Las Vegas exotic dancer two years prior who was able to take the bulk of the proceeds.

Marvella had secured these benefits, also utilizing the services of the Shook and Meisel firm, which would not accept a fee from her because the NBA's insurance company chose to deny those benefits to Marvella and her son. This resulted in a fee-generating recovery under Utah law where the contract was executed.

The United States District Court in Salt Lake was the venue of the action only because the contract provided for this limitation. Marvella had to travel there for a hearing, and finally a settlement was approved by the Court, handled by Shook and local counsel. In addition to the life insurance benefits, Attorney Shook was able to secure benefits from the NBA survivor benefits package for Marvin, but they were modest due to the number of claimants and the value of James' contract. They were of some benefit, of course, and Marvella relied upon the monthly payment for her and Marvin's basic needs.

Meanwhile, young Marvin had become quite the accomplished athlete and had developed into a baseball *phenom*, who had led his junior high team to the regionals. The following year, at age 14, he was admitted to Melbourne Magnet High School, not only because of his athletic abilities, but also because he was an A and B student who had a flair for mathematics. His first year at Mel High, as a freshman, he led the JV team again to the district playoffs.

Marvin stood at 6'1" tall and weighed 180 pounds. He was extremely quick, could hit with power, and was a scary good infielder. He was a handsome young man with a great smile and had many friends and many female admirers, but he had not been involved in any relationships with the girls. He had honored his mother's wishes not to do so.

It was Friday, July 8, 2001, a warm—but not too hot—typical central Florida summer day. Marvin had turned 15 the previous Monday and was playing baseball in a summer league with his mother in attendance, of course.

After the game, his best friend, Travonte wanted Marvin to ride home with him and his brother, Tyrell. In reality, a side trip to see Travonte's girlfriend was really the plan.

After acknowledging the compliments and accolades from the other parents, Marvella stood waiting as Marvin and Travonte walked up.

"Mom, is it OK if I catch a ride with Travonte and Tyrell? We're going to go by Burger King on the way home."

Marvella was OK with this because she knew the boys, and they had never given her a reason to be reluctant, so she accepted the separation with the minimum of anxiety, but her "mom radar" was active.

"OK Marvin, that's fine, just make sure you are home by 7 to do your chores."

Marvin gave her a hug and walked away with Travonte. She left and drove home.

Meanwhile, the boys were picked up by Tyrell in his aging 1990 Nissan Sentra. The car still ran good with 200,000 miles, and, even well-used, it boasted oversized rims, a great sound system, and tinted windows. Mechanically, though, the vehicle was a little questionable. It could only be started by inserting the key and then wrenching the wheel violently back and forth to trigger the starter.

Ten miles away—another world away—Harrison Davis was with his golf buddies at the 19th Hole lounge at Oeste Palma International Golf Club in western Brevard County knocking down multiple silver bullet martinis after an afternoon of golf.

Oeste Palma International Golf Club was built and located in southern Brevard County, off the Melbourne I95 exit. Due to its location, the complete facility included a private airstrip. Its investors, all being from South Florida, could either fly in or drive up I95, just an hour and 15 minutes to the SR 192 exit.

The cost of the land was so reasonable that it could not be passed on. Much of the course was to be located in the wild bordering the headwaters of the St. Johns River and estuary, a truly unique and environmentally sensitive area.

Recognizing its development potential was unlimited, Harrison led the group of investors in the fiveyear project. Their vision of a world-class course demanded the finest of everything, including a magnificent clubhouse. And once finished, they were not disappointed. The club and course now draws players from all over the world.

Silver bullets, as he referred to them, were his drink of choice. They were, of course, vodka martinis straight up. He liked them a little dirty, with some small quantity of the olive juice, along with at least three olives.

He had played a typical round, just breaking 95, but was particularly proud of himself for scoring a par on the last three finishing holes. This had resulted in his victory for the $50 Nassau bet, and, therefore, he was feeling no pain, as they say.

Working the bar that day were Dennis and Dave. Dave was recently hired and the younger of the two, but both became increasingly alarmed watching Harrison drink when they found out that he was driving home. They had to be careful how they broached the subject, since Mr. Davis was a member and also on the Board of Trustees.

Harrison Davis, it seemed, actually had the power to get anyone fired who worked at the club. He was the CEO of a regional health maintenance organization that serviced all of Florida and much of the south. He was chairman of the Chamber of Commerce, and on the Board of Governors for the local State University, and a member of the Lions Club. He was also politically connected and counted many "friends" in high places. He only had to pick up the phone to get the governor to take his call. He was also a fully functioning alcoholic.

Dennis and Dave again found themselves in the uncomfortable position of having to "gently" suggest to Harrison that he not drink anymore.

His buddies were of no help. Drinking with Harrison was great fun. He was clever and witty and had great stories. They seemed to get better with each silver bullet he downed. Harrison was flying high and could not be stopped easily.

Dennis decided he had to speak up. "Mr. Davis, do you want me to call a cab?"

Davis heard the offer and chose to ignore it.

Dennis gathered his courage and asked again. "Excuse me, Mr. Davis, but would you like me to call you a cab?"

Davis was now a little on the pissed-off side and responded curtly, "No, Dennis, I don't need no fucking cab. As a matter of fact, I'll take one more for the road."

Dennis looked plaintively at his companions who were of no help, and finally said, "Yes, sir, coming right up."

Making that silver bullet number nine, Dennis thought to himself. *Well, I've done my job.*

He returned with the one for the road and delivered it to Davis. Davis looked up and responded, "Well, thank you, Dennis. It's good to see a guy can still get a drink in this place."

It seems the topic of the day was Davis' brandnew 2001 Audi Quattro that he had just purchased.

"Damn thing was only 75 grand, but man will it move," was his last comment as he took his togo cup and stumbled out the door.

"Gotta go guys. Got the Missus waiting, and we're going to some godawful function tonight."

Dennis decided to speak up one last time. "Mr. Davis, are you sure I can't call you a cab?"

"No, Goddammit, I don't need no fucking cab. Stop asking me. I'm running late, and I don't have no time or no need for a fucking cab. I've got to go. I'm late, Goddammit."

None of his friends said anything.

Davis made it to the door, got to the valet stand, and his car was brought up. It was truly a beautiful machine—and black, of course. It was sleek looking and boasted every option.

Davis threw down a $20 tip and away he went. The valet, young kid named Mike just said, "Thank you, Mr. Davis. Drive safely, sir."

Davis said nothing as he slid in behind the wheel and rolled out of the parking lot. He headed north on Nova Road leading to SR 192 and then went east.

Also traveling east was Naomi Goldstein, driving her 1976 Ford Granada on her way to the Palm Bay Senior Center to play bingo. She had missed the turn at Heritage Avenue and had to turn east at the next intersection continuing to travel east.

At the same time, Tyrell, Travonte, and Marvin were traveling west on SR 192 and west of the I95 entrance. The speed limit out there was 55, and it was being observed.

Meanwhile, Davis had just covered the five miles over Nova Road in three minutes, had turned east onto SR 192, and accelerated the Quattro to a quick 80 miles an hour. He quickly came up behind Mrs. Goldstein, executed a pass and immediately was confronted by the Sentra traveling west in the westbound lane.

Seeing the impending headon collision, Marvin screamed, "Look out!"

Tyrell immediately yanked the wheel to the left to avoid the Quattro. Unfortunately, though, Davis also sensed the danger through his alcoholinduced fog and pulled the wheel to the right.

Marvin saw it unfold before him. He knew in an instant that it would be bad, but when it happened, after the flash and the crash, everything went into slow motion. He watched as Tyrell and Travonte slammed into the windshield. The Sentra rolled to the right, and he felt and heard a "snap" in his lower back before he blacked out.

The collision occurred just over the centerline in the eastbound lane with an enormous shattering crash. Both vehicles ended up on the south side of the road.

Tyrell's Sentra was completely demolished and ended up on its roof. The Quattro took the collision much better and absorbed the energy with the vehicle stopping on the roadway, but still facing east.

Mrs. Goldstein, seeing the collision, was in shock and traumatized, but managed to stop her vehicle about 50 yards west, well short of the point of collision.

The collision was horrendous. The Sentra was now only a mess of crumpled aluminum foil barely resembling a car. The front of the vehicle was totally destroyed. Tyrell and Travonte both suffered massive head trauma and died instantly.

Marvin, who was belted in in the back, lost consciousness as his back snapped at the L4 and L5 vertebrae, rendering him a paraplegic immediately.

The Quattro suffered severe frontend damage. Davis, who was belted, was dazed due to the airbag deployment, but fared much better. He was alive and, although stunned, did not lose consciousness. He was not seriously injured, suffering only whiplash and bruising to his chest and sternum, as well as some facial cuts.

His to-go cup had spilled and was on the floor.

No one was ejected from their vehicle, but the crash was so loud that it stunned Mrs. Goldstein. She pulled her vehicle up to the crash and got out. Walking up, she heard Marvin moaning. The boys in the front were silent.

Both vehicles were smoking. They had hit and disengaged. The Sentra was still in the roadway, more to the south of center. The Sentra's damage was catastrophic. The Audi had rotated right after the impact and was in the ditch. Davis was still in his vehicle but not moving.

Coming east about two minutes later was a Fed Ex truck driven by a Marcus Smith. He dialed 911 and got out to see if he could help. Climbing out of his car, Davis was intercepted by Smith who persuaded him to just sit in his car and not move.

No one was moving in the Sentra.

South and east on I95 was Deputy Billy Wilson of the Brevard County Sheriff's Office on routine road patrol. A 15year veteran of the department and a former military policeman while stationed in Germany, Wilson was well-prepared for what he was about to see. He had seen highspeed, high-energy car crashes on the Autobahn and had had occasion to supervise the removal of many signal 7's (dead persons) and the cleanup of signal 4's (car crashes).

He turned his cruiser around and gunned the Crown Vic north and was on scene within two minutes. He parked his cruiser just east of the Sentra, exited, and surveyed the carnage. He walked over to Davis and the FedEx driver who were at the Audi.

Smith interrupted the deputy, "This guy's still alive, Deputy. I don't think anyone in the other car is. I came up just after it happened. The little old lady in the Granada said she saw it."

"Thank you, sir," was Wilson's reply. "Just stay put, I'll be right with you. Help is on the way."

Wilson walked over to what was left of the Sentra. No one was moving. The two boys in the front were obviously dead. He put his index and middle finger against the carotids and felt nothing. He did the same for Marvin in the backseat and detected a heartbeat. He got on his radio and called in the closest paramedic and his captain at the substation.

Since it was technically on a state road, he called the Florida Highway Patrol and alerted the nearest trooper.

Cruising north on Wickham Road, just east of I95, was Trooper Odalys RosoMartinez. She drove immediately to the accident after being dispatched. Her sergeant, a 20year veteran, Billy Thomas, also was dispatched.

Billy, who was raised in the south and looked and spoke like a country boy, was not the most enlightened deputy on road patrol.

Trooper RosoMartinez arrived on scene within five minutes—just as the paramedics arrived. Another deputy had taken a position east of the crash scene and began diverting traffic.

Trooper RosoMartinez approached Deputy Wilson and asked, "Were you first on scene?"

Wilson, who was studying the carnage, turned and looked at the trooper who stood 5'2" tall at most, shook his head, and muttered to himself, "It figures."

"Well, yes, trooper, I was first on scene."

"So what do we have, Deputy?" was her next question.

"Well, we got a little old lady eyewitness in the Granada, one survivor over here in the Audi, two dead brothas in the Sentra up front, and one more in the back that appears to be alive.

"The old lady says the Quattro tried to pass her and ran headon into the Sentra. The driver of the Audi is not saying much except that he has a headache. He wants us to call his wife and a doctor. I called his wife, and she's on her way."

"Thank you for that, Deputy."

Deputy Wilson spoke up, "I take it you're taking this one, trooper?"

"Well, Sgt. Thomas is, and he'll be here shortly," she responded, "but I'm thinking we'll be taking it because this will be a traffic homicide investigation."

Wilson was secretly relieved, knowing that Thomas was on his way and that he didn't have to handle this crash investigation, especially since it was obvious what had happened. He was also thankful he wouldn't have to work with this obviously incompetent woman hired only because of her sex and surname.

Meanwhile, RosoMartinez, who was appalled at Wilson's comments, made her way over to the Audi to speak with Smith and the driver, Davis, and asked, "What happened, sir?"

"Ma'am, I was driving east and all of a sudden that car was in my lane. I tried to miss it, but he drove directly into me, and we hit front to front."

"Thank you, sir. The paramedics will be right with you."

She turned to walk away. Thinking she had detected the odor of alcohol, she turned back to him and asked, "Sir, have you been drinking?"

Davis looked up at her and said, "What?"

She repeated her question.

"Ma'am, I don't have time for this. Will you please get me a doctor? I didn't do anything wrong. What's your name again?"

"It's Trooper RosoMartinez, sir, and I would like an answer to my question."

Davis looked up, saw Trooper Thomas approaching, and ignored RosoMartinez.

He spoke up, "Sir, are you in charge here? I demand to see a doctor, and I need to have my wife called."

Thomas walked up behind RosoMartinez and said, "Let's talk, Odalys. So, what do we have here?"

"Looks like the Audi was trying to pass the old lady in the Granada, and it was a front-to-front violation of rightofway collision, sir. She is a little fuzzy on whether the pass was completed."

"That's what it looks like to me, too, trooper," he replied. "So what else do we need to know?"

"Well, sir, I think the guy in the Audi has been drinking, sir. I can smell it. He's also wearing golf shoes. You know, the ones without spikes."

Thomas was impressed by her observations, but decided he would take over.

"I tell you what, trooper, go interview the little old lady, and I'll take the guy in the Audi."

"Yes, sir." She immediately went to the Granada and began talking with Mrs. Goldstein. She took her field notes and got her witness statement forms and began her part of the investigation.

Meanwhile, Thomas, a 20year veteran and son of a retired Georgia state patrolman, took over. This looked obvious to him, and the report wouldn't be too involved.

The paramedics were working on the Sentra occupants. The front passengers were deceased, but Marvin was alive. A fire truck had arrived, and the jaws of life were noisily peeling off the top, or what was left of the top, of the Sentra. Marvin was removed and triaged, then backboarded and transported to the ER at Holmes Regional Medical Center in Melbourne.

Trooper RosoMartinez was quietly and privately fuming. She knew Wilson and Thomas were buddies and didn't appreciate his "dead brothas" comment, but said nothing. She just did her job and let it go.

Thomas and Wilson were huddled up and discussing matters. "Looks like the Sentra is at fault, Billy," was Thomas's opening salvo. "The point of the collision is more in the eastbound lane."

Deputy Wilson was pleased, since he saw it the same way. As far as he was concerned, this investigation was going to be short and sweet.

Thomas spoke again, "So, Billy, you think Mr. Quattro over there has been drinking?"

Wilson's reply was quick and to the point, "Yeah, maybe some, but so what? We don't need to muck this thing up with some halfassed DUI investigation. By the way, you know who that is?"

"No, Billy, I don't. Enlighten me, man," replied Thomas.

"That's Harrison Davis, solid citizen number one, president of the Chamber and CEO of Floridian Health, not to mention allaround friend of law enforcement."

"No shit, Billy. And who is that with him?"

"That's his wife, I think, and she wants to take him to his doc down in West Palm. Since you are now in charge of this crash investigation, you deal with her."

"OK, Billy, I'll take it from here. What do you want me to do?"

"Just take care of the traffic; we'll clear the scene."

"No problem," Wilson said.

Thank God, he thought. He didn't need to get in the middle of this shit-storm and was relieved he didn't have to deal with the issue of Davis and his wife.

Trooper Thomas approached the Audi and spoke to the couple. "Ma'am, I'm Trooper Billy Thomas, and I'm in charge of this investigation."

"Thank God," Mrs. Davis replied. "Please let us leave. My husband is OK, but he has a headache and wants to see our own private physician. You have his statement and all our insurance information. We called our insurance company, and they're on the way. I need to take my husband away from all of this. We can talk later on tomorrow, if you wish."

Thomas noticed that Davis wasn't saying anything and was just letting his wife do the talking.

"And your name, ma'am?"

"I'm Gretchen Davis. I'm his wife. I'm also a lawyer, but I'm just acting as his wife at this point."

This lawyer comment alarmed Thomas, but he decided not to push the potential drinking issue and to release them.

"You may go, ma'am, with your husband; but you might want to go to the hospital and get checked out."

"No, thank you, sir; he's just shaken up a bit. We'll decline going over to the hospital."

Trooper Thomas watched as Davis and his wife walked slowly away. She was saying something to him, but he couldn't make it out.

Gretchen Davis had her husband by the arm and was walking away from the crime scene with him. Out of earshot of anyone around, she said, "Harrison, you dumbass, just keep walking and don't look back. Try not to stumble, you moron. The trooper is watching you, and we've got to get out of here right now."

"Yes, dear," was Davis's only reply.

Thirty minutes later, after being dispatched pursuant to Mrs. Davis's call, Conveyance Mutual Benefit Claims Adjuster Howard Donohue was on scene, photographing and measuring everything.

He noticed the plastic cup on the floor of the Audi, which he grabbed and sniffed. It smelled of alcohol. He threw it out and mentioned it to no one.

Troopers Thomas and RosoMartinez were taking measurements and photos. Donohue interviewed Mrs. Goldstein and the FedEx driver, Smith. He called the contract tow truck for the Audi, and it was loaded on the truck when the troopers gave him the release.

Next, he spoke to Thomas. "Looks like the Sentra was the cause of this disaster, trooper."

"Yeah, it appears that the Sentra was left of the center lane, but the crush damage is so extensive, especially on the Sentra, I'm thinking your boy may have had some speed on him."

"Aw, come on, trooper," he replied. "There's no way our insured's speed had anything to do with this."

"Well, at this point, I intend on placing fault on the Sentra. Your boy is fortunate to be alive."

"Well, trooper, he was driving a vehicle that is twice the weight and immensely better designed than that piece of shit Sentra they were driving."

"I have to agree with you, Mr. Donohue. I will be releasing the car to you."

"Thank you, trooper." Donohue walked away.

Damn, that was close, Donohue thought as he climbed into his Ford Explorer. *Gotta be careful what I put in my report.*

Chapter 2

It was exactly 5:30 p.m. when Mary Jo got the call. The call had come from Davises' agent, and she assigned her most trusted agent in the northern counties, Howard Donohue, to the claim immediately. Harrison Davis was one of her highprofile insureds, and no expense or resource would be spared to savage the claimants in this case.

She had just walked into the lush Wellington home in suburban West Palm and had just dropped her purse and phone on the granite kitchen counter. It had been a typical week of meetings, mediations, and a video conference with corporate and her senior adjusters regarding their claims reduction performance for the second quarter. Pouring herself a Jack Daniels on the rocks, Mary Jo kicked off her heels and relaxed in her recliner.

Claims superintendent Mary Jo Stalinowsky with flaming red hair was a rising star in the company. She was coming up on 20 years and had worked her way up the ladder to her present position after her graduation from college with a degree in business management.

Her father, James Stalinowsky, was a longstanding Conveyance Mutual Benefit agent since the mid1970s with his main office in Plantation and other offices in the surrounding West Broward County area. She was recently divorced. Her ex, an insurance defense lawyer now in Miami, left her. On her own for three years, she had recently bought her Wellington home. She had no children but did have two nieces who lived in Broward with her sister and her husband.

Mary Jo was not a bad looking woman and, recently, underwent breast augmentation. She dressed in tailored business suits and was enjoying the attention that her new look had invited. Her "stock" was on the rise, and she was rumored to be in line for ascendancy to the corporate home office in New York.

Since her divorce, she had not been officially sexually active and had chosen to rebuff the advances of her newfound male attention that had recently surfaced. The only exception was her boy toy, Julio.

She was well known in the legal community in Brevard, Indian River, St. Lucie, Martin, Palm Beach, and Broward County, had proved herself in being one step ahead of the plaintiff's lawyers she encountered.

She could sniff out any weakness almost completely by instinct, but she had unlimited resources at her disposal and could find out anything about anybody and savagely exploited the weaknesses of any claimant or attorney.

In a word, she was ruthless. She would smile and cut your heart out with impunity. She was well schooled, learned from her father and her exhusband, but her total lack of compassion or mercy came from somewhere else. Speaking of her ex, she successfully navigated her divorce with her pension and profit sharing intact and had avoided alimony payments because of the intel she had on him, which, if discovered and revealed to the Bar, would have resulted in disbarment or worse. In a word, she had "dirt" on everyone and knew how to use it. She was deadly, pitiless, cruel, and heartless.

Plaintiffs' attorneys had christened her with various nicknames—"Typhoid Mary," "Queen Mary Jo" and "Mary Jo, Queen of Death" just to name a few. Attorney Jack Russell Shook found out that her middle name was "Jo" as in "Mary Jo Stalinowsky" and quickly christened her "Joe Stalin" or "Little Joe," after the most ruthless despotic Russian killer of the last century. Mary Jo had heard the names and enjoyed all of them except the "Stalin" label. She knew it had come from Shook and didn't like him. If she didn't like you, you had a problem. On the other hand, Shook had been successful on some of his claims with Mary Jo and had three verdicts against her that exceeded $1 million.

For this claim, Mary Jo told Donohue to report verbally as soon as the scene was cleared and was waiting for his call. In cases like this, she always had her field adjusters report verbally before any written report was prepared. After hearing the down and dirty, nittygritty details, she would instruct her adjusters on what to put in the report and what to leave out. Depending on what she heard, she would decide at what level she would move on defense.

In routine cases, most of the reports were fairly straightforward. The strategy was quick and painless. Illegal credit checks would be run on the potential claimants to see how desperate they were for money. Surveillance was always utilized at some level, as was the use of the preferred "go-to docs" for a socalled independent medical examination.

The vehicles involved had to be sequestered and examined quickly by one of the experienced property damage adjusters; and, in cases like this, she immediately would use an accident reconstruction specialist to completely examine the wreck and the scene. In a word, no "expense" would be spared to protect the company from some kind of significant claim.

She had her top five South Florida insurance defense firms at her disposal as well. She pitted them one against the other to see who could produce the best claim results and make sure that they all knew about each other's performance.

She was proud to be associated with Conveyance Mutual Benefit as a no-fault carrier. It was the fifth largest in the country. It boasted the mutual company for the preferred insureds, and the Conveyance Fire and Casualty company for the average Joes. The Conveyance Mutual Home Company provided homeowner's coverage, of course, but it was the Mutual Company that reigned as the flagship.

It was about 8 o'clock that night when she got Donohue's call. She was on a first name basis with Donohue.

"So, Howard, what do we have?"

"Two dead young black males in the front seat, and one severely injured young black male in the back. He is over at Holmes Regional. Both vehicles have been removed."

"OK, now give me the bad news."

"Well, our insured was probably drinking, and the troopers suspect some excessive speed, but it's unknown how much. Our insured has left the scene with his wife, and no DUI investigation was conducted. I threw a to-go cup out the door, which I found under the seat. No mention by the troopers."

"Where is the car?"

"HookedUp Towing has it, and they are taking it down to the Palm Beach yard.

"What we have is a little dicey. Our insured was driving east on SR 192, east of the Beeline and had just passed a little old lady driving east in her '76 Granada. She says he was speeding.

"The other vehicle was a '95 Sentra traveling west. There was one effort to avoid the head-on collision—the Sentra pulled to the left. The POC (point of collision) was mostly in our insured's lane. Our insured is Harrison Davis. He was driving his 2001 Audi Quattro."

"Hold off interviewing our insured until tomorrow. I will get Harry Ranson over to the yard to process the Audi. Don't do a written report until I tell you to do so. Keep your field notes, but no mention of alcohol or speed. Got that, Howard?"

"Yes, ma'am. I got it."

"Get me the potential claimant information no later than tomorrow by noon. We've got two dead kids and one seriously injured, so we can expect claims are coming."

"Yes, ma'am. You'll have it by noon tomorrow."

"So, who is doing the traffic homicide investigation, FHP?"

"Yes, ma'am."

"Well, that means it will take at least two months, maybe three. Get the short form accident report and email it to me by noon tomorrow."

"Yes, ma'am."

"Who is the trooper in charge?"

"It's Billy Thomas, ma'am."

"Perfect, Howard, I'll get back to you on Thomas. Anything else?"

"No. I think you've got the picture, Mary Jo."

"OK. See you tomorrow."

Mary Jo hung up the telephone, and the wheels in her head were spinning. *Got to cover Davis's ass on this one*, she thought. *Don't need any monstrous claims to slow me down at this point. I've got that interview in New York next month.*

She sat back, lit a cigarette, and finished her drink deep in thought. *I wonder what dirtbag is going to climb out of the closet on this one. No matter. Whoever it is, we will stomp him into the ground like an unwanted cockroach. I don't see the need for the team yet, but the night is young. Maybe I'll get them involved just for fun. Depends on who the plaintiff's lawyer is.*

Chapter 3

Marvella was home cooking dinner when she got the call. Marvin should have been home at least an hour before. She had had a tougher than usual week and was tired but grateful that the weekend was here. She had worked at the Senior Center for five years and her pay was modest—not bad for an administrative assistant, which was well within her capabilities.

It was trooper RosoMartinez on the phone. She had a little problem understanding her accent, but the message was clear.

"Ms. Jackson?"

"Yes, this is Ms. Jackson. Who is this?"

"Ma'am, this is Trooper RosoMartinez. I am at Holmes Regional Medical Center. I want to make sure I have the correct person. Is this Marvella Jones, the mother of Marvin Jackson?"

"Yes, it is, trooper," She was now starting to panic. She could feel the fear growing inside.

"Ma'am, your son has been in a traffic accident. He is alive, but is seriously injured. He is in the emergency department right now, and I believe they will be taking him to surgery shortly. You need to meet me here as soon you can get here."

"What happened?" Marvella shouted in a panic.

"Ma'am, he was in a car accident. You need to get here as soon as you can. The doctors need your permission to operate, and I need to talk to you."

"I'll be there in 10 minutes." She hung up the phone.

After grabbing her purse and running to the door, she paused. She retreated to the kitchen, turned everything off and left.

She pulled up to the ER off NASA Boulevard and ran to the door, frantically looking for the female trooper. RosoMartinez met her there as she came in.

"Are you Marvella Jones?" the trooper asked.

"I need to see my son, please," Marvella pleaded.

"Follow me," Roso-Martinez replied. They both walked quietly through the doors into triage. Marvin was unconscious and was attended by the ER doctor and two nurses. They were working on him, and the nurse in charge saw Marvella's concern.

Marvella felt her fear and terror growing within her.

"Ma'am, he's OK, but he has suffered a serious back injury. He'll be taken to surgery right away. Please come with me, so that you can sign the necessary consent forms."

Marvella touched her son's arm and stopped for a moment. The reality of the situation began to engulf her. *He will be OK, but he has to go for surgery.*

She retreated to the hallway with the nurse and the trooper. She signed the forms without even looking at them. Within a minute, Marvin was wheeled out of the ER and off to surgery. She was worried and felt sick but no longer panicked.

She looked up, and the next person she saw was Chaplain Fountain who took her to the meditation room and prayed with her.

Trooper RosoMartinez waited outside patiently. She understood what was happening and gave Marvella the space she needed before talking to her.

Marvella appeared out of the hallway with the Chaplain about 30 minutes later, and they began to talk.

"Ms. Jones, I called you because of the identification found in Marvin's backpack. This was a high-energy head-on collision out on SR 192, west of the I-95 exit. I regret to inform you that the two boys in the front seat are deceased."

"Trooper, please, tell me have their parents been notified?"

"Not as of yet Ms. Jones, maybe you can help me with that."

"Dear God, Trooper, I cannot make that call."

"I will handle that, Ms. Jones, it's my job."

"Thank you for that Trooper."

"I need to call Marvin's grandmother, she needs to be here."

Trooper RosoMartinez respected that and gave her some more time before finishing her report.

Marvella retreated to the OR waiting room and tried to calm down. Nothing seemed to help. She was assured that Marvin would be alive but did not know the extent of his injuries. It brought back memories of James' death years back, and then it hit her.

She had to call Shook, and she had to call him now.

Chapter 4

I-95, from PGA Boulevard North to the Melbourne exit is a road travelled many times before. "Hell, I could close my eyes and tell you where I am at any time. As a matter of fact, you tell me what you are looking at, and I will tell you where you are."

Time flies—and sometimes it drags—but 25 years had passed since Jack Russell Shook left the State Attorney's Office.

Time is often wasted, but not for Shook. Time is everything to him. It's all he has. It's his life and his stock in trade. We all have too much of it on our hands and not enough of it to finish our work. It runs out, but you never get more the next day. It's been said that time heals all wounds, but there are some fools who just kill time. Not Jack Russell Shook, though. For him, there never seems to be enough.

Some men just stumble about in life, and some are robots. Shook stumbled occasionally, but he was more than just a robot; he was an intuitive who saw things coming and was almost always right. A lot of people said he was a cynic, but he was really just a combination of experience and intellect.

The answering service for Shook and Meisel was turned on at exactly 5 p.m. every weekday and stayed on for 24 hours, for the weekend and every holiday. It was expensive, but having a live person answer the phone calls during off hours always seemed to be worth the cost, and it seemed that the clients appreciated the ability to reach their lawyer at any time, day or night. This time, the call was for a serious matter, and the answering party had marching orders to find the attorney on call immediately and to connect the client, or soontobe client, directly to the responsible attorney.

He was not in his office when the call came. Instead, that Friday evening at 8:30 p.m., Shook was at home and had no plans for the evening. He was alone winding down the week when his flip phone went off.

Marvella said, "Mr. Shook?"

"Yes, Marvella. What happened?"

"It's Marvin. He's been in a terrible car accident. I'm at Holmes Regional, and he's in surgery."

"Oh my God, Marvella. I'll be there in 90 minutes. Where will you be?"

"I'm in the surgical suite waiting room. The trooper is still here somewhere."

"OK. I'll be there as soon as I can."

Shook hung up the phone and grabbed his jacket. Holmes Regional was only 90 miles away up in Melbourne, and he was on the move. As he drove, his mind was turning. He had met Marvin in the past and recalled that he was a bright young man with his father's athletic abilities. He was greatly concerned. He privately agreed with Marvella's decision to move up the road to Melbourne Beach. It was much quieter, less traffic, great schools . . . but now this.

Upon his arrival, he met with Marvella and was able to speak to the trooper. He was surprised to meet her. She was about 5'2" tall, maybe 110 pounds. He was impressed with her professionalism. He got off on the right foot with her by asking, "So, trooper, where did you go to school?"

"Florida State. Why do you ask?"

"I'll bet you have a Bachelor of Science with a major in Criminology and Corrections."

"How did you know that?"

"Well, it just so happens that I have that degree from FSU as well, but I stayed and went on to law school." Shook smiled as he said it.

The trooper was immediately impressed. The ice had been broken.

The trooper laid out the basic fact pattern. He got the case number. She said the basic accident report would be finished tonight and that it could be picked up tomorrow afternoon. Though, Trooper Thomas was preparing the homicide report. Shook knew it would be months before it was completed.

He was able to get the location of the vehicles. He was surprised to learn that the Quattro was taken to West Palm. The identity of the other driver was disclosed, but it didn't register with Shook who he was.

He stayed with Marvella until Marvin was out of surgery. It was midnight, and he was able to listen in while a doctor told Marvella about his injuries. He would be a paraplegic. The low back was fractured badly, and the surgery could only stabilize the back, not repair it. Marvella was crushed.

Marvin's grandmother was now with Marvella, and they were able to console each other. Shook had made some calls prior to midnight and had gotten in touch with his investigator, Dragman, a.k.a. Douglas Drakenleader. He was ready to go first thing in the morning. Shook drove back but decided to drive to the accident site. It had been cleared, so he took photos and called Dragman. He was still up at 12:30 in the morning.

"Hey, dude. I'm at the crash site. We need to photograph and process it first thing in the morning. I'm calling the engineer, Henry Hillman, in on this right away."

"OK, Jack. You want me to call him, or will you do it?"

"You call him, dude. I'll meet you at the crash site at 8. See if Henry can meet us there."

Dragman sensed the urgency of the situation and replied, "I'll call him now."

"This is going to be a big one, Dragman; and get ready for this, the other driver is a Conveyance Mutual Benefits insured."

Dragman paused and then said, "Oh, shit. That means we got Stalinowsky on this case, doesn't it?"

"Yes, it does, Dragman. We've got to be ready. I guarantee she's already on the case and plotting our client's destruction."

"'Nuf said, man. I'll see you tomorrow."

Meanwhile, 70 miles away in the Davis' mansion, Gretchen was still up, angrily sitting in the dark with a still smoldering cigarette. She couldn't sleep. *Idiot*, she thought, *I've had about enough of his shit.*

She and Harrison had only been married four years. It was her second and his third. His ex was still in town and had warned her of his drinking, but Gretchen just ignored it. It was now getting old, and she wanted a divorce. She had been seeing another lawyer who she went to school with on the sly. She ignored what she had been warned about Harrison and his fabricated celebrity persona, excessive drinking, and trips to Nassau on his gambling junkets—not to mention the fraudulent tax returns that she had cosigned in protest. She had had enough.

Now she found herself alone, yet again, covering his tracks. He was sound asleep, still passed out in the car where Gretchen had left him in his stinking alcoholic stupor. *I can't do this again*, she thought. But this time was different. This time, there were two dead kids, and she was pissed. *It's time to act. I can't do this anymore. I've got to set the wheels in motion.*

As a lawyer, Gretchen was clever and calculating. She had already begun planning her escape and would amass all the evidence against her husband that she could—quietly. She already had all the tax information. Now, she just needed pictures to give to Michael Kahn, a Palm Beach lawyer with an incredible success rate.

She walked out to the garage and there sat Harrison in the front seat, his chair reclined back and his head tilted up and back. He looked comatose. She moved around his body, snapping photos of him from every ugly angle. *Drunken asshole. What a picture.*

Leaving him there, she turned off the lights, knowing that's where he would stay until noon tomorrow.

Chapter 5

It was Saturday morning, and Shook had gone into Starbucks drivethru on SR 192 and had just arrived on scene. Dragman was already there. Shook climbed out and walked up to Dragman who was in his truck with his notes. Dragman started talking, and Shook just listened.

"Already got it measured and charted. POC is exactly 2605 feet east of the centerline of I95 and New Haven Boulevard. The collision occurred just left of centerline if going eastbound. This means Davis was not completely in his lane of travel. There's a lot of dropped debris at POC, and there's clear-cut gouge marks left by the Sentra. The Audi overturned the Sentra and moved it north of POC and to the east by at least 100 feet."

Shook loved this stuff and had a good grasp of the physics involved, despite getting a C in college algebra. This meant the Audi was speeding.

"I noticed the speed limit is 55 mph. Dragman, how fast do you think Davis was going?"

"I'll bet it was at least 85."

"OK, dude. Anything else?"

"Well, look at this on the north side, 308 feet west of the POC. There are tire tracks through the grass that moved back on the roadway. There're skid marks east of that when he hit the brakes before the ABS took over. I've got it all charted. This means he was on the brakes well west of the POC. I'll bet the bastard was going over 80. So, it also meant that he ran off the road when he passed the Grenada and then pulled it back onto SR 192 before the impact.

"We also have the old lady in the Granada. She saw the pass and must've seen the speed."

"I like it, Dragman, and I appreciate you getting here early. Where's Henry?"

"He can't get here until this afternoon. He's actually down in Key West on a case. I'm picking him up at 1 o'clock at Apex Aviation in Melbourne."

"Good work, dude. We got to get him out here to do his own measurements and get him out to see the crush damage on those vehicles."

Shook smiled but suddenly looked up and past Dragman. "Who the heck is that?"

Dragman got out of the car and looked over. "Crap. It's that asshole, Donohue."

"OK Dragman, that means you've got to sit on this place until Henry gets here. That prick is liable to start covering up shit. I'll pick up Henry myself and get him here. You park your truck just north of those skid marks, and, as soon as he gets up here, I want you to film everything he does. Yeah, plug that camera into that cigarette lighter and film him as he works."

"No problem, boss. Should I say anything to him?"

"Sure, don't be an asshole, dude. Where is Wheeler?"

"I don't know, boss, but I can find him."

"Well, call him now and get him here. It's going to take two of you to sit on the scene."

"No problem, boss. I'm on it. I think Donohue sees us. I'm sure he does. As a matter of fact, he's on the phone."

Donohue had just pulled up and parked in a QuickChek parking lot that was east of the accident site.

Meanwhile, one hundred miles away out in suburban Palm Beach County, Mary Jo was still asleep when her cell phone went off. She ignored it at first, but Donohue redialed four times until she finally got up, angry that her phone was being blown up. When she recognized the phone number, she picked up.

That asshole Donohue can't do shit without bothering me, she thought.

"What do you want?" Mary Jo asked, her voice groggy from sleeping.

Donohue hated the way she talked down to him but understood he had to take it and replied, "I'm on scene. That Shook guy is here with his investigator, that old prick Drakenleader."

"OK, what are they doing?"

Donohue gulped and then finally spoke. "Well, it looks like they're looking at me. I think they've noticed me."

"Where is Ranson, Howard?"

"He's in Atlanta. I called him last night. He can't get here until Monday."

"That's bullshit. I want him here now. Just document everything, photograph everything, and get your measurements. Don't talk to them unless they talk to you. I'll call Ranson. Keep me apprised of everything they do."

Leaving Donohue on his own, Mary Jo called Harry Ranson.

"Harry?"

"Yes?"

"I need you to get to Melbourne now. We've got a traffic homicide down here, and our insured has unlimited coverage. The plaintiff's lawyer is already on scene with his investigator."

"But, Mary Jo. I'm up here on vacation with my family."

"Goddammit, Harry! Don't give me that family vacation shit. If you want our work, you need to move now! You know no expense will be spared. Get to Hartsfield now and be in Melbourne today before 5:00!"

"OK, Mary Jo. I'll be there as soon as I can."

"That means by noon today, so move!"

Harry Ranson hung up the phone and broke the news to his wife. She was not happy.

"Look, Honey, last year she paid me six figures alone for her work. I gotta go."

Meanwhile, back at the scene, Donohue got his wheel out and started walking the road charting everything, muttering to himself.

Shook and Dragman sat in Dragman's truck and watched.

Mary Jo got up and put on the coffee. Her mind was racing. *OK, Shook,* she thought. *What can I do to you?*

The next thing on her mind was the insured's car. *Got to move that Audi, get it over to our Broward lot.* Anything to protect her client. She was on the phone in a flash with Donohue.

"Where's the Audi, Howard?"

"It's out on the Southern lot," he replied.

"OK, I'm calling our two guys to move it. It will be at the Broward lot. That prick Shook won't see that coming. Just stay there and do your work. You pick up Ranson at the airport later. I'll call later with his flight information."

She hung up the phone, sat back, took her first drink of coffee, and lit up a cigarette. *OK, Mr. Shook. You think you got me?* she thought. *Maybe I need to put the Fucerinos on this one.*

The Fucerinos were actually Melvin and Calvin Fucerino from Broward County; they did her dirty work. She had used them on Shook in the past, and they knew about his exwives and his kids.

Shook was a troubling enemy lawyer, since he always paid his bills, paid his taxes, never had been audited, never used drugs, had a clean record with the Bar, and never had been disciplined—in sum he was a problem trying to get to.

He once had a Ukrainian client that he had decided to have a personal relationship with because she was a delightful woman who happened to be beautiful. He immediately terminated his employment with her, got her another lawyer, and off they went. In short, he played by the rules. His only possible vice was women. They once tried to set him up with a hooker out of Miami, who was beautiful, but he somehow saw it coming and rejected her.

He did have one little bit of scandal in his life. He had a son without marrying his mother. The child's mother had been convicted of money laundering back in the late '70s and ended up serving some time. Shook began a relationship with her that resulted in a child, but they were still friendly. She lives in Miami with her fifth husband who just happens to be an orthopedic surgeon. Her life had completely turned around.

Mary Jo knew the whole sordid history. The baby mama had actually been married to a former police chief who was now retired and living on Andros Island with his new girlfriend. She was once associated with Doc Gaylord, who went to prison, found religion, and became a TV preacher. *Life is strange.* But, aside from that, she had nothing on him. He did like to drink, but never went over the edge, and he was a blatant heterosexual and serially monogamous.

His investigator, Douglas Drakenleader, or Dragman, had been with him since the '70s when he was his lead investigator at the State Attorney's Office.

Drakenleader was once arrested for the murder of a drug dealer in one of Shook's old investigations back in the late '70's but was exonerated. He supposedly fed the perpetrator to an alligator. His cop buddies loved him for that. He was a celebrity. He and Shook reunited after that.

Drakenleader was a former New York cop, well known and deadly efficient, who knows everybody and had sources everywhere. He had just turned 70 years old but still loved his work and loved to fish. He was divorced, of course, but had many admiring girlfriends.

Shook had also hired a former longtime Conveyance Insurance adjuster, Ken Wheeler, who had been with them for five years. He knew a lot, even where some bodies were buried, and was still active with the remnants of the "Claimsmen." The Claimsmen were a loosely formed group of insurance adjusters and their friends who met monthly. They were serious drinkers, and Wheeler was afflicted with the alcoholic gene. He was, however, a great investigator and knew how to hack any claim. Mary Jo avoided him. She couldn't be seen as an alcoholic.

Now, though, Mary Jo had to get moving on the case. New York would not like a huge claim right now, and her chances of getting promoted to the home office was always on her mind.

Right now, the extent of the special unit's activities was well disguised. When she did have to book some of the expenses, she ran them through an offshore account. It did provide her with the means to create a serious slush fund, which she used for the unit's activities. Sooner or later, though, she knew her special unit would be exposed.

Chapter 6

It was noon when Engineer Henry Horatio Hillman of Pompano Beach walked into the terminal fresh from his flight from Key West. Shook called him "senator," because of the obvious connection with the former Minnesota senator and failed presidential candidate, Hubert Horatio Humphrey.

He was a presence and a force. The presence was his size. He was a large dude, overweight actually, but it was evenly distributed. He had a full beard and looked like he just walked out of the Alaskan wilderness. The force was the locomotive between his ears—his brain. He was an engineering genius. Shook met him for the first time back in the '80s when he opposed one of his clients. Shook vowed to never be on the other side of any Hillman case. They had been friends ever since.

Hillman smiled as he walked up to Shook. Shaking Shook's hand, he inquired, "So, Jack, what do we have now?"

"It's a big one, Henry. Two dead kids up front. My client was in the back, paralyzed. Our client is the son of James Ballin' Jackson."

"The former NBA star?"

"The very same." Shook was impressed with his trivia acumen.

"So, what's the hurry—aside from the obvious, Jack?"

"Well, it's a Conveyance Mutual case. The other driver is a political bigwig; probably has huge insurance limits, and their adjusters are sitting on the scene right now doing a staredown with Dragman. Dragman beat them there this morning. The accident happened last night at about six."

"I see, so who's got the case? FHP?"

"Yep, they do, and I'm hip to the fact that they probably were there last night."

"So what do we have, my man?"

"Well, our client's a passenger in back of a high mileage '90 Sentra. The defendant was driving a 2001 Quattro, passed a little old lady on a two Lane Road just west of I95 on SR 192. They do a little "dance" trying to avoid each other, but the collision was in the center of the roadway, more to their side than ours, and we've got some interesting skid marks and tire marks over on the shoulder near the scene, which Dragman thinks shows some serious speed."

"I like it. So, where are the vehicles?" Hillman asked.

"The Sentra is here locally in Melbourne, but the Quattro is in West Palm."

"So, how much do you know, Jack?"

"Well, I was at the hospital last night with the trooper, and she was informative."

"She?"

"Yes, *she*, Henry. RosoMartinez is her name. She looks brandnew."

"Let's go, dude, time's awasting, the scene may be altered."

"Still got the Titan, I see."

"Yeah, Henry, I just can't part with it. Still got the diesel F250?"

"Sure do, baby."

Shook and Hillman climbed into Shook's Titan, and off they went.

They arrived about 20 minutes later. Donohue was in his Explorer doing paperwork. Hillman jumped out and went immediately to the eastern end of the scene and photographed everything. He started measuring the skid marks through the shoulder, the reentry to the roadway, and all the way down to the POC. Shook walked with him holding his measurements notebook. He said nothing.

The total time on scene was about 90 minutes. They retreated to Shook's truck. Hillman spoke first. "I've got to agree with Dragman. The Audi was definitely speeding. I'll need to see both vehicles to see the crush damage to give you an opinion, but it looks like 30 over at POC. Let's go to the yard, and we'll check it out. Incidentally, it's a high-end Audi with an onboard ECM computer, aka 'little black box,' which will definitely prove the speed."

The drive south was quiet. Hillman was busy with his charting and calculations. Dragman followed close behind.

Flipping his binder closed, Hillman said, "We've got to get that 'black box,' Jack. It's critical to the case." They immediately pulled south of I95 and were in West Palm within an hour.

Harry Stark, the yard keeper was up front in the guardhouse when they went through. Hillman knew him well. "So, Harry, what's up?"

"Hey, Hillman. I'll bet you're here to see that big Six Series Audi Quattro, right?"

"Well, yes, we are, and also the '90 Sentra."

"Well Henry, I'm impressed with your radar, dude."

"No radar, man. Conveyance had the Audi moved. It left two hours ago. Jack's Towing picked it up, put it on a flatbed, and took it out."

"So where did they go?"

"They wouldn't say, but I'll bet south."

Damn, Shook thought, *the enemy is already on this one and knows we're here.*

"OK, so where's the Sentra?"

"It's back in Melbourne."

"Well, turn this thing around. I've got to see it now, since they are playing games."

They drove back up I95 to the Brevard lot.

Once there, they drove past endless rows of crushed and damaged vehicles. Shook could only imagine the carnage this lot represented. They found the Sentra, and Hillman was out of the car immediately.

The Sentra was totally destroyed. You could not recognize it as a Sentra, or anything else for that matter.

"Where was our boy sitting?" he asked Shook.

"Driver's side rear," Shook said.

"The top had been peeled off, and the front seat was a bloody mess."

"He had his seatbelt on, Jack, my man; look how it's stretched."

"Good."

I don't need no damn seatbelt defense on this one, he thought.

Fully processing the Sentra, Hillman climbed back into the back seat in the Titan with Dragman.

"So what do you think, Henry?"

"High energy, high velocity impact. Davis was at least 20 mph over at POC. He probably was 40 to 45 mph over when he first applied his brakes, maybe more."

"Shit, that means he was doing 90?"

"Yep, you need to find that Quattro. I've got to see it."

"OK, man, got it." Shook turned his attention to Dragman. "Dragman, get over to Jack's and find out where she sent the Quattro."

"I'm on it like a fat man on cake."

"I'll take Henry home."

They drove out and separated. Dragman drove south and west to Uncle Bill's Towing. He knew Bill well.

Bill was actually Bill Turner, a former Broward County sheriff's deputy and, therefore, friendly with Dragman. He also fished and had been in a couple of the tournaments sponsored by the Palm Beach Fishing Club of which Dragman was a longtime member. Turner was also good buddies with the secretary, Larry Driscoll, Bubba's little brother.

"The world is round," he thought as he drove up. Bill was in the office.

Dragman smiled, "Hey, Bill, my man."

"Oh shit, it's Dragman."

"Gotta talk, Bill."

"OK, let's go into my office if we need privacy."

"We need privacy, Bill."

They retreated to the inner sanctum of Bill Turner's office and closed the door. Turner spoke first. "I'll bet this is about that Quattro, right?"

"You're sharp, dude. You are right. So where is it?"

"Now look, Dragman, if it comes back to me that I told you, Mary Jo will kill my business. Are we clear on this?"

"Bill, it will never come back to you. We just need to know where it is, so we can inspect it and get the black box out. We'll construct another scenario on how we found it. You will never be implicated. No fucking way."

"No fucking way?"

"NFW, dude, plausible deniability. She will never know."

"OK, man, it's down in a warehouse at 154th Street, west of 441, Broward Street. Address, 26287.

"Thank you, Bill. Remember if there's ever anything we can do for you, just tell me, and it is done."

"I appreciate that, Dragman. There is one thing."

"Name it."

"My kid got busted again. He's in the Palm Beach County jail."

"What's the charge?"

"It's drugs, man. He's on those fucking pills."

"Bill, you know Shook can't be involved directly, but we'll get someone good on it Monday, OK?"

"Thanks, Dragman, good hunting."

Dragman pulled out and down Belvedere Road. "Gotta check it out right now. The players hide the most on us. What's so damn important about that Quattro?"

Shook was passing Glades Road when his phone went off. He saw it was Dragman. "OK, man, where is it?"

"They're hiding it out at some warehouse down off Broward Boulevard on West 154th Street, west of 441."

"OK, man, so what's the skinny?"

"Well, Bill is jammed up on this. We can't divulge this information. We've got to backtrack it to someone else or maybe a court order."

"Hmmm, they're worried on this one. "Little Joe" has her set of knickers all twisted up on this. Let me check on it, dude."

"There's one other thing, Bill, my boy."

"Oh, oh, what the fuck is it?"

"Bill's kid is in jail again. He asked for help."

"What is it, drugs again?"

"Yup, you got it, boss."

"OK, no problem. I'll get someone good, some young hungry lawyer. Let me think about it, Dragman."

"Well, I told him we would have someone here by Monday, so I need a name, boss."

"OK, call him back. Tell him it's Ben Baxter. I'll handle it with Ben. Let's go completely gratis on this one, it's worth it."

"I've got one of his other cases. We'll put him to work on it. I'll bump him on the fee, kick his cut up to 50/50, he'll be cool with that; and no connection on the criminal referral."

"That's pure genius, boss."

"No, I'm not, I'm just paying attention, dude."

"Anything else today, boss?"

"Nah, you're good to go. I bet you're going fishing, right?"

"Yeah, boss, I am. I'm running out to pick up Larry. We're going up to Buckhead to spend the night and then out at first light."

"You staying with Buck?"

"Yeah, he invited us up period."

"You tell the Buckman I said hey, OK."

"Yes, sir, see you Monday."

Chapter 7

E rika sat in her office alone in complete solitude examining the document before her. She read it, and it touched her to the core. She knew it was coming, but she thought there might be one last chance that providence might intervene and that she could avert what she now faced.

A Florida Bar suspension order signed by the clerk reflecting various decisions by the court with her name on it—a matter of public record for the whole world to see, including her friends, her colleagues, her family—was shocking to her. Her enemies would now laugh and be vindicated. She could hear them chuckling and saying "I told you so" to anyone who would listen. *That crazy bitch was getting just what she deserved.*

Now that she was alone, she felt truly alone. The whole world could now laugh and point their finger and whisper behind her back.

She knew she was completely isolated. The language on the first page of the order was unmistakable and clear:

The court on its own motion suspends Respondent from the practice of law until further order of the court, effective 30 days from the date of this order so that Respondent can close out her practice and protect the interests of the existing clients. If Respondent notifies this court in writing that she is no longer practicing and does not need the 30 days to protect existing clients, the court will enter an order making the suspension effective immediately.

There it was, a complete suspension with no end date, to remain effective indefinitely on a document headed by the Supreme Court of Florida, with her name on it, Erika L. Rodriguez, announcing to the entire world with no exceptions that, despite the recommendation by the referee, she was now officially humiliated in front of her species.

True, it wasn't disbarment, but a clear humiliation nonetheless, dated July 30, 2001.

Now what? She thought as she sat in her chair and began to tear up. *No, dammit, no crying. I gave that up long ago.* After a few minutes, she gathered herself and began reflecting on the last 10 years, which had just gone up in smoke.

As a single mom with two boys, she worked for lawyers for years and realized quickly that she was just as smart as them and could do the job even better than a man. She was a young woman at 35. She had gone a long way from Ponce, Puerto Rico to the States after her graduation from the university there. A goodlooking woman with a pretty smile, great Spanish eyes, and a friendly nature, she found herself wanting to be a lawyer but without the means to do it. There was a two-year stint as an insurance adjuster, before she was admitted.

She had applied at the big state schools, but couldn't get in. She didn't take standardized tests well and, despite two efforts at an LSAT, couldn't get the necessary score to be considered. Undeterred, she applied to private schools, and Nova Southeastern accepted her.

It was the best option. Actually, it was a good school, and it was local right there in Fort Lauderdale. She had two exhusbands paying child support, and she worked parttime, and she had some help from her father, which gave her just enough money to survive on while she collected student loans to finance the effort.

In the end, she was successful. She graduated in a little over two years and owed just under $75,000 in loans, but she did it. She took and passed the bar on her second try and began practicing law in October 1996. She got a job as an assistant public defender in downtown Fort Lauderdale and immediately had 100 clients.

She did well, but her meager salary of $40,000 was not enough to survive on, so she joined a group of lawyers across the street from the courthouse, a loose association of Professional Associations, and was able to keep most of what she earned. She had a volume criminal practice and was essentially a sole practitioner, but she proudly opened her office with great expectations.

She did have a weakness, and it was alcohol. She managed to avoid any significant problems over the years, but she enjoyed having a drink with friends and sometimes drank too much. It really started in law school where she had fallen in with a group of "party animals."

She didn't realize it at the time, but alcohol is an occupational hazard for lawyers, and there are only few who can successfully manage its consumption. The profession seemed to be in a state of denial about this because every professional event, which included local bar meetings, judicial investiture, always has an open bar and everyone seems to drink, even the judges. It all started innocently enough, and then things began to happen.

She found that the more clients she had, the more money she made. This seemed to be a fairly simple concept, except that you have to service clients, and sole practitioners stay busy to the point of being overwhelmed. She did her best to service her clients, but not all of them were taken care of. Every day, she found herself down at the bar with her bar friends drinking after work. Soon, complaints began to come in, and the Bar sanctioned her for neglecting some of her clients. It happened slowly, but she had five complaints in three years.

She needed the money to run her business and her life, and she found herself in that cycle where she took on more than she could handle. She had other lawyers who would cover her from time to time, but their help began to dry up, as she couldn't cover them, being so busy. The judges were sympathetic at first, all except one, a hard nose named Jonas Hickok who was a redneck at his core and a ladies man, of course, married to his third wife.

Hickok had made a pass at Erika a few years back, and she rejected him, politely, she thought, but rejected him nonetheless. She missed a court date about six months later, one that she thought was covered, and Hickok issued a warrant for her client for her failure to appear. The client was arrested. No courtesy call from the judge's office, and the client was livid.

Secretly, Hickok enjoyed the power that he wielded and smiled to himself knowing that Erika was about to suffer. Also, he did not really care too much for Hispanic lawyers but kept that to himself.

The final act was completed now, the Supreme Court publicly reprimanded her, since it seems that Judge Hickok had found three more instances where she had missed the court date. This was a humiliating experience for Erika. You travel to Tallahassee, you stand before the Supreme Court in session, which is televised, and you are shamed publicly by the Chief Justice.

You can't say a word; you just have to stand there and take it. After it is over, you are dismissed from the court and told to leave. That moment was burned into her memory. It was a nightmare.

But then came the DUI. She was still drinking, and then the inevitable happened. She left the bar after having the usual one too many, got in her car to go home to tend to her kids, and was immediately stopped by the Broward Sheriff's office.

This was not a chance stop; her misfortune was orchestrated. Sitting in the bar was a young obsequious little prosecutor who routinely sucked up to Judge Hickok. He had seen her leave and made an anonymous call to alert the cops about a drunken lawyer leaving the bar, driving a powder blue Mustang.

This report had immediately gone out to the Broward County Sheriffs on duty and a nearby unit pulled out from a side street to monitor the reported "powder blue Mustang."

The deputy activated his dash cam video and captured Rodriguez's tires touching the fog line over three times. At that point, she was stopped. The deputy who got her out of the car smelled alcohol. She refused—politely at first—to perform the roadside exercises and to take a breathalyzer. Erika was then arrested.

She spent the night in the Broward County jail. She never realized how bad the air was in the Broward County jail. It was stifling, huge, and so impersonal. She suffered a cavity search by a correctional deputy, who laughed at her good fortune as she performed the search. The next morning, she went before the first appearance judge and bonded out. She was completely humiliated.

Feeling completely defeated, she reached out to her old friend, Greg Crutchfield, a well-known lawyer in Rockledge, who referred her to the Shook firm in Palm Beach, who referred her to Mike Kahn.

This was a bad period for her. She missed some more court dates and, despite Kahn's efforts, she refused a plea bargain that required jail time, went to trial, and was convicted. She went on probation and spent 30 days in the Broward County Jail. Then came the Bar complaint, which resulted in a 30-day suspension recommendation by the referee and then the Supreme Court order.

There she was, in August, unemployed, unable to make money with two boys who looked to her for guidance and life, and she was unable to provide for them. She did not know what to do. She began to take inventory. She had $3,000, a paidfor used Mustang, and some jewelry. She was at rock bottom.

As she sat wondering how long she would last with everything she had, which she quickly calculated to be two months, she recalled that she had a busted Rolex at home that she had been told that she could sell. She got on the phone after searching the internet and found a buyer in downtown Fort Lauderdale. She would see him in the morning.

She could drive now that she had served her suspension for other than business purposes and drove home. She decided she would not tell her boys what happened. She ordered Chinese and had a good dinner with them.

The next day, she was at a watch broker with her busted Rolex. She collected $2,100, cashed the check, and went to her office.

No one spoke to her at the office. After all, she now had to wind down her practice without help and consider her next move. As she sat in her office alone, she thought to herself, *Well, this is the busted watch summer vacation.* She was at her lowest point, and then it happened. The receptionist was here to tell her that she had a call from Palm Beach, some guy named Doug Dragenleader.

Dragman.

"I'll take the call, Marie." The call was put through, and she picked up. "Doug?"

"Yes, Erika, it's me."

"It's good to hear from you, Doug, but things aren't really good for me now, and I can't take any more criminal cases. What can I do for you, my friend?"

Doug was a friend she had known for years. She knew of his past and how he had recovered to be the head investigator for the Shook and Meisel firm up in Palm Beach. She always liked him and wished he were younger. He was in his 70s now but still working.

"Listen, Erika, that's not why I'm calling. I read the suspension order. We know all about it. Jack Shook has been briefed, and he wants to see you tomorrow. I think he's going to offer you a job as an investigator. The pay will be good, more than you make now, with an expense account and a car allowance and insurance for you and the kids. He can see you tomorrow morning at 10 o'clock in Palm Beach. Can you make it?"

Erika was silent for a moment and then said, "I'll be there at 10. And, Doug, thank you."

"No problem, Erika. I know what you can do. It will be up to you to decide to get your license back, but there will be no shortage of work if you are willing. There is just one condition: you can't screw up."

"I'm willing, Doug. See you tomorrow."

Erika hung up and began to weep quietly again to herself. Suddenly things didn't seem so dark. She walked out her old office after gathering some personal belongings and never looked back.

Chapter 8

Ranson was late, of course. He didn't walk into the terminal until well after 2. Donohue was annoyed that his Saturday was now going to be spent chauffeuring this dickhead around, but such is his life.

"Hey, Howard, so what is the latest?"

"Harry, we got to go soon. Mary Jo wants you to check out this Audi. We had to move it. The plaintiff's lawyer is already on the case."

"So where is it at?"

"It's down at the Skunkworks warehouse."

"Well, shit, Howard, if I had known that, I would have flown into Lauderdale."

"Yeah, well, she made her move after we got to you. Relax, I'm driving."

Harry Ranson, Conveyance's goto inside guy, was a registered professional engineer. His specialty was accident reconstruction.

He was a handsome guy who looked great when he testified. He worked with Mary Jo a lot and knew what she wanted and how to please her. His fees were astronomical, and he resisted plaintiffs' lawyers doing discovery on his billing history. It was too late, however. The book on him was out. He was bought and sold by the insurance industry. He was good, and he was deadly. He also had no ethics, so he and Mary Jo got along famously.

Since the car was at the Skunkworks facility, he surmised he would be the inside guy who would cover the wreck first, and, if anything questionable had to be done, he would do it before a disclosed expert was on the case.

They walked into the facility about an hour later, and Ranson surveyed the remains of the Quattro. He sat at the desk for a while and pulled up the vehicle specs—stateoftheart engineering with a "black box" that is an onboard event recorder. Not wasting any time, he pulled out the diagnostic computer, hooked it up, and downloaded the data for the 60 seconds prior and up to the impact.

Top speed: 92 mph, five seconds prior to the impact. Energy braking: eight seconds prior. Not good. The insured was 37 mph over the speed limit.

Ranson processed the rest of the wreck, photographing and calculating the crush damage. He got it down to about 20 over at impact. If the Sentra was going a slower speed, at or near the speed limit, the force was similar to running into a concrete wall at about 100 mph.

That is a high-energy collision, he thought. *Got to call Mary Jo and see what she wants.*

He caught her at home and relayed the bad news. She was not happy. "All right, Harry, I guess you're off this one. I'll pay your fee, of course."

"Well, what about the event recorder?"

"Take it out, beat the living shit out of it, and put it back in. Make sure you render it useless."

"That's a problem. Some damage is doable, but the only way to kill it is to drown it, preferably in bleach and water."

"Well, Goddammit, drown the fucking thing. Is anybody there with you?"

"Yeah, Howard is here."

"Well, don't worry about Howard."

"OK, but you know we could switch it out."

"Yeah, I know, but then you would have to alter the numbers and there would be a paper trail. No, just beat the shit out of it and drown the motherfucker, OK, Harry?"

"OK."

"That will totally disable it, right?"

"Yes, it will, Mary Jo. They are very delicate."

"OK, well do it."

"It's done. I will mail my bill."

Mary Jo hung up the phone and sat back. She grabbed another cigarette and lit it up. "Checkmate, Shook, you sarcastic prick," she muttered to herself.

Meanwhile, sitting outside and across the street from the Skunkworks Warehouse sat Kenny Wheeler. He recognized Donohue's companyissued Explorer and sat on it waiting him out. It was about 4:30 p.m. when they came out. It was Donohue and Harry Ranson. He took a picture as they climbed in his SUV.

"It figures," Wheeler mumbled. "Shook is going to love this shit."

He dialed his number. "Hey, bossman, I'm down here set up on the warehouse, and guess what!"

"What would that be, Kenny?"

"Howard's down here with that prick, Harry Ranson."

"OK, just make sure they don't see you."

"They won't. That fucking Howard is a blind man. Never liked him. I never understood why they hired him."

"They hired him because he does anything they tell him to do and he keeps his mouth shut."

"Yeah, I guess, you're right. I just never liked him." Wheeler was a little embarrassed that he didn't see the obvious.

"So boss, you want me to get inside?"

"How you going to do that, Wheelman?"

(Wheelman was his moniker, and Shook was his boss. Dragman was his other boss, and Meiselman was his last boss.)

"Don't ask me, boss. Don't ask, don't tell, and no one will know."

"Is there anyone else there?"

"Don't ask, don't tell, boss."

"OK, Kenny, but just remember rule one."

"Yeah, I know, boss. Don't fuck up."

"You got it man. All I need is a photo ID to show that it's them. That's all, nothing else."

"Got it, boss."

Kenny hung up the phone and decided it was time for a cocktail and a steak. *I'll come back later*, he thought.

In the truck were his tools. He could pick any lock and disable any alarm system. This should be a piece of cake. Then he saw the cameras. *Oh shit,* he thought. *Got to disable them, too. Damn, this is a secure facility. What the fuck?*

His mind was racing. *Maybe we'll just walk in. I'll get one of my boys to walk in and act like he's lost, looking for directions. Yeah, yeah, that's the ticket. So we've got to do it during the day. We need a FedEx driver or something.* He thought about calling Shook back but decided against it. Instead, he went to get dinner.

The drive up to the Tiger Lounge only took about 15 minutes. The place was packed. The clientele was upscale mostly, and Wheeler knew two of the girls. They served dinner that wasn't bad. He ordered a strip and baked potato along with all you can drink, and a lap dance, of course. Dinner was OK; the lap dance better.

It was about 8:30 at night when he'd finished, and the lighting was poor. He had parked way out back and didn't notice the two guys behind him. Suddenly, everything went black.

Chapter 9

Hillman was at home relaxing. He had just finished dinner when his cell went off. It was Shook.

"Hey, Henry, we set up on the warehouse, and guess who's there and just left?"

"Tell me, man."

"It was Ranson."

"OK, dude, that means it's no holds barred. What's with this warehouse anyway?"

"I don't know, man."

"So, what do you think?"

"Well, I've got to run the specs on that car. It's very stateoftheart. It's . . ." He paused for a moment. "Oh, shit!"

"So, what's the matter, Henry?"

"It's a brandnew Quattro, right?"

"Yeah, so what?"

"Well, guess what! There's an event data recorder on it."

"Yeah, you mentioned that before."

"We've got to get that black box."

"I guarantee they already have the data."

"So, what should I do? Henry asked."

"Well, you got to get to it. I guarantee they will fuck with it."

"Well, if they do, I can get an order dealing with spoliation."

"Well, yes, but you've got to prove it."

"Damn, that means I've got to file this thing Monday and get an order."

"Hold off on that, dude, maybe you should just call Little Joe."

"It's Saturday night. She's not going to answer."

"Call her anyway."

Shook had her cell number on his email memory and found it quickly. He dialed the number.

Mary Jo was up and had just finished her evening bath. She had blown off her latest boyfriend, not Julio, of course, and wanted to be alone.

The phone rang, and she checked the caller ID. It was Shook. *That sonofabitch. How dare he call me on a Saturday night.* And then she caught herself. She couldn't help herself. She was always attracted to Shook.

"Well, hello, Mr. Shook, what can I do for you?"

"Thank you for coming to the phone, Mary Jo. I appreciate it, and I'm sorry to bother you so late."

"OK, Jack, what's up?"

"Well, we got another case."

"So what? And why call me now?"

"Well, I need to look at your insured's vehicle."

"What vehicle?"

"Come on, Mary Jo, you know perfectly well what I'm talking about."

"You need to tell me, Mr. Shook," (Now he was Mr. Shook.)

"The Quattro. Your insured is Harrison Davis."

"You'll have to call me Monday, Jack. I need to be in my office if I'm going to give you some meaningful information."

"Well, I'm just telling you right now that I'm putting you on notice to produce the vehicle with no destructive testing. I'm emailing you right now."

"OK, Jack, anything else?"

"No, not right now."

"Good night, Jack."

"Good night, Mary Jo."

What a dissembler, he thought as he hung up, *but all things considered, it's best she doesn't know what I know.*

Mary Jo was deep in thought as she hung up the phone. *Damn that Jack Shook. I wish I could get to him. The average lawyer wouldn't do anything until he saw the accident report. Why does it have to be him? That's it, damn it, I'm pulling out all the stops on this one. His weakness is women. This setup has got to be perfect. Gotta make sure the Fuccerinos are on this one, but I don't want to call them until Monday. They would think that entitled them to some kind of overthetop bonus. It's too bad they're worth it.* She lit another cigarette and sank down in the overstuffed chair by her bed, scheming a way to get to Mr. Jack Shook.

Chapter 10

Harrison Davis spent the entire day sleeping off his hangover. He was starting to come back to normal. He got up at 4 p.m. and dealt with Gretchen. She was completely pissed off and left, saying she was going over to her buddy Nikki's for a while.

It always seemed to bother him that she had single girlfriends, but what the hell? He let her go. It wasn't worth the fight.

At 60 years old, he was overweight, had heart disease, and was diagnosed with diabetes. He took all sorts of meds, but he refused to stop drinking. "Everything was under control" was his mantra. Though, he felt lousy today. His neck hurt, his chest hurt, he had a headache, but, otherwise, he felt OK. He had no thought or any concern for the kids he had just killed or the one who was seriously injured and in the hospital. He just didn't give a rat's ass.

He was privately glad that Gretchen had left. All he wanted was peace and quiet. He had to be sharp on Monday. The auditors were coming in from Jacksonville, and the numbers needed to look right. They were planning to go public next year, and the runup was crucial. He also had a United Way event the following Thursday, so he had no time to deal with lawyers or doctors or this little problem.

He had called his agent and assessed the Quattro. It was totaled, so he was going to pick out a new one tomorrow to replace it. No problem, but the color should be different. He was supposed to play golf tomorrow, as was his usual custom on Sundays, but he just didn't feel like it.

Gretchen had thrown the Post at him. He wasn't page one on the local section; he was page 2, so the phone had been ringing all day. He couldn't answer it. He had to deal with the fallout on Monday and let his administrative assistant fight off the inquiries. She was good at it. *Let her earn her pay for a change.* I mean, the oral sex was great for Davis, but she needed to earn her pay doing something more constructive.

I need to step up the community service angle now. I'll be criticized for sure, he thought.

Meanwhile, Gretchen was not with Nikki; she was with her latest boy toy, Jerry Fox, at his place over off of Peruvian. Nikki would cover her, of course. Jerry was her personal trainer and was well endowed. She loved the sex and was getting a little reckless.

"Don't care anymore," she thought. "I'm done with that alcoholic windbag, Harrison. He can eat shit and die for all I care. When I get finished with him, he'll be selling insurance door to door, but I need to be more careful." She had a dirty little secret herself and was in denial. She loved to snort a little coke with her girlfriends. Her husband has suspected this and once accused her of being bisexual because she spent so much time with her single girlfriends, some of which routinely did coke.

She had called for an appointment with attorney Mike Kahn. She spent Saturday gathering up her stuff, which she stored at Nikki's. She knew he cooked the books, and his personal income was reported low by at least 30 percent. His expense account was over the top, and he reported only the bare minimum. She could not understand why he felt the need to cheat and worried that the IRS wouldn't buy her innocent spouse defense.

This would be the battleground, but she had the upper hand. The photo of Harrison Davis in a dead stupor after killing two kids was the clincher. She was ready for battle. Her appointment was Monday at 11 o'clock.

Chapter 11

Marvella had spent the entire weekend at the hospital. Marvin came out of surgery at midnight, but he was still in a coma. She spent the night in his room. The nurses had provided a recliner for her next to his bed in ICU. Clovis had been taken home. She was distraught but could see no purpose in her staying at the hospital.

There she sat, listening to the machines, feeling helpless and depressed. There was nothing she could do to help her baby. The two boys, Tyrell and Travonte, she did not know. They were older, both about 19 or 20 years old, but she didn't have a clue about them.

One strange twist was that Marvin was wearing his seatbelt, and he was the one rendered paraplegic but did not die.

She was tired, exhausted actually, and didn't want to talk to any more doctors. Marvin was in a druginduced coma. His body had suffered such a terrible trauma, but a coma was supposedly the best way to deal with that. She had spent a good part of the day talking to a rehab specialist, who tried to brief her on what to expect.

"He'll be in the hospital for at least two weeks, and, if no further surgery was necessary, the next step is a rehab center," the specialist explained.

Marvin would be in a rehab center for at least 60 days before he could come home. *And then what? I'm just not ready for this*, she thought.

Marvella was a deeply religious woman, and Pastor Timmons, who had come and spent a couple hours with her in the afternoon, comforted her. It was hard for her to understand why this had to happen to Marvin. His life was so full of promise and now this. Why did this have to happen to her child? He was such a good child. It just didn't seem to make sense. How could this have been part of God's plan?

It was close to midnight, and the lights were off, but the machines emitted just enough light to make it difficult to sleep. She sat there in the dark watching her baby, deeply depressed.

Chapter 12

Ed was home on Sunday when Mary Jo called him. This was going to be a big one, and she was counting on him. She had made it clear that she could use any one of a number of A-listed insurance defense firms, but she decided on his firm because of their "special" relationship.

Ed listened quietly and thanked her for the referral and assured her that no stone would be left unturned on the claimants or their lawyers and that he understood the urgency of the situation.

Ed was actually James Edward Baldwin, a senior partner with the law firm of Baldwin, McQuaid, Cook, and Smith with main offices in downtown Fort Lauderdale, as well as an office in West Palm Beach and Melbourne. Ed's main claim to fame was his legendary ability of "bundling" campaign contributions for insurance-friendly politicians.

Ed knew Harrison Davis, of course, and was going to see him Thursday night at the United Way function scheduled at the Radisson in West Palm. He thought he should call him Monday and let him know he was on the case. The Conveyance adjuster had already briefed Davis on the fact that he couldn't talk to anyone except law enforcement about the crash, and, if they called him, he was to call them to get counsel present.

Davis had a duty to give an interview and cooperate with the troopers as long as they conducted the accident part of their investigation, which was privileged under Florida law. Nothing he said could be used against him in any subsequent civil or criminal proceeding.

After that part of the interview, if they told him they were now conducting a criminal investigation, he needed a lawyer present before saying anything.

The trooper in charge, Thomas, had only handled the first part of the investigation. Davis had told him he was traveling east on SR 192 when, all of a sudden, the Sentra pulled out in front of him. He was going the speed limit. He tried to evade the Sentra, but it drove into his path.

Ed was very familiar with Thomas. Thomas had accepted the explanation and did not switch hats for a criminal investigation. There were no questions about alcohol despite the fact that RosoMartinez had alerted Thomas to the issue.

Ed was privately happy to get this case. It would produce serious billings. It had two death claims and one seriously injured claimant. Jack Shook was already on the case, and more lawyers would surface for the other claimants. He quickly calculated that the fees on this would easily go over half a mill, and probably a million, if someone went to trial.

Ed was 66 this year and was going retire. His partners were buying him out. They had exercised their option to buy his stock under the buy/sell agreement, and he was planning a run for the State Senate next year in '03.

His buddies in the State Senate and the Republican Party statewide had assured him of their support.

The boundaries for his district, which ran from Broward into Palm Beach, were "gerrymandered" further east and west as needed to collect the perceived affluent voters who would vote Republican for a change, and it was now or never for "Big Ed."

There were other problems, of course, the first being Ed himself. He was really not much of a people person, and he did not relate well to the common man, much less anybody else. The Democratic incumbent was well entrenched.

Ed didn't care, however, because he was so full of himself that he was nearly delusional. He had convinced himself that the new district boundaries would carry the day.

This was payback, of course. Ed had spent the last two decades actively involved in behindthescenes fundraising and lobbying for the insurance industry and their candidates.

He was one of the coauthors of the original 1986 version of the "Tort Reform Act," which made it very difficult for any deserving claimant to get fair and full compensation for his injuries, especially when it came to the "intangible" damages, such as pain and suffering, loss of enjoyment of life, and mental anguish. He was proud of his efforts, and he was now going to be rewarded.

His latest project was privatizing prisons. After the election, he would get into it in a big way but was engineering the necessary campaign contributions from his friends to ensure the result.

He was, at least to all concerned, and to the general public, a solid citizen. He had been married forever. He had chosen his wife well. She was a good woman and a wonderful mother. She was responsible for the kids, not Ed, and she was immensely tolerant. His kids were grown, and they turned out good, but there was a scandal in his past.

Ed was the breadwinner and provider. He had done well. He was also arrogant and corrupt. Ed was far from perfect. He had had numerous affairs— one with Mary Jo 15 years earlier when she was still married. They had parted company on good terms, however. They were like two scorpions. Each had dirt on the other, so it was a standoff. They developed a mutual respect based on fear.

He was not too smart about women in general. As a matter of fact, he was stupid on occasion. He had "hooked up" with some Hispanic hookers at a conference in Miami a few years back and had got into a dispute over payment with one of them and had to explain it to the MiamiDade police.

No report was made, and he brought the matter to an end by buying her off for $10 grand.

By far his biggest disaster was having an affair with one of his new associate lawyers about eight years ago. This was big news for about a year, since she sued him for sexual harassment after the firm discovered that she was basically useless; she wouldn't take orders from insurance adjusters.

He denied the affair officially, but she filed the lawsuit. It was settled confidentially right before his scheduled deposition. The plaintiff's lawyer was Greg Crutchfield out of Rockledge, who was associated with Shook and Meisel.

The payoff to the fired female associate was $1 million. There was insurance coverage to pay it, but the premium was so expensive that the firm decided to drop it when they all agreed to restructure their partnership/stockholder agreement the following year. In short, his partners were glad to see Ed go—they'd only put up with him because of his rainmaking abilities.

Ed also knew Davis. They were both members of various golf clubs, including Oeste Palma, and he had once served on the board. He had played golf with Davis many times, and Ed had sat at the bar with him on many occasions, trying to keep up with him.

Ed drank, heavily. He never got a DUI, although he had come close a number of times.

Shook and Ed had "locked horns" on cases over the years. Shook's pet name for Ed was "Mr. Ed" after the '50s sitcom series featuring a talking horse.

Shook had tangled with Ed in court years back and quickly discovered that Ed was not really a trial lawyer. He was a figurehead who ran his law firm with guile and with fear. Ed was smart, however, and treacherous. He had decades before been hired by the original architect of the firm, Frank McGrath, who was now deceased. Shook also despised Ed because he once shot a neighbor's dog for barking too much.

Frank was the undisputed dean of the local insurance defense bar, who began his practice back in the '50s. He hired Ed right out of law school. He also hired Lucas McQuaid.

Lucas was the trial lawyer of the firm. His abilities were instantly recognizable. He related to jurors; he related to everyone. He was a great communicator. His straightforward and unambiguous approach to everything related well. He could simplify even the most complex of subjects. He also had integrity. If he told you something, you could believe it. He didn't play games. He was plainspoken and highly intelligent. He could instantly read people. He could handle himself in any situation. He was talented. He had a great speaking voice but did not pontificate, like Ed. Ed was famous for his "bloviating."

Lucas had a great sense of himself. He was a reasonably good-looking guy, who had a presence. His wardrobe was legendary. He did not look like his well-moneyed opponents. He wore no jewelry except a cheap watch and a wedding ring. His hair was short, and he had no facial hair. He wore suits that had threads hanging off the back and, sometimes, did not match. And he wore his legendary Bass Weejuns that had been resoled at least three times. They looked a little battered and in need of a polish. On one occasion, Shook offered him a new pair during a trial recess once settlement discussions were made. Lucas declined. Shook made a comment about them to the jury, and Lucas did not object and played the comment perfectly, turning it into humor.

Lucas was one of those lawyers that you feared. Whenever he spoke, he was doing damage to your case. He was legendary in his cross-examination of doctors.

He and Shook were friends. Not good friends, but friends built on mutual respect. Shook kept his comments about Lucas's partner to himself when speaking with Lucas.

Lucas had weaknesses, too. He drank and he womanized. He drank every day after work. He was probably a fully functioning alcoholic. He womanized when he drank. Shook was amazed at how Lucas could function so well in trial the next day after drinking in the evening.

Lucas also had a temper. He had lost it with a lawyer who foolishly tried to challenge his integrity one day in court. Later in the week, he confronted the lawyer at an evening function in the parking lot, and it got ugly. Lucas hit him once, and it was over. The other lawyer did nothing about it.

Shook also had found out from Ken Wheeler that Lucas had been diagnosed with "intermittent explosive disorder." Shook didn't think any such diagnosis existed until he verified it in his DSM, after all, all good trial lawyers have the updated version, when they encounter and obviously disturbed human being.

In short, Lucas was a great lawyer, but he had his weaknesses. Shook never took full advantage of those weaknesses except to force him into crossing his experts in the morning while hungover. He wondered if, one day, he would be forced to instigate an incident that triggered the rage that was just below the surface. He tucked it away, never to be used.

The two junior partners in the firm were Howard Cook and John Smith. They were the "worker bees" of the firm who spent 60 hours a week working and directing their six young associate lawyers who worked six days a week, sometimes seven, with their "billable hours" war. They were each able to bill 90 hours a week, although their real hours were about 50 to 60.

Shook had spent a year working for an insurance defense firm back in the late '70s before he formed Shook & Miesel, LLP. He had wanted to see what the opposition was up to and how it functioned. He took his orders from the insurance adjusters and claims superintendents. For a year, he was immersed in the personal injury practice. Defending insurance companies was the best way to learn how to sue them. He learned his lessons well and made his exit. Sam Harkness mentored him, and when he left remained on good terms with him.

Lucas was privately pleased that he had Shook on the other side of this one. He had a decent case. Liability was on his side. The dead kids had violated his insured's rightofway when they tried to pass; their vehicle was a mechanical deathtrap. He was going to win this one, and he would get the credit he so richly deserved. Life was good. From such arrogance, the games began.

Chapter 13

Melvin Fuccerino, pronounced "fookerino," was home when he got Mary Jo's call on his cell Sunday evening. Her number was on speed dial. Shook found out about Melvin and his brother Calvin a few years back and instantly dubbed them the Fuccerino boys.

"Well, hello, Mary Jo," he answered.

And then Mary spoke. "Melvin, I've got a new case for you. Howard will call you tomorrow with the details. This one will be under our usual protocol: full credit checks, full background including exspouses, girlfriends, boyfriends, full criminal and substance abuse. No holds barred, Melvin, you understand?"

"I understand perfectly, Mary Jo. Do we have a lawyer yet?"

"Yes, Melvin, we do. It's that prick Jack Shook. Incidentally, I want you to do a full run-up on him again. It's been a few years. See if you can get anything going with his exwife and do something with that felon Latino femme fatale that he made a kid with. As a minimum, we need to set him up with hookers, drugs or something. Use your evil little imagination, Melvin."

"I understand completely, Mary Jo. So Howard briefs me first, and I report directly to you, right?"

"Yes, Melvin, that's the deal. Nothing to my office—and nothing in writing. Remember, this conversation never happened. I need to know everything about this woman who is the mother of Shook's client who is about 15 years old. She's black and lives in Melbourne Beach somewhere, and there doesn't seem to be a father. She must be vulnerable and desperate for money. You understand?"

"I'm on the case. Howard calls me tomorrow."

Melvin hung up the phone and sat back and smiled. Another big one from Conveyance. Big money, big return.

Melvin and his brother, Calvin, operated out of Broward County, doing business as Investigations, Inc.

Melvin was a former Miami Dade cop who resigned about 10 years ago amidst a federal investigation into missing drugs and contraband seized during his eight-year stint as a cop. He narrowly avoided being charged.

Calvin was formerly a Dade County bondsman who joined his brother in the business. They did a lot of "straight" domestic surveillance and insurance work.

The work done for Mary Jo was all illegal, of course. Some of the work they did dealing with credit checks were federal crimes. It's against the law to run credit checks on claimants. The Fuccerinos used a car dealer down in Plantation whom they bribed.

It is also against the law to falsely report criminal behavior. The setups of plaintiffs' lawyers was one of their many specialties. It's also criminally punishable for "bad faith" claims activity. Melvin and Calvin knew all this, of course, but flourished in its execution.

Ken Wheeler, the former Conveyance adjuster who worked for Shook's firm, became aware of them and their activities but could not produce any evidence to expose them. He also was reluctant to do so. It was better that

Shook and Meisel were aware of it but chose not to mention it, because it was best for Mary Jo to go on thinking she had not been detected.

Wheeler also had signed an employment contract when he was hired by Conveyance that provided that he could not disclose any of the information gathered and "work product" performed from his employment with Conveyance.

About 20 years prior, some exemployee was sued under this nondisclosure agreement, which was upheld by the court. The company had used this ruling to intimidate everyone ever since.

Shook was aware of the nondisclosure agreement, but considered it a nonissue if Conveyance was engaged in illegal activities, especially if it was part of a consistent pattern. He chose not to push the issue because he really did not have the "smoking gun" he needed to prove it and just quietly accepted the reality that he faced.

He also did not know that they had a "book" on him and had tried to entrap him with that really goodlooking escort a few years back. He accepted that it was well known that he had a child with Linda Driscoll after she was released from prison back in the '90s, but accepted it as part of his "mantra." Linda was doing well, living in Miami, married to her doctor husband.

After all, Shook still lived in the same house down on Clark Avenue in Lake Clarke Shores with his dog and cat and spent a lot of his time with his youngest son, who lived with his mother most of the time in Miami.

Shook had never remarried. He had a series of relationships, but avoided the "cruel hoax" of what marriage has become in our time. He could have married a number of times, but something always happened to derail the nuptials. Shook always thought that if you give someone long enough, they would reveal themselves. The real person will emerge. He was recovering from his latest disappointing relationship.

Everyone has an agenda for their lives, and everyone has a story. Shook was not involved with anyone at the present, and he liked it that way.

Shook chose to be married to his job. He loved his life. He was a true trial lawyer who relentlessly pursued justice for his clients and, in the process, made a good living for himself.

Chapter 14

Dennis had Sunday off this weekend and spent the day with his wife. As a professional bartender, Dennis Woodbury had spent most of his adult life in the beverage industry. He worked as a bartender while in college, worked for AnheuserBusch as a district manager after college, but, eventually, came back to his first love. He was at the top of his game. He made a sixfigure income at the club as head bartender. He was quick with a joke, and the members loved him.

He had read the newspaper article about the accident involving Davis, and he was quietly angry about the whole Friday night episode when Davis abused him for suggesting that he had had enough. He quietly disliked Davis. He was an obnoxious blowhard who "threw his weight around" and generally abused the staff. It didn't matter if it was the guys in the Pro Shop or the waiters, he was always complaining about something. He was tolerated because of who he was, his money, and his being on the Board.

Dennis was a shrewd guy, however, and could see what was coming even before he got the call from the club's beverage director Sunday morning. He knew the call was coming. He had privately downloaded Davis's bar tab off the computer onto a thumb drive and made a hard copy. He tucked it away, took it home, and deposited it in his wall safe.

Harry Bennett, his boss and beverage director, rarely called him at home, but this was different. He checked the caller ID on the phone, which was the Club's office, and he took the call.

Dennis answered with a simple "Hello."

"Dennis, this is Harry, how are you doing?"

"I'm well. What can I do for you?"

"Well, I want you to know that I just got a call from the Club's lawyer, who told me to download Harrison Davis's clubhouse statement and put it away."

"Yeah, so what?"

"I'm here to tell you that you need to keep our members bottling and alcohol consumption confidential. You understand? Dennis?"

"Yes, boss, I know what to do and what not to do, but have you talked to David?"

"Yes. I already did, and he understands. I just wanted to make sure you and I were on the same page, OK?"

"I understand, boss."

"OK, Dennis. See you Monday at noon."

Dennis hung up the phone and sat back, smiled, and shook his head. *Here we go*, he thought.

Dennis privately disliked Harry Bennett, but he tolerated him because he enjoyed his job and the pay was good. He wondered if Bennett had called the three other members in Davis's foursome who were at the club drinking with Davis Friday night. He decided it best not to ask.

"So, what are they going to do now? Are they going to sanitize Davis's monthly statement?"

He thought about it and realized, yes, they were, and it pissed him off. It would probably show one or two drinks, or the other drinks would be transferred to someone else's tab. Something would happen. He would check it Monday.

He sat back and smiled again. He was very pleased with himself that he had already downloaded the Davis's account bill. He wondered how and when he would use it. He would talk to David on Monday and have one of their "graveyard" conversations. He was 30 years younger and untested, but he was close to Dennis and took his "cues" from him. Dennis was his mentor, and David would follow his lead.

David Hanks was a new generation guy. A tall, handsome dude who was learning the ropes. Everyone liked him. He did what he was told. He had a future, and he knew it. No reason to mess it up because of some loose-lipped drunken asshole like Davis.

Dennis wondered if Marcia had seen the news article and waited for her to bring it up. She never did, so he didn't either. *Better to keep her out of this loop, too*, he thought. Marcia Whitney was technically his boss as club manager, and he did not want to anger her.

Sunday afternoons during the summer were boring for Dennis. No football—just baseball to watch. Dennis had a "Fat Boy" in the garage and decided to take it out. It was a lovely day. He did his best thinking on his bike, and he needed to think about this for a while. His move north to the new club out on Nova Road was perfect for him.

He was pleased with himself that he had the smoking gun safely tucked away. Dennis didn't know it at the time but would soon learn that Jack Shook was on the case. He knew Shook from his days when he bartended at the old Schooner Club. They always got along and were actually friends. Shook gave him unused Dolphin tickets regularly, and they shared a love of motorcycles, not to mention goodlooking women.

Shook had complained to the owner when Dennis was forced out, because of some complaints about Dennis' occasional "offcolor" politically incorrect jokes, and Dennis was aware of his efforts.

The world is round, baby. Life comes full circle. This immutable rule in life was about to come full circle.

Chapter 15

In the office on Monday, there was no Ken Wheeler. He had vanished without a word since Jack and he talked on Saturday when he was sitting on the warehouse.

He's probably off the wagon again and going on a bender, Shook first thought, and he shared that with Dragman.

"No way, boss," Dragman said immediately. "Something bad has happened. Ken would never do this. I'm calling the Broward Sheriff's Office and see if I can find Captain Willis." Dragman harkened back to the days back in the '70s when it was then Detective Ralph Willis who made all the right moves to get some justice for Larry Driscoll when he was shot by some asshole cop down in Broward.

Shook was starting to get concerned, because of Dragman's insistence that something must be very wrong. Ken wasn't at home, and no one had heard from him since Saturday. *Let Dragman handle it, we'll get some answers soon.*

Marvella was due to come into the office at 11 a.m., and Tiffany was getting ready for her arrival.

Tiffany, Shook's legal assistant, was Tiffany Ann Treadstone. She had been with Shook for six years and was irreplaceable. She ran his practice.

Tiffany was paid well, because she was worth it and always projected a great image for the firm: good looking and smart, with a sense of humor.

Shook always signed his memos "JRS" and Tiffany was "TAT." He once commented about her initials being "TAT," and her immediate response was that it was fortunate that her middle name wasn't Irene. She was an original—a real person with a great sense of humor who was good at what she did.

Marvella promptly arrived at 11 a.m. and signed all the necessary contracts and releases. Shook got the full report and reported to Marvella what they already knew. Tyrell and Travonte's mother had called Marvella asking for a lawyer. Marvella gave her info to Shook. They had called the day before. He would refer her to Greg Crutchfield. After all, they used to work together.

Marvella was truly fortunate to have Marvin's father's health insurance through the NBA as a survivor. He would get the best of care.

All of that worked to the advantage of the defendant, Davis, and his insurance company, because of the collateral source rule. He explained it briefly to Marvella. It actually had the effect of reducing the defendant's exposure for past and future medical expenses.

Marvella left at 1 o'clock and went back to the hospital. Marvin was still in the ICU, and she needed to be there.

Shook was impressed with her strength of character and her resolve. She left, turned back, and looked him right in the eye. "Mr. Shook, you know I trust you with my life. Now, you have Marvin's. I know you will do the right thing. I prayed over this last night, and I'm sure we're doing the right thing."

Shook was not particularly religious, but he was spiritual. He understood that she meant it right from her heart. "I appreciate that, Marvella. I'll do everything in my power to get to the bottom of this and do my best for Marvin."

"Whatever you need, I will do it. If you need anything, I will be here in a heartbeat, Mr. Shook," Marvella replied as she left his office.

Shook was left standing with Tiffany as she left, and he noticed Tiffany's eyes were red and glassy. She was emotionally moved by Marvella's last words.

Shook spoke, "I'll be paying close attention to this one, Tiffany, and so will you."

"No problem, boss. I know what to do."

"Yeah, I know, just don't fuck up," Shook said.

Shook went looking for Dragman, figuring it was time for lunch, when he found him in his office on the phone. Dragman waved him in. He wrote something down feverishly, and then hung up.

"They got the car parked at the Fort Lauderdale airport but no Wheeler."

"What the hell was he doing there, Dragman?"

"He wasn't there. The car was stashed there. Its purpose is to throw us off the track into believing he has flown off somewhere. There is no record yet of him ever being there, and they are going over security video right now to see when it was driven in. I've been told to stand by. They're going to email it to me."

"I'll have Tiffany order something in for us. What's your thinking Dragman?"

"I don't ever want to think about it, but he was sitting on that warehouse when he disappeared. He was trying to figure a way inside, and he vanished. If anything happened, it's got to be connected."

"Yeah, but you are talking abduction or worse, Dragman. That's over the top for this kind of case. Let's give it to Willis and tell him what he was up to. We'll get the S.O. to get info on that warehouse."

"I'm on it, boss, like a flies on a roast. I'll be in Willis' office in an hour."

Shook sat in his office ruminating after Dragman left. "What's going on here? They must know that we know, but what if it's just coincidence? Now, there's no such thing as a coincidence. I've heard of a few, but I have never seen one."

Across town and by the lake just before the north bridge, Gretchen was meeting with Mike Kahn. She was "loaded for bear" and spent three hours disgorging the last five years spent with her husband that she had grown to detest. She had the emails, the tax returns, and the photos, which included the last one of Davis passed out in a drunken stupor in the garage.

Kahn had read the article on the Post and was on top of the facts. He decided Davis needed to be put under surveillance and that Gretchen had to stay with him for at least another two months until they were ready to file. He took his retainer and signed her up. *Ten grand is just a drop in the bucket on this one,* he thought as he left the office.

Meanwhile, it was late in the afternoon when Billy Thomas got the text in the Gardens to meet Donohue for beer. His shift officially ended at 4 o'clock. He had to finish up a crash report and clear the scene. He was late and got there at 5:30 p.m. Donohue was still there when Thomas walked in wearing street clothes. He actually disliked Thomas, but he couldn't show it. He could make anyone think he was their friend.

"Hey, Billy Ray, what's up?"

"Hey, Howard, good to see you."

I'll bet, Howard thought.

"So sit down, my man, I see you're incognito."

"Yeah, I get anonymous really good these days."

Yeah, I'll bet, Billy Ray thought.

Thomas rolled in wearing jeans and a Hawaiian print shirt and a beatup Dolphins hat. He was also wearing sunglasses. He was definitely unrecognizable.

"What are you drinking, Billy Ray?"

"I'll just take a draft, and then I've got to go."

"No problem, dude." He was privately pleased that he didn't have to spend any more time than necessary with this asshole. The shorter the time, the better.

They both made small talk, but both wanted to finish the business and move on.

"You got my envelope?"

"Yeah, Billy Ray, I got it, but I can't give it to you here."

"Well, where is it, Howard?"

"It's outside, dude."

"So, let's go. I gotta get going."

"No problem, but it's best if we don't leave together."

"I agree. You go first. I'll see you at my truck in 10 minutes."

"Sounds good. Let me pay my tab."

After paying his tab Howard left and spotted Thomas's wellused F150 over in the back of the parking lot. He grabbed the envelope and checked its contents. *Yep, 10 grand in 50s.* He walked back to the rear.

Ten minutes later, Thomas came walking out right on time. The envelope was passed under a newspaper with nothing said. Thomas got in the truck, fired it up and drove west on PGA Boulevard.

Donohue retreated to his car and made his note on his log and sent an email to Mary Jo. "Mission accomplished with 'TF.' The cats in the cradle."

This was the buzzword phrase that he always used when he reported a payoff to Mary Jo. She demanded it and demanded to know. Mary Jo had set up this elaborate little system, and each recipient of a payoff was coded. Thomas was "T," and FHP was "F." Donohue had been the bagman since he joined the "unit."

They don't pay me enough to do this shit, he thought, as he drove into the night.

Meanwhile, Shook was at home when Dragman called.

"We got the surveillance tape at the airport. His Silverado rolled in on Sunday at 4 p.m. You can't see who was driving. He's wearing a hat and sunglasses. Another car drove in behind. They left it in long term, boss."

"OK, Dragman, we need to get into that warehouse now."

"Willis is going first thing in the morning. I'm going to meet them there."

"OK, dude, keep me posted. Shook was worried when he hung up the phone.

Chapter 16

It was 8 o'clock in the morning when Calvin pulled up to the front gate of the warehouse. Willis was there along with Dragman and two marked units. Detective Ralph Willis had located Calvin through the owner. Calvin was renting the warehouse under the name of Markham Properties. He had agreed to meet Willis there in the morning.

Calvin knew who Dragman was but didn't reveal that bit of intel. Dragman had no idea who this guy was.

He clicked open the fence, and they all drove into the parking lot.

As they got out of their cars, Willis spoke first, "Mr. Fuccerino?"

"Yes, that's me, but just call me Calvin, please, detective."

"OK, Calvin, I appreciate your cooperation. We need to get inside for a few minutes."

"No problem, detective," and the automatic door opened with ease.

They all walked inside to see a half empty warehouse, holding only six classic cars. There was an old '60s vintage Corvette, two '70s Camaros, a '63 Plymouth Sport Fury Golden Commando, a '36 Ford Coupe and a '55 Chevy truck, restored.

There was no trace of the Audi.

Willis spoke up, "Calvin, have any cars been removed from here since Saturday?"

"Not that I'm aware of. Why?"

"We're working on a missing person's report, and we had info that a wrecked Audi was brought here last Saturday."

"Well, detective, I don't know anything about that. As you can see, we use this warehouse for storage and repair of our classic car business."

Dragman walked around the warehouse and took a few pictures, his mind was spinning. The inside was finished off with an office, and there was a hydraulic lift and a huge workbench filled with tools. Something was seriously wrong with this picture. He knew the Audi had been towed here.

Willis spoke up again. "Calvin, I noticed the surveillance cameras outside. Where's the control box?"

"It's in the office, detective."

They adjourned to the office and ran through the video memory. There was nothing seen on the memory for Saturday, but it was all fast-forwarded. No record of any delivery of a wrecked Audi. This was beginning to get odd. The surveillance had been turned off when the Audi arrived and left.

Willis thanked Calvin, and they left. Outside, they huddled in Willis's car.

Dragman spoke up. "Ralph, I'm telling you right now that a tow truck from Jack's Towing delivered that Audi here Saturday."

"OK, Dragman, but it's not here now, and it's easy to disable the video before you bring it in."

"Yeah, but the driver had to meet someone."

"OK, Dragman, you run that down for me and let me know. Right now, all we have is a missing person and hearsay based on hearsay. He's probably shacked up with some broad somewhere."

"OK, Ralph, I'm with you on this. I'll get back to you."

Dragman left, traveling north on I95, and checked in with Shook. Shook directed him to the towing company to get the lowdown and get it fast.

Turner was in the office when Dragman walked in. He was not happy to see him.

"Where's the Quattro, Jack?"

"Look, Dragman, I've got nothing else to say. I told you what I told you guys based on our agreement. I can't say anything else."

"Jack, look, man, we got a missing person now, and I don't want to get the cops here. You've got to tell me."

"Look, man, I told you what I told you. Don't jam me up, because I'll deny everything. There are no records. My business is at stake here."

"Well, tell me one thing, Jack, did you guys move that Quattro again?"

"Hell no, Dragman, and that's the truth."

Dragman left and drove to the office.

Meanwhile, Calvin Fuccerino was on the phone with his brother as soon as Willis and his entourage left.

"That asshole, Drakenleader, was here with the cops, man."

"What?"

"You heard me. That means that that lawyer Shook somehow knows that we had that crashed Audi here."

"Well, Wheeler worked for Shook, dude, we already knew that."

"So what do we do?"

"Well, if I tell the redhead, she'll shut us down, and I need the fucking money, man."

"She ain't going to shut us down, we know too much."

"Yeah, we know too much."

"So where the hell is he now, Melvin?"

"Last night I called Cancun and talked to my man. He's in the safe house in Miami, and they're injecting him every day. He's now officially a heroin junkie. They been giving him LSD, speedballs too. He doesn't know shit and is never going to remember shit."

"Incidentally, Calvin, why the fuck didn't we just eliminate him?"

"Orders, Melvin. The redhead is on board with his abduction and over-dose. He'll be in a Mexican prison within a week, and he'll think he's Paco Sanchez, drug dealer. He'll die in a Mexican prison."

"Why did she want that rather than a vanished witness?"

"He used to work there, Melvin, and he violated the confidentiality agreement. She wanted to teach him a lesson. She figures if he does escape one day, then there's no connection to Conveyance, and she and everybody else walks. It's called plausible deniability.

"That's some coldblooded shit, man. I hope we're wellpaid, Calvin."

"Yes, this is our biggest payday ever, dude. Just stay with the plan and we walk with serious six figures."

"I'm down with that, dude, but what about this detective, what's his name?

"You mean Ralph Willis?"

"Yeah, man, what the fuck?"

"Simple, we cooperate. We stick with the story and stay low. We never saw the dude. There's no evidence he was ever here."

"So, who did you get to steal his truck and dump it if it's in South Miami?"

"Just some old friends, man. They took five grand and laughed all the way to the airport."

"OK, dude, I gotcha. Just don't fuck up, OK?"

"No problem. I got this."

"So how did you pull this off, man? I mean what the fuck, sooner or later someone will take his fingerprints?"

"Well, since you asked, it's all so simple. First, his prints were sanded and they amputated two fingers. Next they got him in prison as an escaped Mexican drug dealer who really is dead with no family alive to connect the dots. Next, it was just a matter of a ten grand bribe."

"Where'd the money come from, man?"

"It came out of our budget, dipshit, and it's all cost."

"Damn, I'd really hate to cross that Stalinowsky bitch, Calvin."

"Yeah, me either, but not to worry, we won't and life goes on, baby. Just remember, asshole, it never gets to her. It's cut off at Howard. It's called plausible deniability.

"Plausible what?"

"Deniability, asshole."

"Got it."

"Good, keep it that way."

"OK, we'll just make damn sure no one finds him."

"You have nothing to fear, dude, he's gone."

"So who let the driver in the door when the truck arrived?"

"I did, man, and no one else was here."

"Well, here's what I'm telling Mary Jo. We moved the car, and it's in the west warehouse. Jack's driver will just be mistaken about the address he delivered the wreck to."

"Better yet, just get Jack to say the address was the west warehouse. That way we are clear. Better yet, get that damn thing into the Broward storage yard tonight and get Jack's driver to say that's where it was taken.

"Better yet, get them to do it and say that's where he took it in the first place."

"Yeah, yeah, that's the ticket. And I'll tell that Red Devil where it is."

"Red Devil. I like it, Jack."

"Melvin dialed Mary Jo's cell phone, and she answered. "Mary Jo, you need to know that a Broward detective and Shook's investigator showed up at the warehouse this morning looking for the Quattro."

"What?"

"You heard me, Mary Jo."

"Why a cop, Melvin?"

"Apparently, Ken Wheeler is missing, and they had some intel that the car had been delivered there. The car is gone, and we're dropping it at Brevard Salvage this afternoon."

"Jack's tow driver will be told to say that's where he took it, right, Melvin?"

"Exactly. Just letting you know, Mary Jo."

"OK. Is the Quattro ready for public inspection, Melvin?"

"Yeah. Harry took care of that. It's ready, Mary Jo."

"OK, get it to Broward Salvage. Now!"

"Got it."

Mary Jo hung up the phone and called Donohue. "Howard, get over to Jack and pay him off. Make sure he is informed that his driver took the Quattro to Broward Salvage, not to the warehouse. I'll make sure the salvage yard is clear on the handle."

"Got it, Mary Jo."

Howard drove immediately to Jack's Towing and caught Jack in the office. Jack was not happy to see him but feigned his typical goodnatured greeting. "Hey, Howard, what's up?"

"You know what's up, Jack. Here's your envelope. By the way, your driver delivered the Audi to Broward Salvage on Saturday. Make sure of that, you savvy?"

"Me savvy, boss," Howard grinned as he said it.

"Gotta go, man."

Jack was a little nervous with the development, but it offered him a way out. *No problem*, he thought. He opened up the envelope and counted his cash. *Five grand, not bad.*

Howard left and drove east on Southern Boulevard. He emailed Mary Jo: "Mission accomplished with JT. Cat's in the cradle."

Chapter 17

It must've been 8:30 a.m. when Paco found himself partially blinded by the sunlight coming through the prison cell window. He opened his eyes and was immediately blinded. He closed them, but the light was still there. He waited, and it slowly disappeared.

He was able to sit up, although he was shaking. He felt like he had the chills and couldn't stop quivering.

He tried to stand up. He couldn't. He fell directly back onto the damp concrete floor. A dirty mattress was on the floor over in the corner.

Laying there, Paco finally was able to focus. He was in a cell. He knew not where. He was alone. It measured six foot by eight foot with a steel door. He had a window. Insects were crawling on the floor. The toilet had no lid and was stained almost black.

He managed to sit up and sat against the wall. He began to hear voices and noises. It became louder, and, suddenly, the food port opened, and a tray was pushed in. Nothing was said to him, but the voices were speaking Spanish.

He managed to pull himself up, take the metal tray in a shaking hand, and sit back down without spilling the yellow flour tortillawrapped red beans. He ate it in seconds. There was a hunk of stale bread and a cup of water. He ate it all.

He sat back and surveyed his surroundings. He was starting to come around. A few minutes later, he stood and gazed out between the bars of the metal grate that covered the window. He could see buildings and hear voices outside speaking Spanish. *Where the fuck am I?* he thought.

About 20 minutes later, the food port opened, and a voice said, "Dame la bandeja cabrón."

Holy shit, thought Paco, *I'm in a Spanish jail. This asshole just told me to give him the tray, and he called me an asshole.*

Paco instinctively put the tray on the food port and said, "Gracias."

It disappeared, and the food port slammed shut.

Paco sat in silence and began to fantasize about a hot, steaming cup of coffee—lots of cream, lots of sugar.

A few moments later, the door opened, and a guard stood before him. "Párate pendejo."

Paco knew immediately that he needed to stand up. The guard stood back and shouted, "Salte y haz la fila."

Paco knew enough Spanish to get outside and get in line. Once outside his cell, he saw the cellblock. It was huge and double-decked. As he looked, he saw a man looking at him and say, "Hey, gringo, who the fuck are you?"

Paco looked back and realized he wasn't sure what his name was. Suddenly, from behind, a voice yelled out, "That's Paco Sanchez, cadrón. Don't fuck with him."

Paco turned around and studied the source of the voice that came from the rear and said nothing but instinctively felt the need to nod at the man.

They were marched into an open yard, and Paco walked slowly into the clear. He was surrounded by high walls and guards around the top. He was in a prison and wondered, *How the hell did I get in here? What did I do to deserve this, and where the fuck is this place?*

Again, from behind, the same voice came to his ear, "Hey, Paco, how long have you been here, cadrón?"

Paco turned and came facetoface with the inmate who seemed to know his name. He was small, maybe five foot five at the most and pudgy. He seemed to know who the hell he was and was full of questions.

"OK, man, how do you know my name, and who the hell are you and where the fuck are we?" asked Paco.

The small, fat little man looked stunned and took a step back. "So, you finally came out of your shell and woke up?"

"Are you shitting me, man? What are you talking about, and who the fuck are you?"

"I'm Willie James, man, and you're Paco Sanchez. You've been walking around this place for weeks mumbling some shit about being lost and saying nothing much else."

"So, what is this place, Willie, and how do you know me?"

"Welcome to Fuente Grande, Paco, and you and I came in together from Cancún. You weren't saying much, so I figured you were just some junkie that got lost. The guards have told me that you're Paco Sanchez and that you were a serious dude. You look like an Anglo, which is why he called you a gringo. My cell is next to yours."

"I've got to sit down, Willie, and take all this in. Let's walk over here to the shade and talk this over."

"Look, Willie," he began, "I really appreciate your interest, man, but this is all news to me."

"I can see that, Paco, so what the fuck can we do about it?"

"What do you mean?"

"Well, we gotta get out of here, and I know you must have people that can help."

"Listen, Willie, I need help and the only person I can trust is you. You've got to let me soak all this shit in, Willie. I agree we need to get the fuck out of here, but, hell, I just found out where I am; and, to be brutally frank, I don't think I'm really Paco Sanchez."

"What do you mean, man? Of course you're Paco."

Seeing the obvious benefit of accepting this moniker, Paco backtracked. "Yeah, yeah, yeah, I guess I need to trust *someone,* and it might as well be you. Yeah, I'm Paco."

"That's more like it, man. You need to snap out of this crazy shit you been pulling. It's not getting you anywhere."

"What do you mean?"

"Well, the guards say you are Paco Sanchez, with the Corev Cartel that uses the Altermundistas for cover. They say you and El Guapo were good friends, and they finally got you. They don't fuck with you, though, because they are tied to El Guapo. You must be a bad motherfucker, and they don't want to piss you off."

"No shit?"

"No shit, Paco, and you know it. Now how the fuck are we going to get out of here?"

"Let me think about this, man. It may take a while, but, really, all I need is money to bribe the guards."

"So, who do you know, and how can you help, cabron?"

"Well, I'm tied into a group also out of Cancún, but we just run hookers, all kinds, from streetwalkers to the most beautiful women you can find on this planet."

"So, what did you do to get thrown in here?"

"I double-crossed a couple of cops who didn't get their money. Truth is, I didn't double-cross anyone. I didn't get mine, so I couldn't get them theirs. They're pissed, and I'm here."

"So, what am I charged with?"

"You escaped from prison, man, and they caught you. You must be one strungout junkie not to know that. You've been on the run for two years, they say."

"I have no lawyer, and I have no pending charges?"

"No, they may try you for escape, but your sentence is 60 years anyway, so what's the point?"

"So, our only option is to escape?"

"That's our only option, Paco, because I just can't be locked up. I'm leaving, and you should, too, because you're going to die here unless you escape."

"What do I have to do to get a cup of coffee around here, Willie?"

"No problem, Paco, how do you like it?"

"Lots of cream, lots of sugar."

"You'll have it tomorrow morning."

An hour later, they were led into the cellblock. They only had two meals a day, so they had to make it count. They got dinner through the food port. It looked like a burrito and had some kind of meat in it.

The heat in the cellblock was intense, but it cooled down after midnight when it actually got cold.

The next morning, Paco got coffee. He sat and was deep in thought. *I guess I've got to ride with this Paco shit for as far as it will take me*, he thought. *Willie didn't like the "I'm not Paco" routine. Somehow, I don't think the regime here is going to be impressed with the "you got the wrong dude" defense. We are way past that.*

Chapter 18

It was a Wednesday night, and Ed Baldwin was at the club, sitting at the bar. Dennis was on duty, and they were joking with each other. Dennis was in rare form tonight. His jokes were really good when the women were not there.

Privately, Dennis disliked Ed intensely, but he couldn't let him see it. It was just another "bigshot" that he had to suck up to. He was a member and former Board member, and the price to pay for his welldeserved salary was to put up with these arrogant assholes—Ed was at the top of the list.

Ed's bill each month topped five grand, and it was paid in full with a firm check. Life was good with members like Ed. They were easy. Just act like you're their best friend, tell them jokes, and listen to their bullshit. No problem for Dennis; he was the master of this routine.

There was only one other person at the bar, and they were down at the other end when Ed motioned Dennis in close and, almost in a whisper, said, "Dennis, I understand you were on duty the Friday that Harrison Davis was here and then in that car crash."

Dennis was taken aback but didn't show it. *Gotta be cool*, he thought.

"Well, yes, Eddie. I was," he replied.

"Well, you know that it wouldn't be good for the club if it also got out how much he had to drink, right?"

"Well, yes, I guess it wouldn't be too cool to have that information made public."

"No, it wouldn't. Now, we're counting on you to keep all that confidential. I know you know the consequences of serving someone who was already intoxicated, right?"

"Of course, yes, I can do that, Ed. You can count on me. But what do I do if the cops show up?" Dennis was privately pissed at the implied threat.

Ed was a little disturbed by this comment but answered quickly, "Confidentiality is one of the cornerstones of this club, Dennis, and I'm sure you know that. I want you to understand how important and grateful we all are for your understanding."

"Of course, Ed."

"And, just to let you know how grateful we are, a gentleman will be by to show you our gratitude. His name is Donohue. He'll be here and about 30 minutes."

"Oh, OK, Ed. You can count on me. I'm with the program. No problem."

"Thanks, Dennis. I knew we could count on you."

Ed got up and left. As soon as he got in the car, he called Mary Jo.

"Mary Jo, the bartender is on board. Just have Donohue pay him a visit. I think about five grand will do it."

"Thanks for the call, Ed. I'll take care of it."

Donohue was home when his cell went off. It was Mary Jo. *Damn*, he thought. *Doesn't that bitch ever stop?* He took the call.

"Howard, take five large and get it to a bartender at the Oeste Palma International Golf Club in western Melbourne right now. His name is Dennis, and he's there. His code will be 'DB.'"

"Yes, ma'am, I'm on it, but it'll take me about 90 minutes." He hung up.

It was about 10 o'clock when he pulled up to the valet. They seemed to be expecting him.

"I'll only be a minute," he said.

He walked into the lounge, and it was about half full. He was privately pleased with himself that he had brought a jacket. He walked up to the bar at the empty end and asked for Dennis.

"You got him, sir. Are you a guest of a member?"

"You might say that. I've got something for you."

He slid the newspaper across the bar that was folded with the envelope inside.

Dennis took it and smiled.

Howard said, "Goodbye, Dennis." Then, Howard strode out the door. Dennis immediately walked into the men's room and closed the door and privately examined the contents: Five grand in fifties.

Hmmm, he thought to himself, *this is getting interesting*.

Howard pulled out of the driveway and emailed Mary Jo on her private email: "cat's in the cradle for 'DB.'"

Chapter 19

A month had passed, and Gretchen was at The Breakers with Harrison. It was the United Way soirée, and Harrison's company was one of the main sponsors.

A lot of movers and shakers were here: politicians, doctors, lawyers, big-time corporate. Harrison had had a few drinks and was in rare form. She thought about warning him, but she stopped. *Let him hang himself.*

Privately, she enjoyed having that feeling of quiet confidence, knowing that she had him by the balls. Two counts of manslaughter by an intoxicated motorist for starters, two fifteen-year felonies. Thank God she took those photographs of him passed out drunk in the garage. What an asshole.

It's hard to be such a deceptive bitch, she thought, *but you gotta do what you gotta do.*

No one except her best friend, Nikki, knew about her plans—and certainly not her boyfriend, Jerry Fox.

Speaking of him, she had to see him again, no later than tomorrow. *I need him. I have needs,* she thought.

Meanwhile, she had to listen to all the bullshit and smile and pretend to be interested in the spectacle.

Harrison had his cadre of clapping seals present, including that little bitch administrative assistant of his. She had her radar up.

The rest of the cadre was made up of each division chief, certain board members, and the CFO and his wife. The usual suspects. She wondered what would happen to all these phonies when the fecal matter hit the oscillating fan.

Enough of that. I'll get the house, the cars, the retirement, permanent alimony, hell, anything I want, she thought.

Meanwhile, Shook was in his office preparing for the evidentiary hearing filed on his "true bill of discovery" against Conveyance Mutual Benefit, demanding injunctive relief to produce the Audi in question. It had been over a month since Wheeler's disappearance. He really wanted sworn testimony from someone, preferably Mary Jo, about what happened to the damn thing.

His complaint named Mary Jo, or a person with actual knowledge, or the summons which would be served on the agent for service of process of record.

Wheeler was still missing, and Dragman had been by to see Jack at Jack's Towing again, who, all of a sudden, disclosed the location of the tow as Broward Salvage. Everybody was closing ranks.

He knew something had happened to Wheeler. His truck was still at the airport under surveillance. This was not good, and he was thinking the unthinkable—that somebody had killed him, but who and why?

Everybody was gone, and he had a pile of pink phone message slips to run through. He still used a manual receptionist and the "live" after-hours answering service.

Browsing through the messages, he found one from his buddy, Mike Kahn, marked "urgent."

There were various others, including one from a young bank teller that he had been flirting with who had called him. Her name was Yovanda Ruiz, and she was Hispanic, as was usual for Shook. That was his weakness: big, beautiful brown Spanish eyes. He resisted the temptation and decided on calling Kahn back.

"Jackie, what's up, dude?" Kahn said.

"Nothing much, just working as usual, Mikey." He called him "Mikey" when he called him "Jackie."

"Listen, dude, I've got something for you that you've got to keep graveyard for about two months."

"OK, Mike, I'm interested."

"I represent Gretchen Davis, Harrison Davis' wife. She is about to file on him. She's got some very damaging shit on him, and I've got to keep it confidential until we finish the case. I can't go into it now, but, trust me, it's some really nasty shit."

"Like what, Mike?"

"Can't do it. I'm just alerting you that it's coming. She's got to cut her deal first, and then the hammer will fall."

"OK, I'll be all ears. I appreciate the call, but I'm really curious."

"I can't divulge anything now but stay tuned."

"How long is this going to take, Mike?"

"I'd say three to six months tops."

"OK, but I'm concerned. You heard that Wheeler is missing, right?"

"No, I hadn't. What's that all about?"

"Well, we had gotten some intel that your client's soon-to-be ex's car had been moved to Broward, and Wheeler was sitting on it when he disappeared."

"No shit?"

"No shit, Mike. We're very concerned. I don't suppose you've got any info that might help?"

"No, Jack, nothing on that, and that's the truth. That's some over-the-top shit, though."

"Well, if you hear anything, let me know, OK?"

"I will, Jack, I will. Stay tuned."

Kahn hung up, sat back and digested the call. *What the hell is this about?*

Shook had gone through his pile of messages and came to Yovanda's. *What a name*, he thought. *I've got to call.*

He dialed her number, but she didn't answer.

Well, at least I returned her call, he thought. *I'm at least 20 years older than she is. She's really too young, but, damn, she is good looking and friendly . . . She's probably on a date. No woman that good-looking would be home on a Thursday.*

Chapter 20

A week had passed, and it was Thursday, and it's 10 o'clock. Shook's in his office—still no Wheeler. The phone rings, and it's Baldwin. Ed speaks first. A week had passed since talking with Mike Kahn.

"Shook, you piece of shit, how are you?"

"Always a pleasure to hear from you, Ed. Killed any dogs lately?"

Ed ignored the comment.

"What can I do for you?"

"This bullshit—true bill of discovery—that you filed is on my desk."

"So what, Ed?"

"Well, if you wanted to see the car, you could have seen it any time. All you had to do was ask."

"Yeah, right, Ed. I'm glad to see that you still have a firm grip on bullshit. I did ask, and I was stonewalled."

"Asked who?"

"You'll find out, Ed. You might want to talk to your client. Also, where the fuck is Wheeler?"

"What are you talking about, Jackie, my boy?"

"Don't call me Jackie, asshole. Talk to your fucking client, and then talk to the judge next Monday."

"I'm not available Monday, Jackie."

"Of course you're not. I'm sure you've got something very important to attend to. Me, I'm going to be in front of Judge Murphy at 9 o'clock. Have one of your typical fucked-up days, Ed, I got to go."

"Listen, Jack, don't hang up. Don't you know we could be friends?"

"I can't imagine that, Ed."

"Jack, I can get you $1 million if you just stop that shit and come to your senses."

"That's strange, Ed, it used to be 30 pieces of silver."

"You're hopeless, Jack."

"No, Ed, you're the hopeless one. See you in court."

Shook hung up and smiled. It was so nice to talk to Ed again. He knew that Lucas would be there, not Ed. Then again, Judge John C. Murphy, a damn good judge whose only negative claim to fame was an altercation where he was accused of striking an assistant Public Defender, was up for reelection the following year, so maybe he would put in an appearance. He enjoyed handling cases in Cocoa. He could have lunch with his old buddies, Greg Crutchfield and Joe Caruso, at "Lellos."

Truth is, he despised Ed. He stood for everything wrong in the practice of law. He always threatened you, called your pleadings bullshit. He lied about everything. He would not cooperate with scheduling hearings. His witnesses, especially his experts, were paid liars. He hated him, and he enjoyed beating him.

Ed had hung up, too, and was sitting at his desk, pissed off. *Goddamn that Shook. When I'm finished with him, he'll be flipping burgers at Burger King,* he thought.

He screamed out the door at his secretary. "Doris, Goddammit, get Mary Jo on the line."

She complied, of course, and Mary Jo got on the line.

"Mary Jo, we got to do something about this Shook shit."

"Couldn't agree more, Ed. Why are you calling me?"

"Well, do you have the 'unit' on this one?"

"That's a stupid question, Ed. Of course, I do."

"Well, I mean completely on this case?"

"Yes, Ed, completely."

"So, you got the Fuccerinos on this, right?"

"Yes, I do. Why are you asking me this?"

"Well, last one we did with them, they kept telling me that they only take orders from you."

"Well, that's true, Ed, so what?"

"Well, what are they doing about Shook? Last time you tried something, it didn't work out."

"Yes, I remember. Calvin tells me that they got another idea. They got to some cute little bank teller at Shook's bank, and she's very cooperative."

"Well, keep me posted, Mary Jo."

"Of course, Ed."

"What about this hearing Monday?"

"Well, I'm sure as hell not going to testify, and neither is anyone else. It's available for inspection out at Broward Salvage. Make him look stupid."

"He says he asked, and no one would tell him."

"Well, you know how to handle that. Send him a 'safe harbor' letter under FS 57.105 and see what develops."

"Good idea."

"Of course, it is, Ed; and, oh, by the way, I thought you were supposed to be the lawyer."

"It's handled, Mary Jo," he said and then hung up the phone.

Damn, I hate it when she talks to me like I'm an idiot, he thought.

Ed's next call was to Calvin. He got on the phone. "So, Calvin, we got this Audi covered?"

"Yes, Eddie, my boy, we do. It's at Broward Salvage, and the black box is fucked up."

"How is it fucked up?"

"Water damage, Eddie. It must have been rained on."

"What's with this bank teller, Calvin?"

"She's on board. She's a child compared to Shook and knows how to play the game. She's on and has already received her deposit."

"So, how much, Calvin?"

"Ten grand."

"Damn, that seems to be the going rate. Who gave it to her? Donohue?"

"Yes, it was Donohue."

"How did you do this, man?"

"Well, we surveilled Shook for two weeks and saw this little flirtation going on. We sent in the black widow and gave her the ten grand right after that."

"Good work, Calvin, keep me advised."

Ed hung up and sent Shook a fax. Ed falsely claimed that he was told that the car was at Broward Salvage, and the next they were going to seek fees if he actually had the hearing.

Shook got the fax and had Dragman on the road within 30 minutes. He picked up Hillman in Pompano. Hillman had his mobile diagnostic computer with him when they found the Quattro. The black box was dead. He photographed everything and estimated the crush damage to correlate with a point of collision speed to be 75 mph.

Shook wrote a corrective letter and did not cancel the hearing. He knew they got to the box and that Henry was on tap to testify.

The weekend was uneventful and a rather slow one for Shook. He ignored the toxic fax he received from Ed.

Dragman was beside himself about Wheeler. The truck had been towed and inventoried and processed. Nothing to report. No strange prints, no nothing.

Monday morning finally arrived. The drive to Viera was always challenging, and parking was an issue.

The hearing on the bill of discovery was colorful. Ed sat back, and Lucas did the talking. They provided the car and did not understand what the problem was.

Hillman testified about how he tried to inspect it the day after the accident and that it had disappeared.

Shook put in his email to Mary Jo, in evidence, that had no response.

Hillman testified that the onboard data recorder had obviously been tampered with.

Lucas had nothing except excuses.

A bill of discovery was granted. The order provided that the spoliation was proven, and he would entertain sanctions.

Shook left the hearing with a victory, and Ed left muttering to himself.

"I've had enough of this Shook shit," he mumbled as he got to the elevator. "This motherfucker is going down."

Shook got back and put the finishing touches on his complaint.

Dragman had stopped calling Detective Willis. He was getting nowhere. They were concentrating on the case, as well as other work.

The discovery package went out with the complaint. He called Greg Crutchfield, who confirmed they were filing on behalf of the two dead boys. Ed's firm was on the case as well.

Chapter 21

It had been two months since the accident, and Gretchen was out with Jerry. It was one of those typical late September Friday nights. The temperature was still in the mid-80s at 10 o'clock at night, and Gretchen was on her fourth white wine at the Rendezvous Pub on the beach in Vero.

Jerry was knocking down tequilas with beer chasers, and Gretchen had started taking some tequila shots with Jerry.

Sitting over in the corner at the end of the bar was David Hanks, a black dude. It was dark, and he was wearing a Miami Marlins hat, watching through his sunglasses.

David, a junior bartender at the golf club, was hanging with his buddy, JT, and his girlfriend Miranda.

"See that well-dressed and well-lubricated woman in the corner?" he asked JT.

"Yeah, so what?" JT said.

"That's Gretchen Davis, wife of Harrison Davis, big-time member of the club."

"Really . . ." he replied.

"She really looks friendly with that guy, whoever he is."

"Yeah, JT, she is definitely friendly, to say the least."

"I don't think Harrison would be too pleased with this."

"So, who's that guy sitting over there in the other corner?"

"I don't know, JT. Why do you ask?"

"Well, he's got his phone on them, and it looks like he's videoing the whole scene, man."

"No shit?"

"No shit, David. Just watch but don't look too obvious."

Hanks pulled the brim of his hat down and studied the stranger sitting in the corner. He was a black dude, well-dressed, and it looked like he was waiting for someone. He also was on the phone.

"You're right, JT. He really is studying Gretchen and her boyfriend. And that dude has headphones."

"So, what are you going to do about it?"

"Nuttin'. Absolutely nuttin'. There's absolutely no fucking way I'm getting involved. Davis' wife is a lawyer, and she would have my ass barbecued. Besides, she doesn't even know I exist. I've only seen her maybe three or four times and I'm just the help, man. I'm invisible to her. I'm just a fucking waiter at the club. I am nothing to her."

"So, why not rattle her chain, man? She looks like a truly spoiled bitch who could use a reality check to me."

"No, I'm staying out of this shit, JT. I'm just glad that it's dark as shit in this place."

"Hey, the guy's leaving. He's out the door."

"Yeah, OK, but what the fuck? Ignore it, man."

Gretchen was feeling no pain and had decided it was time to leave. She stumbled out the door with Jerry and wandered off into the night.

Unbeknownst to Gretchen, she was being surveilled. The well-dressed black dude, Brandon Dinkus, was actually an operative working for Investigations, Inc. out of Lauderdale. Gretchen had violated the well-known and well-entrenched first rule of screwing around: it's called the "100-mile rule." You needed 100 miles to be between you and your wife or husband to avoid being seen. And, oh, by the way, even then, you could still be seen.

Gretchen was driving tonight. Her black 450 Lexus started to pull out of the parking lot and stopped. It retreated into a back corner of the lot and parked.

Brandon hung back. He sat in his plainJane fourdoor crown Vic and didn't move. He waited five minutes. The Lexus was parked back in the shadows, and nothing was happening.

He got his tablet out and tested it. It was powered up. He had just gotten it. The video capabilities were phenomenal—the latest technology. He exited the Vic without activating the interior light and walked around the back down to the back row behind the Lexus.

There, he found Gretchen giving Jerry oral sex. She was undressed from the waist down.

Brandon walked to the passenger side of the car, very slowly, and turned on the tablet; it amazed him that the video quality was so good with so little light. He was actually standing behind them to the rear, but he had the tablet perfectly positioned. She was working on Jerry's erect penis with great enthusiasm. There was moaning and Jerry kept repeating, "Go, baby, go."

Suffice it to say that this was worth every dime of the exorbitant fee being paid to capture this shabby little slice of Gretchen's life.

The thought of chrome on trailer hitches was running through Brandon's mind when he stepped back away from the car and quietly walked back to his. He had captured the whole sordid episode without being detected. This was a beautiful thing.

His mission was to wait them out and follow them. He checked his work while waiting. It was beautiful. *Gretchen was really taking the chrome off the trailer hitch, baby*, he thought.

About 10 minutes later, the Lexus' lights came on, and they moved out of the lot. Brandon waited for a few seconds before he followed. He passed them off to his coworker, James Henry, who was parked down the street.

James pulled in behind them. They turned right and headed south down U.S. Route 1. James was in pursuit and reported that Jerry was now driving. Gretchen had been sitting in the passenger front seat but had laid down to the left and was not visible. James marveled at Jerry's ability to drive while getting his "mobile hummer."

Damn, that Gretchen sure likes to give head, was James' only other thought.

They drove through Vero and Stuart and continued south.

Jerry pulled east off U.S. Route 1 just before the Jupiter bridge over the inlet and pulled into the Jupiter Beach Hotel and Spa on the ocean.

James and Brandon hung way back as Gretchen and Jerry valeted the car and walked in together. Gretchen had a small bag; Jerry had no luggage.

James was elected to go into the lobby and watch the registration. The lobby was crowded, so he blended in. He was able to get within earshot of the room number, 712, seventh floor on the ocean. Gretchen signed the guest card. They collected their key and walked to the elevator.

Brandon's tablet recorded the walk to the elevator. They got in and disappeared. *Mission accomplished so far. Now, we need to wait them out.* He retreated to the parking lot and checked in with James.

"This is great shit, man. I got some film of Gretchen going down on this guy. Who the fuck is he to her anyway?"

"His name is Jerry Fox, and he's her personal trainer, Brandon. We've been tailing them for weeks, and this is the best shit we got."

"I hope they don't spend the night, man. I want to get some sleep tonight."

"Hey, go ahead and sleep. I'll take the first shift. If anything happens, I'll call. Just make sure you answer."

"Thanks, James. I'm on scene."

It was about 12:30 a.m. when they reappeared and had the Lexus brought up. *Damn, that's a very expensive crib just to have sex in*, Brandon thought.

He woke up James and led the procession out after Gretchen and Jerry.

Jerry was driving again, and Gretchen put her head in his lap.

Damn! Enough already! Brandon thought.

They drove back to Jerry's apartment out on Village Drive, and Gretchen drove home.

Wait until Mary Jo sees this shit. Then, he and James called it a night.

It was 8:30 in the morning when Brandon called Calvin.

"Hey, boss, just wanted to make sure you were up before I called you."

"So, what you got, Brandon?"

"We got her cold. I even got her giving Jerry head in the parking lot in Vero before they drove to the Jupiter Beach Club where they checked in for two hours. I got some good video of them sucking face in the lounge, and she was in his lap when he drove up to the valet and back to his place where she dropped him off."

"Damn, that is some good shit. So, Mr. Davis is certainly getting his money's worth?"

"So, who's paying for this anyway, Calvin?"

"Believe it or not, the 'unit' is on this. It's actually his insurance company."

"No shit?"

"No shit."

"So why in the world is his insurance company doing this?"

"Well, it's simple, Brandon. The client was certain that his wife was up to something, and she's the one who drove him away from the scene of the crash when he was shitfaced. He reported it to the redhead, and she put us on Gretchen."

"Damn, what the fuck kind of insurance coverage is that, man?"

"It's the kind we can't buy, Brandon."

"OK, I'll be in the office at 10 a.m. I'll bring the shit."

"Good, see you, man."

Calvin hung up the phone and sat back, smiled, and thought to himself, *This is going to be good. This is better than even Mary Jo ever dreamed. There's no way this bitch is going to turn on us when she finds out what her husband has tucked away. She will be delighted, and my fee will be paid without question. Life is good.*

Chapter 22

It was late August. Marvin was still at the rehab center, and Wheeler had vanished from the face of the earth. Gretchen had provoked a fight with Harrison at the house when he came home shitfaced two weeks ago, and she called the cops. He was arrested and taken to jail. She has a nocontact order on the criminal case and a domestic violence injunction against Harrison. She now had exclusive use and possession of the house in Breakers West, and Harrison could not come within 500 feet of his own house or Gretchen. Harrison had retreated to Nassau, to avoid service of process, and he wasn't coming back anytime soon.

Gretchen filed for divorce first and still had Michael Kahn as her attorney. Harrison hired Walter Rose and filed a counter petition. Things between them were about to get nasty. Gretchen and her lawyer still had no idea about the surveillance and were feeling very selfassured.

Meanwhile, it's just another typical day for Shook who was in his office preparing for the day.

The mail normally arrived at 10 o'clock in the morning, and Marvin's traffic homicide report was finally in. Trooper Thomas's report laid the responsibility firmly on the Sentra. The Sentra had "violated the Audi's rightofway," causing the Audi to move to the right, and then the left, which caused the collision to occur in the center of the roadway.

The report was silent about the speed at the point of collision (POC) and under "Driver Defects" relating to the Audi, the trooper had checked off "none."

The bloodwork had come back on the driver of the Sentra, and there was a general report of THC in his system. Shook already had Tyrell's medical records and lab work, and he knew there were trace amounts of metabolites. It was not a major problem.

It puzzled Shook why Thomas made it sound more important than it was; and there was no mention of the reason for the lack of blood or urine on the part of Mr. Davis despite Florida's law that requires all drivers to be tested in the event of a death.

Even more troubling was the assertion that Marvin was not wearing his seatbelt. He wondered why Thomas would report this when Hillman had reported that the seatbelt was "definitely in use," because it was severely stretched. He was privately glad that he had bought the salvage on the Sentra and had the vehicle stored away at a warehouse out on West Belvedere Road.

The report also made a very big deal of the Sentra's vehicle defects. The tires were either bald or nearly bald. This was true, but this really was not a significant factor due to how the collision occurred.

The report also made no mention of the skid marks west of the POC, the reentry roadway scuff marks, or the entire trail off the shoulder. There was no mention either of the eyewitness's side of the events. In short, the report was a disaster for Marvin. He wondered why Thomas would do such a lousy job on this case. He was perplexed.

To top it off, rumors had begun to surface in the legal community that Judge Murphy would be faced with opposition next year when he faced reelection. This perplexed Shook at first as well, since Murphy carried a generally good reputation for fairness, objectivity, and impartiality. He sensed that Ed was up to his old games of intimidation but would not go public with his support for Murphy's opposition, whoever it was going to be.

Judge Murphy was a decent judge and a decent man, but he was not without some personal history. Somewhere back in the dust lurked his diabolical exwife who worked against him six years ago when he was reelected, but he overcame her treachery.

The day was growing late, and he had other things on his mind, namely meeting Yovanda at the Schooner Club after work. She had asked him to pick her up at the bank after she balanced her drawer, and the time had come. Things were getting to the point of "critical mass" with her, and she was becoming far more friendly.

He climbed in his black Five Series Mercedes that he had just purchased, and which he was still becoming acquainted with its finer points, and pulled it out of the garage.

Yovanda was out front when he picked her up, and she jumped in and gave him a big kiss.

Hmmm, thought Shook. *What's going on here, she seemed overly friendly.*

It was Thursday night at the Schooner Club, and the bar was full. Meisel was going to try to get by but was down in Fort Lauderdale at a deposition, and Jeff was on duty.

They sat over in the corner next to the east end of the bar by the window. Shook had his Wild Turkey on the rocks with a splash, and Yovanda had her daiquiri. She was looking fine when she leaned forward and, almost in a whisper, said, "Jack, there's something I've got to tell you."

OK, Shook thought. *Here comes the brushoff.*

"I've been trying to think of a way to tell you, but I just didn't know how."

Yep. Here it comes. "Well, go ahead, baby, I can take it. I'm a big boy. What's on your mind?"

"Well, I just wanted to tell you that, about a month ago, this man came up to me in the bank and said he needed to talk to me. He said it was very important and that it would be a big deal for me. He asked to talk to me after work, and I said 'OK.'"

"OK," replied Shook, "so what was it about?"

"It was about you. He said he was doing some background investigation on you and that he needed my help. He told me that, if I helped him, he would pay me a lot of money."

"OK," said Shook, a little stunned but curious. "So, what did you do?"

"I told him I would think about it at first, but I thought about it and changed my mind."

"Did you tell him you would help him?"

"No, Jack, I didn't. I told him I wouldn't help him, and he acted a little mad. He left, and I never saw him again."

"So, who was this guy, Yovanda? What was his name?"

"He only said his name was Jim and that it would be in my best interest to help him."

"What did he look like, baby?"

"He was average looking, a little fat, wearing a rumpled jacket, no tie. A white guy. He drove a white Ford Explorer."

"So, you've never seen him since?"

"No, I never have."

"So, why did you wait to tell me this, Yovanda?"

"Well, to be honest, I was a little scared to tell you, because I really didn't know you; but, since we started seeing each other, I thought the time had come to tell you."

"Well, I appreciate that, Yo."

"Tell me, Jack, what's all this about? Who was that guy, and why would he do this?"

Shook privately had his suspicions but decided not to share them with Yovanda. "I don't know, honey, but if he ever comes by to see you again, please let me know, OK?"

"OK, Jack."

The rest of the evening was spent with a wonderful meal in the dining room and a truly memorable finish later at Shook's place. Yovanda decided she wanted to spend the night, and Shook did not dissuade her.

He dropped her off after breakfast the next day and drove away. He had slept well last night and now was in deeper thought.

Who was this mystery man, and what was he up to with Yovanda? I guess I just need to get used to this shit. It could be anyone, the way I live my life, he thought.

Chapter 23

It was four o'clock in the afternoon, and Dragman found himself sitting outside the Oeste Palma Golf Club in the parking lot. He had confirmed with the head valet, Joe Murray, that Harrison Davis was playing golf and probably would be coming out around five. It was Friday, and he usually played golf on Friday, according to Joe.

Dragman was not a golfer, but he had sources everywhere. Joe was one of them. Joe was a member of the Space Coast Fishing Club, and Dragman was at least acquainted with him.

Harrison's usual abode was now a rental home in a gated community just west of the Turnpike off Okeechobee Road. He was not driving now and had a limo take him everywhere.

Dragman was sitting quietly, deep in thought about Wheeler. He was gone, vanished from the face of the earth. He had a daily routine, which began with his call to Detective Willis. He had rattled every chain he could, but it was as if Wheeler had just evaporated into thin air.

He refused to believe Willis's report that he went out to one of the strip clubs out on Broward Boulevard, got hooked up with the wrong people, and simply disappeared. He had a report that someone fitting his description had been there and the security video had identified a guy who may have been him, but that lead had ended in nothing.

He wasn't about to let go, dammit. *Wheeler is my friend, and I'm not going to walk away,* he thought.

It was right at five o'clock when he saw the limo move to the valet station. The driver was on the phone. Joe looked out to the parking lot right at Dragman and nodded. Dragman was on the move. He had the summons and the process server with him. They got to the valet station just seconds before Davis did.

Davis walked up, and the process server looked at him and said, "Mr. Davis?"

Davis turned and said, "Yes?"

The process server took the summons and complaint and tried to give it to Davis. Davis saw it coming and refused to take it. The process server touched him with the papers and announced, "You've been served, sir."

Davis said nothing. He had just let the summons and complaint fall on the walkway, jumped in the limo, and sped away.

Standing back a ways was Dragman, filming the whole episode. He walked up to the papers laying on the walkway and filmed them. They left them there.

Joe saw the whole episode and asked, "What should we do with the papers?"

"You can leave them there, if you want, but you might want to check with the club manager," Dragman replied.

Dragman and the process server left immediately. Joe was on the phone into the club. He was met with a pissed-off club manager who was growing weary of this ongoing Harrison Davis bullshit.

Dragman walked into the club and was on the phone to Shook. "Hey, Jack."

"What's up, Dragman?"

"We got him, and I got it on film. He wouldn't take the papers. They are laying on the sidewalk at the valet station at Oeste Palma."

"What an asshole, Dragman."

"Yeah, he was pissed, but we got good service."

"Thanks, dude. Go home and wind down."

"Can't wind down, man. Gotta get ready for tomorrow. I gotta be at Buckhead at six in the morning."

"Better you than me, dude. Good luck fishing."

Shook hung up.

Chapter 24

S hook was in his office, at about 10:00 a.m. He had the television on, watching two jetliners crash into the World Trade Center Towers. It was Tuesday, September 11, 2001. Tiffany was with him, and he turned to her and said, "well, Tiffany, the world can't get much crazier can it? I mean, Wheeler's still missing, Harrison Davis is hiding out in Nassau with Ukrainian hookers, his lawyers have moved to quash our service on him after bribing the Valet, and I had to get Teresa Leonard on the case to find him, and now the country is under attack!"

"Yes boss, things are getting weird."

"Please don't call me 'boss' Tiff, it's just you and me here."

"Okay, Jack, but what can we do?"

"About the country, we can do nothing until election time. About Marvin's case, it just pisses me off that I have to play games with these lawyers, and now the whole country is getting a wakeup call."

"So, what's the plan for Teresa, Jack?"

"Well, Davis is such an idiot that Teresa will lure him back to the states, and we'll serve him on video."

"She called me last night. She is meeting him at the Desert Inn, in Vero, on Friday night."

Chapter 25

I t's Friday about 7:00 p.m. and Teresa is at the bar, chatting with the Bartender, Dave Rittenhouse, who moonlights at the Desert Inn on alternate Friday nights.

"So Teresa, who is the victim tonight?"

"Well David, it's a big wig dodging service that I tracked down to Nassau."

"So good lookin, who are you working for?"

"Jack Shook."

"Shook's on this?"

"Yes."

"I pity the poor bastard who tangles with the Shookman."

"Yeah David, this is a big one. Jeff is set up over by the pool entrance to video the whole thing."

"I love watching you work Teresa."

Dave, sat back, and reflected on his experience with this lady. Damn good looking, brunette, beautiful athletic body, intelligent, well spoken, and at ease in any situation. *This ought to be good.*

Well, well, well, there's the victim, right on time. *Ah, isn't that sweet, a big kiss.* David sauntered down the bar, "Good evening, sir, may I get you a drink?"

"Yes you can my man, Silver Bullet, straight up, 3 olives, a little dirty, and please bring the lady another. Okay?"

"Yes sir, may I have a name for the tab?"

"Yes, it's Davis, Harrison Davis, and don't forget it."

Davis turned to Teresa, "Damn you look good tonight, there is just something about a black cocktail dress that brings out the dog in me."

"Well thank you Harrison, I will take that as a complement."

"So, what's going on with you these days?"

Davis looked up and smiled as he took a big gulp of his drink and replied, "Had a board meeting at 1 o'clock, and met with the auditors at 3. I have got to kick some serious ass in my business. I run the largest HMO in south Florida and without me they're fucking helpless."

"Ah, poor baby Harrison, let's see if we can settle you down a little, okay buddy?"

Privately, Teresa detested listening to this bloviating asshole, so full of himself that she could hardly contain herself but she had a job to do.

"So Harrison, I read in the newspaper a couple months back about you getting into some car accident up in Melbourne. What was that all about?"

"Yes, Teresa it was me, and it's all bullshit. I was driving out to my condo in Melbourne Beach and these young punks pulled out right in front of me, in their piece of shit ghetto mobile, and I wiped the little bastards of the face of the planet."

"Yeah Harrison, don't you just hate it when that happens?"

Silently, she was appalled at his description of the two boys he had killed and rendered the other a paraplegic.

"Yeah, and to top it off the little bastard's families are suing the shit out of me and have some scumbag lawyers after my ass. But they don't know what we've got in store for them. By the time my insurance company gets finished with them, they'll be lucky to get a job working for some Public Defender, for peanuts."

Teresa, was now at the end of her tolerance listening to this jerk. He was wasting her time. *Time to do some business.*

"Harrison, I have got some good news and some bad news for you baby. Which would you like first."

"I'll take the good news first."

"The good news is that your Silver Bullet is on me."

"Okay, so what's the bad news?"

"The bad news Harrison Davis, is that you are now served," as she shoved the Complaint and Summons into his hand.

Stunned, he threw the papers back at her and said, "you fucking bitch. I am adding you to my list. You'll never work in this town again," as Davis stormed out the door.

"Very nice Mr. Davis, by the way, we have got you on video too. Have a nice day."

David, who was watching the 'shit show,' came down the bar, smiled and said, "Teresa, I like the way you work."

"Well thank you David and just remember that he identified himself when you asked for his name on the tab, okay?"

"No problem baby, I never want to cross you."

"David, don't worry about it, you and I will always be good."

Chapter 26

D*avis v. Davis* was the next scheduled mediation for Harry Scruggs. Harry had set aside an entire afternoon for this one, even though it was set for mediation and preparation for temporary relief scheduled the following week.

Harry, a retired circuit judge, was handpicked by Howard Dorfman as the mediator in this case, and Kahn did not object.

Dorfman, Harrison's latest handpicked divorce lawyer had a special relationship with Scruggs. They went way back, and Dorfman had a book on Scruggs.

Scruggs, it seems, a former insurance defense lawyer, just barely squeaked by a JQC complaint dealing with campaign contribution violations, paid a $25,000 fine, and was publicly reprimanded by the Supreme Court.

All of that occurred 10 years prior, and everyone seemed to have forgotten it was Ed Baldwin who was involved in that fiasco and that it was Baldwin who had steered Davis to Dorfman and now Scruggs.

Dorfman was feeling cocky. This was a shortterm marriage—six years. The wife, Gretchen, was an attorney and certainly capable of supporting herself.

Equitable distribution of marital property was not disputed, but alimony sure as hell was. He had the "fellatio video" and surveillance report tucked into his bag. Now was the time to drop the hammer on Gretchen, make a deal, and get her out of the house with a couple of bucks in her purse. She could then concentrate on the next poor, hapless idiot who got involved with her.

The mediation was scheduled for 1:30 p.m., and Dorfman had agreed to do it at Kahn's office just to give him a false sense of security. He had scheduled a 12:45 p.m. appointment with Harrison in his office, and he had just arrived and was ushered into his office. After shaking hands and exchanging pleasantries, Harrison spoke first.

"Howard, why in the world are we going to Kahn's office? I feel like we are showing weakness by agreeing to go there."

"Because we wanted Scruggs, and it was a package deal, Harrison. You see, Scruggs is our man, and Kahn doesn't know what's coming."

"OK, but I just don't like it, Howard. Besides, I'm growing very weary of this domestic violence injunction and this bullshit criminal charge of domestic battery."

"Well, Harrison, if all goes well, all of this should go away. By the way, Harrison, I need to let you know that you are not supposed to say anything during this mediation—and I mean say nothing—except when Scruggs is with us privately after the positioning part of this little kabuki dance is over. You understand, Harrison? Not a fucking word."

"Got it, Howard. Besides, I can't stand being in the same county with that bitch, let alone in the same room."

"OK, man, let's go."

The drive over to Kahn's office took only a few minutes, and then they found themselves cooling their heels in the waiting room.

At 1:45 p.m., Howard got up and told the receptionist that if the mediation didn't start in five minutes, he and his client were leaving.

At 1:52 p.m., they were ushered into the mediation room. It was obvious that Scruggs and Kahn had met privately first, keeping them waiting.

Kahn went first after Scruggs to make his introductory remarks, urging the parties to keep an open mind and do their best to settle their differences.

Kahn drew first blood and went all in with the photos of Harrison passed out in a drunken stupor in the garage on the night of July 8.

Dorfman wasn't expecting this but maintained his wellpracticed poker face. He also looked bored when the vague general financial and tax issues were mentioned. He knew that Gretchen had signed the tax returns, and she was a lawyer.

Gretchen sat there, glaring at Harrison and smiling her "smirky" little smile. Harrison didn't flinch but looked away. Gretchen saw that as a sign of weakness. She was going in for the kill, and she was about to be a very wealthy woman. Thoughts of her trips to Vail and hanging out with her other divorced friends at the Sailfish Club, playing tennis at the Palm Beach Tennis Club, and spending endless hours having sex with younger men fueled her little fantasydriven vendetta.

Kahn was finally finished, and it was Dorfman's turn. He started slow, stating the obvious: that Gretchen was well capable of taking care of herself and that it was a short duration marriage that did not warrant alimony.

Dorfman then went for the jugular. "Ms. Davis, I must say that you're looking much different today than you did on the night of September 15. Just in case you have forgotten what you were wearing—or, should I say, not wearing—we've got a little disc and some photos here that, along with this report, will take you down memory lane."

Dorfman slid an envelope across the table and announced, "We'll be in the next room waiting for you, Mr. Scruggs."

"So nice to see you, Gretchen."

Harrison couldn't contain himself as he looked Gretchen right square in the eye. The concern in her eyes had replaced the glee that she had been experiencing just a few minutes before.

Dorfman stood up and said, "Harrison, come with me."

Harrison complied, and they walked out of the room.

Scruggs was startled, and Kahn was speechless.

The big mailing envelope was opened, and photos of Gretchen nude from the waist up, engaged in fellatio on Jerry, were passed around. Kahn digested the report.

Scruggs got up and excused himself. "Mike, I assume you would like to speak with your client privately, right?"

"As a matter of fact, I would, Harry."

Meanwhile, in the adjoining conference room, Dorfman was having a "sit-down" with Harrison.

"Harrison, what the fuck is this?"

Davis could only mutter what he was told by Baldwin. "I'm not supposed to say anything unless he is present."

"July 8 was the day you were in that car crash that killed those two kids, right?"

"Yes, that's the day, but I'd don't remember these photos being taken."

"Well, of course you don't, you're passed out. Holy crap, Harrison, your dear sweet little cocksucking wife is threatening you with a manslaughter by intoxicated motorist charge."

"Call Ed, and he will fill you in, OK? You're making me nervous."

"OK, Harrison."

Back in the conference room, Kahn was sitting with Gretchen going over the report. Kahn was privately amused, but he did not show it. He was well practiced in the art of deception and, of course, so was Gretchen.

"What should we do, Mike?" she asked.

"Here's what we do, Gretchen. We get up and walk out and don't say a word. I'll tell Harry that we're terminating the mediation as being unsuccessful."

They both got up and walked out.

Kahn spoke briefly to Scruggs. "Don't tell Dorfman and his client that we're gone for at least 15 minutes."

Meanwhile, Dorfman was on the phone with Baldwin. "They got a series of photographs showing Harrison passed out in a car in the garage, Ed."

"Damn, that little bitch is smarter than we thought. She's going for the big payday, isn't she, Howard?"

"Ed, what are we doing about this?"

"Cancel the temporary relief hearing for certain, Howard. I'll let you know what our next step is, OK?"

"Well, OK, Ed, but sooner or later they're going to get to the golf club and get that bar tab, which is all on the computer."

"Well, Howard, the bill is sent monthly, and, in case you don't know, he is listed as having two drinks attributed to him. All we need to say is that Harrison was so exhausted and upset that he just stayed in the garage, because he couldn't stand listening to that cocksucking bitch anymore."

"I like it, Ed."

"So how many drinks did he really have?"

"Don't ask, don't tell, Howard. Just make sure Harrison doesn't say shit, understand?"

"Understand. By the way, you want to talk to Harrison?"

"Yeah, put the moron on the line."

Harrison was handed the phone, and Ed spoke first. "Harrison, don't say shit about anything, you understand?"

"Understand, Ed." He hung up.

Meanwhile, Kahn was meeting with Gretchen. It was fortunate that she had cleared out all but one of the 12 bank accounts and had all of the individual and joint credit cards. His client would be fine.

Gretchen sat quietly listening until they were about to separate and she could leave. "So, what now, Mike?"

"Well, for one thing, please be discreet with that Jerry guy. I'm thinking we up the ante now, Gretchen. It's time I call my good buddy, Jack Russell Shook, and give him some high-quality intel. Your husband is about to have the heat turned up to redhot."

"But, what if they charge him with manslaughter? If they do, my claim for alimony goes out the window."

"No, it doesn't, Gretchen. Just leave it to me," he said as he ushered her out the door.

His next call was to J.R. Shook, Esquire.

It was 3:30 in the afternoon when Shook got the call. He was still in his office. Tiffany had transferred it back to him in the library.

"Mike Kahn on two, Mr. Shook."

"Hey, Mikey, what's up?"

"I'm calling you back, Jack. It's about the Davis case. Just went to mediation in the divorce, and it's allout war. They got film on my client giving head to her personal trainer."

"Nice, Mikey, sounds right up your alley, dude. You and Meisel get all the good shit. Me, all I get is some hopeless idiot turning left in front of oncoming traffic."

"Spare me, dude, you make decent money doing what you do. So, if you're finished poor mouthing, let me make your day."

"I'm all ears, Mikey."

"Davis was shitfaced when he had the accident. He had just come from Oeste Palma and was riding high."

"No shit."

"Yeah, no shit. My client went to the scene to retrieve him, and there was a cooperative trooper who let her take him. She took him home, and he passed out in the car and spent the night in the garage. My client took photos of him in the garage passed out.

"There is a problem, however. My client tried to get his bar tab, which would be on his monthly statement, but it was sent to his office. I suspect that someone has altered or deleted it."

"Hmm, Mikey, I like it. I appreciate the heads up. Can I get a set of the photos?"

"Yes, Jack, I'll email them to you."

"Great. Anything else?"

"Well, you're going to be limited by what she will say because of the privilege, but she is sick and tired of him. He's a drunken asshole, and she's over it."

"Thank you, Mike. I look forward to the email."

He hung up the phone and sat back in his chair. *What the hell is going on?* he thought. *Why in the world did Thomas cut him loose at the scene? This doesn't make any sense.*

Shook left the library and walked into Dragman's office. He delivered the good news.

"So, what do you think, Dragman?"

"I never liked that dipshit, Trooper Thomas. I always wondered about him."

"Well, is there anything you can do?"

"Let me check, Jack, but wasn't there another trooper there at the time?"

"Yeah, there was. I met her at the hospital that night. I forget her name, but she was very young. Let's get to her and see if she can shed any light on this."

"Good idea. I'll get right on it. But, let me tell you, I smell a rat on this, just because that prick Baldwin is involved."

Shook left the room, pondering what he had just learned. It occurred to him that Davis's wife was exposed to possible criminal charges herself for obstructing a traffic homicide investigation. She was, after all, just another notsobright lawyer.

Meanwhile, 1,300 miles away, it was 11 o'clock in the morning when Mary Jo walked into the home office waiting room on the 40th floor of the Chrysler building. She made sure that she was prompt and was not a minute late. Her appointment with Tim Rogers, senior vice president, had been scheduled for a month.

Her flight up last night was pleasant enough. She chose the night flight to make sure there was no possibility of delay. She was staying at the Waldorf, and a Town Car was waiting for her by 10:15 a.m. The trip downtown into Manhattan was no problem.

She was wearing one of her new Versace suits and chose to walk over to the window and survey the city, rather than take a seat. Corporate headquarters for Conveyance Mutual was located at the Chrysler Building, which was at 405 Lexington Avenue, in Midtown, so the 9/11 disaster was further down Manhattan. As she looked out on the vista, she knew she wanted to be here. She had had enough of Melbourne, and West Palm. She had paid her dues. She was ready to go corporate, and the time was now.

Rogers walked into the waiting room and extended his hand. "Ms. Stalinowsky?"

"Yes, you must be Tim Rogers."

"Yes, I am. Please come with me, Mary Jo."

Mary Jo was pleasantly surprised to see no wedding ring on his finger; he was about 50. She needed to be careful, though. No flirting—at least not now.

Her father had told her that she was a shooin anyway and that this was just a confirmation meeting. She was impressed that Rogers had walked out personally to meet her rather than sending in some minion to escort her. They entered his office.

"Hold my calls, Alicia. I'll be with Ms. Stalinowsky for at least an hour," he said.

"Yes, sir, Mr. Rogers," she replied as she closed the door.

His office was even more impressive than Mary Jo had imagined: a corner office, southeast corner, 40th floor. She resisted the impulse to check out the view. The furniture was very modern, and his desk was in the corner. Off to the right was a conference table with 12 chairs right against the window. A video conferencing flat screen was on the wall.

"Can I get you some coffee, Mary Jo?"

"No, thank you, Mr. Rogers."

They sat at the conference table. There was no file on the table. She glanced at the wall and saw that he was a Princeton graduate.

"Mary Jo, we have been watching your career now for about the last five years. Your claims payments records have been number one in the Southeast Division now for the last three years. Your performance ratios in terms of cost and claims paid are off the charts."

"Thank you, sir. I appreciate that, but I didn't do it alone. I've managed to assemble a great team of committed people who work well together to accomplish our mutual goal." She knew that corporate meant management of people and knew exactly what to say.

"Well, Mary Jo, that's obvious, and that's why you are here. Coming to corporate requires that we make sure that you can assemble and manage personnel that are committed to the company's mission. Do you think you can do that at this level?"

"Yes, sir, I'm certain that I can. I've grown up with this company. My father is one of the highest performing agents in South Florida. I've always worked for the company. I started as a field adjuster after college and have been successful at every position that I've held. I am a company person."

"Yes, Mary Jo, I see that. I would like to ask you though, how have you been able to keep these claims payments down?"

"Well, Sir, first and foremost is diligence and people on the ground. If you don't talk to a witness, they don't exist. If you don't touch an exhibit, it doesn't exist. And, if you don't go to the scene, it doesn't happen, and you have to get to them first.

You also have to size up the claimant and his attorney fast. We know who all the players are and have all the numbers on every attorney in our district. We also have the ability to evaluate just how desperate his client is to get money.

We approach every claim with the assumption that the claim is either frivolous or fraudulent and require the claimant to prove otherwise. After all, we're the ones with the money."

"Well, Mary Jo, that's very entertaining, but how do you get the background on the claimants?"

"Well, sir, you may not know that the industry shares all claims activity. We have a record of every claim ever paid by any carrier, and we share that information."

"I see, but what about the big claims that have either aggravated liability issues or catastrophic damages? I see that your district leads the nation in that category. How do you do it?"

Mary Jo had to level here. She could not disclose the existence of the "unit" or the special rules that apply.

"Sir, all I can tell you is that we are diligent. We pay attention. We have the 'docs,' and we have the intel."

"Docs?"

"Yes, sir. We have the docs. I'm proud of the group that we have assembled. Before the examination of any claimant, a chosen doctor reviews all the medical records for the claimant before they ever see the claimant and is briefed by my line adjusters on what we're looking for. We absolutely require that they send us their draft report for review and revision before it is ever released."

"I see, Mary Jo, but what about these big cases?"

"Well, it's diligence, sir, that's all it is."

"That's remarkable. Well, as you know, this interview is your first step to your move to corporate. In a few minutes, I'm going to take you around to meet the CEO and CFO, and the Chairman is here today. We are having lunch brought in today, and we want to have you join us, OK?"

"Of course, sir, it would be my privilege to join you."

"Well, that's our privilege, Mary Jo, not just yours. We have been watching you and have been looking forward to meeting you."

They sat and talked for a few minutes more, and then adjourned to the rest of the corporate floors. She was walked through each department and introduced to everyone. They finally arrived in the massive corporate conference dining room and each took a seat. The accommodations looked like a fivestar restaurant with fine linens, silver, and china. There were waiters and a bartender. She was offered a mixed drink, which she declined. Her father had alerted her to his little trick.

Upper management was truly a collection of what the public might suspect. They were all impeccably dressed, impeccably coifed. The men wore tailored suits. Their nails were manicured. Everyone wore a Rolex. They were of a different class completely. She wanted in. She belonged here. She had paid her dues. They owed her, and now was her time.

After lunch, she was taken downstairs and delivered to the limo. Before leaving, though, Rogers gave her his final thoughts. "Mary, I truly want to thank you for coming. It's been a great privilege to meet you. It will take a few months to get you on the agenda, but you should know within three months at the latest. I want you to know that I'm very favorably disposed to having you join us here."

"Thank you, Mr. Rogers. I do appreciate it."

"Please just call me Tim, Mary Jo."

"OK, Tim, I await your call."

"Have a great flight."

Mary Jo climbed into the town car and was whisked away off to JFK. She sat quietly, deep in thought. *Those bastards better move me here. I've done everything right. I survived my divorce, and I climbed my way to the top. They better let me in the club.*

As she rode along, studying her surroundings and the people on the street, it never occurred to her that she had sold her soul for what she thought she wanted.

It's too late now, and I'm never turning back, she thought.

Chapter 27

Erika was born in Ponce and was the fourth daughter of an engineer. She attended the University of Puerto Rico and studied engineering. She loved her country but found employment opportunities limited. She moved to Palm Beach Gardens at 25 and began working for a State Farm agent.

Being extremely bright and hardworking, she figured the business out quickly. She was hired as a field adjuster for the "Farm" and quickly moved up to a field supervisor.

As a woman in South Florida who was fluent in Spanish, she was invaluable to the company, but the years had gone by without additional advancement, so she went to law school.

She had met Doug Dragenleader along the way, and they became friends. Nothing sexual—just friends.

Doug had a girlfriend introduce them. It seems Doug had a weakness for good-looking, brown eyed, Latin girls. Rodriguez was in that category. She stood about five feet four inches tall and had those famous Spanish eyes. She was trim but watched her weight. She looked great in a bikini but was always understated. She was actually surprised when he flirted with her and found her attractive; she was not spoiled with attention.

She was a single mother of two boys. Both of her exes were not involved in their lives, and she liked it that way.

Dragman recognized her capabilities immediately, and, despite his penchant for using dinosaur English to refer to women in a sexist sort of way, she actually found him amusing. He was harmless and, in many ways, reminded her of her father. Her legal career was now over.

Shook met her and was immediately impressed. She would be a great addition to the firm. They hired her and paid her a handsome salary. She was with the firm for two months now, and she was tapped to go interview Trooper RosoMartinez by Shook.

"Erika, here's the file. This is the Jackson case. Something doesn't make sense here. We now have intel from the defendant's wife's divorce lawyer that shows he was shitfaced when the collision occurred. I spoke to Trooper RosoMartinez at the hospital, and she said nothing about alcohol. That nimrod Thomas did the homicide report; it is silent about alcohol, and Thomas cut the drunk loose at the scene. I want you to find out what the hell is going on, and I think we need to start with RosoMartinez."

"Where is she stationed, Mr. Shook?" Rodriguez asked.

"She's down in Miami, Troop L, I think, Erika. Are you on it?"

"I'm on it, boss." She grabbed the file and walked out the door. She was down south within three hours.

Shook and Dragman were back in the office.

"So what do you think, Dragman?"

"She'll get something for sure, Jack, my boy. Just wait and see."

The next day, Erika walked into the trooper's office in Pompano Beach at 9 o'clock in the morning. She had called and made an appointment.

RosoMartinez walked out when paged. Erika stood and extended her hand, which the trooper took.

Erika spoke first. "Trooper, I'm Erika Rodriguez, and I drove all the way down here to talk to you about Harrison Davis, Marvin Jackson's mother's case. Is there a place where we can talk privately?"

RosoMartinez stopped in her tracks, turned to face Erika directly, and asked, "OK, who do you represent, and who do you work for?"

"I work for the firm of Shook and Meisel in Palm Beach, and we're acting on behalf of the Jackson family," Erika quickly responded.

"Which was Jackson, Ms. Rodriguez?"

"He was the boy in the back who was paralyzed, Trooper," she replied.

"I see, so what do you want with me?"

"Can we just go with first names and off the record?"

"Well, OK. You can call me Odalys."

"OK, Odalys, let's chat."

Outside the main office at the Turnpike rest stop was a group of picnic tables under some shady trees. They sat, and Erika spoke again.

"So I'm from Ponce, how about you?" Her intention was to break the ice. She could feel Odalys' tension and reluctance.

"I'm from Dorado."

Erika switched immediately into Spanish. "So, I understand you were first on the scene and actually met Mr. Shook at the hospital."

"Yes, I was the first trooper, but a deputy was already there."

"Well, we have read the homicide report, and we have questions, Odalys."

"Well, I did not prepare the report, and I did not participate in preparing it," she replied. If you want a statement, you have to drop a subpoena on me, and I have to go through channels."

"This is off the record."

Odalys's mind was racing now. She knew what was coming. They switched back to English, and Odalys spoke first. "I requested a transfer after that crash. I wanted to get away from that asshole, Thomas."

"I see, and why, if you don't mind my asking?"

"Well, he's a Neanderthal, and I don't like the way he talks to me—and I don't like how he works. I'm not afraid of that redneck, but I just don't want to be around him, and I especially didn't like taking orders from him," she added. "So, what is it you wanted to know, Erika?"

"Well, we have intel that the Audi driver was drinking," Erika replied.

"OK, and what do you want from me?" Odalys fired back.

"Well, was he?"

"Yeah, he was, and I told Thomas, and he told me to go handle traffic control or something. No, actually, he told me to talk to the little old lady. I told Thomas I could smell it, and he sent me away from the Audi."

"Anything else, Odalys?"

"Yeah, he called the two boys up front 'dead brothas,' and the Audi driver's wife walked him out of the scene."

"Have you seen the homicide report, Odalys?"

"No, and I don't want to. I'm sure it's a classic," she replied.

"What do you mean?"

"Well, I'll bet there's no mention of the alcohol and he places 100 percent of blame on the Sentra for the accident."

"You are right on the money, Odalys. Why do you think that is?"

"Well, it's Thomas. I saw a number of his reports, and I almost never agreed with them. I decided I wanted out of there and got transferred down here and just got promoted to corporal."

"Congratulations, Odalys. It's good to see one of us moving up," Erika replied. "Anything else?"

"No, just drop a subpoena on me, and I'll tell it like it was, Erika."

"I appreciate that, Odalys."

The two women sat for the next 30 minutes trading life stories. It was amazing how similar they were. Erika was 10 years older and wiser, but Odalys was on her way up. They exchanged cell numbers and parted as friends.

As soon Erika got in the car, she called Dragman and spoke first.

"Just left Trooper RosoMartinez. Nice girl from Dorado."

"Yeah, and what?"

"Davis was drinking. She smelled it, but Thomas sent her away like a little school girl, and she's pissed."

"I like it, Erika."

"She says drop a subpoena on her, and she'll drop the rock on Thomas."

"Thank you, Erika, I'll see you later this afternoon, OK?"

"OK, Doug." And she hung up.

Dragman sat back and buzzed Shook, who was in his office.

"Guess what, Jack?"

"Tell me, man."

"Just spoke to Erika. Davis was drinking, and she smelled it and told Thomas. She's also pissed off at Thomas."

"Damn, I love it, Dragman. Keep me posted."

"No problem." And he hung up.

Shook sat back and thought a moment. *Damn, now we got one pissed off Puerto Rican trooper. It just gets better and better. But what the hell is going on with Thomas?*

Chapter 28

It was one of those crisp and cool South Florida mornings late in February. The press conference was scheduled for 11 a.m., and Ed was feeling a little nervous. His preplanning had been set in motion a year before and his executive committee was in place. His war chest boasted 500k and his major on tap contributor was a PAC out of Tallahassee that specialized in criminal justice. Private prisons were on the way and Ed was about to set it all in motion and ride the gravy train.

Sunshine Corrections, Inc. or SCI was in place and ready to go. He held 20 percent of the stock personally. The rest was reserved for a public offering that would bring in millions.

The State Corrections system was struggling to avoid the drip, drip, drip of scandal and the horror stories were commonplace. The prison population had just topped 100,000, and the Department supervised about 150,000 offenders on some form of conditional release.

The annual budget was at $2.5 billion and climbing. The cost of warehousing these people was enormous.

Florida was in line and leading the rest of the country, second only to Texas in incarceration rates which disproportionately represented minorities, black and Hispanic. This was not unusual just for Florida; the country had five percent of the world's population but housed 25 percent of the world's incarcerated population. Ed saw this as a growth industry, and he wasn't going to lose out. This was his ticket to the top.

Included in Ed's war chest were donations from Harrison Davis, his company, most of his senior VPs, and most of Conveyance's senior Florida managers.

The State Senate was his for the taking, and no one would dare challenge him except the hapless Democratic incumbent that he would crush.

The announcement was only 10 minutes away, and he was collecting his thoughts.

The venue for this momentous event was the seawall just south of Jetty Park with the backdrop of the Intracoastal. His platform was ready. Insurance fraud was at the top of his list, along with welfare reform and more Workmen's Comp reform; all were based on the specter of fraud and how he could confront the evil and that he alone could save money for the taxpayers. They managed to muster about 150 people to witness this momentous event with the flags waving and the signs at the ready.

The DJ was signaled, and "God Bless America" began. Although there was less than thunderous applause as Ed walked through the crowd to the podium, it was nonetheless marginally impressive. He started by thanking all of those assembled for coming out and tried his best to be humble. He began his speech talking about his "journey to justice" and his 40year-long career of "fighting crime, corruption and fraud." He ended with his decision to offer himself to the voters to continue in this quest for justice and to save their tax dollars for only essential services. He had all three networks present, and they were filming the spectacle.

Shook, Dragman, and Meisel sat in their conference room watching the debacle.

"Thank God, he's leaving the courtroom," said Shook.

"Yeah, but, if that prick is elected, he'll do everything he can to destroy the civil justice system," Draglman added.

Meisel was more amused. "He's going to get his ass kicked."

"Don't be so sure, Keith. He's got a lot of money and a lot of juice."

"I didn't get an invitation to the reception tonight at Oeste Palma—did you?" Draglman mused.

"Not likely," Shook replied. "Can we get a spy in there?"

"Way ahead of you, dude. Erika is going as Howard Donohue's date."

"Holy shit. How did you pull that off?"

"Well, she and Howard have known each other for years, and he's been chasing her for years. It was actually her idea, and I concurred."

"Perfect, Dragman. I'm sure we'll get a full report. She's not sleeping with him, is she?"

"Hell, no, Jack. She stays in touch through the 'claimsmen.' She's an honorary member and still attends those private meetings. Besides that, she donated $100 to his campaign."

"Are you serious?" Keith asked.

"Relax, I gave it to her. We've got to keep this prick close."

"I like it, boys. I'm sure will get a full report."

Later that evening, Howard arrived at Erika's in a brand new Conveyance field SUV.

"Hey, gorgeous. What's new?" he called out to her as she walked toward him.

She dodged his greeting kiss, letting it land on her cheek. "Hi, Howard. So what's with the new wheels?"

"Well, it's my new vehicle. Just got it."

"What is it anyway?"

"GMC Yukon, baby, and it's got everything including GPS. Check it out."

"Very nice," she said, giving it an admiring nod.

The soirée at the club was impressive with about 300 people crowding the dining room lounge and veranda. A DJ provided the music, and Erika counted 50 American flags. Ed was pleasant to her, even though he knew where she worked. After all, she had contributed $100.

Harrison Davis was there, sitting at the bar. He had already downed three Silver Bullets. Erika noticed Trooper Thomas and Mary Jo Stalinowsky. They looked right through her.

Yep, I'm invisible to them, she thought.

Dennis was at the main bar and was supervising six bartenders. He had two in the dining room, two on the veranda, and three, including him, inside. The liquor was flowing. Dennis recognized Erika. He had always had a "thing" for her, and she was friendly.

Smiling at her, he greeted her over the music. "Hi, doll."

"Hi, Dennis. It's good to see you again. I remember the days when you were over at the Schooner Club, and you haven't changed a bit."

She was lying, of course, but she knew Dennis was a "force" to be reckoned with and a fertile source of information.

"You're looking pretty good yourself, baby. What can I get you?"

"Margarita on the rocks, Dennis, not too sweet. No salt, please."

"Coming right up, my dear."

Dennis always made the best drinks, she thought as she took her first taste. He made them with a Grand Marnier splash, and that just set them off perfectly.

Sitting over in the corner with two martini glasses in front of him was Harrison Davis. She knew who he was, and, for the next few minutes, she sipped her drink, studying him.

All of a sudden, she heard, "Dennis, Goddammit, what's this shit that you're making? I can't taste shit on this one. Where're my fucking olives?"

Erika glanced at Dennis and looked at him for only a moment. She was embarrassed for him. His job required that he suck up to these drunken assholes, and she could tell he was embarrassed.

Dennis quickly delivered two olives and apologized to Davis.

Erika came to the bar when he returned. "That guy's an obvious drunk and a few bubbles off his plumb, Dennis."

"You have no idea, baby. That prick is going to really piss me off one day."

"How's that, Dennis?"

"Can't say, doll, but one day I will. I can't stand that prick, but, one day, he is going down.

"By the way, what's with you and Donohue? You can't really like that degenerate prick—do you?"

"He's just an old friend," she said, catching Dennis's eye, "and I can't say anything more than that."

"Maybe we can talk more about this after dinner some night, doll. What do you think?"

"I'd like that, Dennis. Here's my number. Call me next week, OK?" She flashed her eyes and blew him a kiss as she walked off.

Dennis was impressed and studied her as she walked away with lust in his heart.

The rest of the evening was boring as hell. Ed's speech sucked, but the clapping seals didn't seem to mind. They were too intoxicated to care and too selfabsorbed to even hear it. Later, Erika noticed that Howard was too drunk to drive. She asked Dennis to call a cab, which was provided to any guest of the club at no charge. The policy had begun just two weeks after Davis' debacle.

She had carefully and surreptitiously watched and listened to Davis' ramblings at the bar. He was a classic obnoxious drunk who not only bored the listener to death with his bullshit, but he would spit on them while talking. What an asshole.

Chapter 29

Paco was just settling into his little corner of the trash truck bin and was more than a little concerned that he was having trouble breathing. Too late now; he was committed. God help him if he got caught. He would never get out of this hellhole, at least not alive. His new BFF, Willie, was securely ensconced in the opposite corner, surrounded by rotting garbage and two rats that were at least a foot long. Damn, you'd have thought that all that money promised from the cartel would have bought them better accommodations.

Willie, somehow, got this hooker to come through, and they were meeting her at the dump some 20 miles away. He didn't know if he could make it. He also didn't know if he could continue the con. All he had to do was get to a phone and call Palm Beach. If he could do that, he knew he was on his way. His first concern was just getting to the dump alive.

The truck was moving, and he concluded that he must be outside the prison walls because he could hear other traffic noise. Horns were honking. They were stopping and moving. He must be on his way. This had been a long time coming, and he wasn't going to blow it.

Willie somehow convinced the cartel that Paco Sanchez was on his way out of prison. He knew he was living on the edge. He knew they were likely people that he did not want to disappoint. So, the key was to not meet them. Just to get to a phone. If he couldn't, he had to get to the border.

Maybe the con would work. They thought he was Paco Sanchez, drug dealer. You do a thing, and that's what you are. You get a job, and you become your job. He knew he had to be convincing, but he was ready. Hell, he started selling weed and Coke in Vietnam 40 years ago. He had met a lot of them on the way. It was time for his best performance. After all, he apparently had a whole new set of friends.

He wondered what the hooker would look like. She was supposedly a high-priced escort, but this was Mexico, so what could that mean? His mind was racing when he noticed that something was nibbling on his foot—another rat.

I can pull this off, dammit. Yeah, yeah, Shook told me once that I sometimes overshoot the runway. I can overshoot this one, dammit.

The truck suddenly began to bounce. It was obviously not on a paved road anymore. The gears were lower, and the engine was whining. Suddenly, it came to an abrupt stop, and then they were backing up. Now, he could hear birds, birds, and more birds. The truck stopped, and the back opened up and the big hydraulic piston pushed them out with about three tons of garbage. It was late in the afternoon, but there was light.

They fell out of the truck and dropped and rolled about 50 feet before he came to a stop. He took cover behind an old, junked washing machine that was smashed but still open on the one side where he squeezed in and didn't move.

The truck moved away, and he began taking in his surroundings. There were people there picking through the garbage.

Time to blend in, thought Paco, *and where the fuck am I?*

He grabbed a plastic bag, emptied it, and began picking up random items. He was not injured and able to move. Off to his left, he spotted Willie, and he waved him over. He came running.

"Let's get the fuck out of here, man. We got people waiting for us down at the entrance of this place, and we got to get moving now."

The dump was enormous. It was the largest trash mountain Paco had ever seen, but they followed the road down past the trucks coming up.

This is the time, this is the place. I've got to do this, he thought.

Willie was lagging behind, so Paco had to push him.

Finally, he rebelled. "Damn, Paco, I must say you're taking this a whole lot better than I thought you would. I never thought you were this tough."

"Come on, Willie, we've got a hooker to meet."

About a mile down the road, Paco spotted the gate. Sitting behind it was an old Ford Galaxy with blackedout windows.

Willy nodded toward the car. "That must be Este."

They nonchalantly cleared the gate and walked to the Galaxy. The driver's door opened and out stepped a young, petite brunette that flashed an enormous smile. Her teeth were snow white. Her eyes were beautiful and deep. She was not provocatively dressed. She was in an Adidas workout outfit. She was beautiful, and Paco could not believe his eyes.

Greeting him, she said, "You must be Paco. Welcome to my world."

Paco was nearly speechless, but managed to say, "Dear God, I must be in heaven."

She walked to him and gave him a hug. He could feel her body—athletic and well proportioned. She embraced Willie, and they all got in the car and drove away.

Nothing was said at first, and then Este broke the silence. "First thing, Paco, we want you to know that we know who you really are. You're Ken Wheeler, and you work for some Palm Beach law firm. You were purposely locked up as Paco by some very powerful enemies of ours, and we had to play along with that deception. All of this is over. We are now going to get you out of Mexico, but you have to help us bring 500 kilos of cocaine across the border."

Wheeler sat speechless and looked at Willie, who was sitting in the front seat. "So, Willie, how long have you been a part of this?"

"From the very beginning. I had to make sure you got the message that you had to be Paco Sanchez to get out of that hellhole."

"Damn, so what's the price of my freedom?"

"You got to remain in character and get 500 kilos of coke to Miami. That's the price."

"So, how are we going to do that?"

"Just south of McAllen, Texas, is a little town where we pick up the product. It's being loaded into a garbage truck, and we're going to drive it across the border. The immigration guard on duty in McAllen has been bought, and even he really thinks you are Paco Sanchez."

"So what? Why would he do that?"

"Because he wants more business and thinks, by helping you, he will become a steady confederate of ours."

"I've got to absorb this shit. Give me a minute. By the way, Este, who are you, and what's your part in this?"

"I'm Este Ramirez, and I want out of Mexico. This is the price I had to pay. You are taking me to Palm Beach."

Wheeler grinned, "Damn, I cannot believe my good fortune."

"Just remember, Ken, the people that put you in that hellhole are very powerful, but they also have very powerful enemies. We need to get this done quickly and carefully. We need to cross the border by tomorrow at the latest. It will take about a day to get the word to the big man that you are not in custody any longer."

"So where are we going, Este?"

"Next stop is Reynosa. By the way, we're stopping to get you cleaned up and fed. We're going to travel by night. We should be there by dawn. First stop is a motel in Leon where we get cleaned up and eat. Then, we drive all night to Monterey and then on to Reynosa. We should make it to Reynosa no later than 8 o'clock."

Ken sat for a while and then managed to mutter to Este, "Thank you, Este, and God be with us on our little adventure."

Este looked up in the rearview, made eye contact, smiled, and said nothing.

Willie sat silent.

Into the night, they drove through the Mexican countryside, perfectly blending into the night.

Ken sat deep in thought. This is no emptyheaded beauty. She was a force. He was immediately drawn to her. He could feel the impulse. The wheel of fortune still spins and providence had intervened.

The great mystery of life is that, when you meet people, you never know how they will affect your life. Right now, his life was in the hands of a young Mexican woman driving a 20yearold car across the Mexican wilderness. We can do what we can to control our destiny, but the wheel still spins. He nodded off to sleep.

Chapter 30

It was 7:30 a.m. when Este pulled into the salvage yard in Reynosa. Ken had managed to sleep and was awoken when the Galaxy transitioned to a bumpy road and then came to an abrupt stop.

He opened his eyes. It was daylight, and he squinted at the light.

Este walked over to an ancient trailer and disappeared. He could see no one. The sky was clear, but red on the eastern horizon. The old saying "red sky in the morning, sailor take warning" ran through his mind. He decided to stay put and not move.

Five minutes later, Este emerged from the trailer carrying three cups of coffee. He climbed out of the car and gratefully relieved her of one cup. It was perfect—strong, lots of cream, lots of sugar. *How did she know?*

"OK, Este, what's the plan?"

"You're about to meet Juan Carlos. The truck is in back. Remember, you are Paco. Play along, but don't be solicitous. They think you're some kind of serious gangster out of Cancún."

"I hope my Spanish holds up, baby."

"It will. Let me do most of the talking though. I'm your private secretary and a bodyguard." She pulled her zipper down on her jacket and the nine-millimeter Glock became visible in her waistband.

"So who is Willie supposed to be?"

"He's just a passenger we are delivering to the other side. We have to get the semi across to our contacts that will unload it and pack it in the container to run it down to Miami."

"A semi?"

"Yes, with Wisconsin plates, loaded with cheese that is refrigerated. The dogs will not be able to smell it."

"OK, baby, let's go."

They walked to the rear of the yard and came upon two armed men carrying automatic weapons. They appeared to be AR-15 rifles.

Este did all of the talking. Paco played the strong, silent type who merely nodded and spoke only once, saying, "Thank you for your service" in Spanish. They climbed in the truck.

As he slid into the driver's side, Willie said nothing. Este fired up the diesel, and Ken marveled at her ability to handle machinery. She primed the engine manually, choked it, and let the ignition heat up before she fired it up. It roared to life, and she slid it into second gear to pull away.

Este ran through the gears like a pro and prompted Ken to ask, "Where did you learn to do that, Este?"

She just smiled and said, "That's just one of my many secrets, Ken."

He nodded. *That's par for the course. This woman is full of surprises. What next?*

It only took 15 minutes to get to the causeway leading to the border. Traffic was heavy. There were a lot of people going across. Este chose Gate No. 3 as she approached, even though the other lanes moved quicker. She pulled up to the gate and said, "That's him. He's looking directly at us. Just be cool."

Este produced her passport and her pass. There was a quick conversation, and they were waved through. She eased the massive diesel through the gears as traffic sped up. "We're being followed, Ken, so don't say a word."

"Where is he, baby?"

"He's behind and to the left, the black F-150. All we've got to do is make the handoff and then disappear into town."

She pulled into a salvage yard and drove back to the warehouse. The doors opened, and she drove through. In the back was a semi, a Kenworth, with the refrigerator generator running. Suddenly, three men appeared who seemed to know Este. She pulled up and stopped, talked with them briefly, and returned to the truck.

"Everybody out," she said softly. They left the car out front. "I've got the key, so let's go."

Ken walked quietly and just waved at the men. They saluted him; he saluted back. Willie said nothing and just settled in.

The Crown Vic was sitting out front, and they all slid in—Ken in the back. Este drove, and out the gate they went.

"Get me to a phone, baby. I've got to make a call."

"Already got it covered, Kenny. It's disposable, and it's in the glovebox, but we can't use that one, baby. They left it for us. We've got to get a clean one."

"Where's the nearest Walmart?"

"OK, have it your way, but we're supposed to be on our way to Houston to catch a flight to Miami. We're on our way, all right, but it isn't to Miami, it's to Palm Beach, and we're not flying commercially.

The stop at Walmart took 20 minutes, and Este emerged with a new disposable phone.

Ken dialed the office. It was about 10:30 a.m., Palm Beach time. Tiffany answered the phone.

"Tiffany, this is Ken. Give me Jack. This is an emergency."

"Oh my God, is this really you, Ken?"

"Yes, Tiffany, it's me."

"Are you OK?"

"Never better, baby. Now give me Jack."

Jack and Dragman were in the office meeting with an expert witness when Tiffany ran into the office.

"Mr. Shook, it's Ken. He's on the phone, line 2."

Shook was stunned but moved to the phone and picked it up. "Ken? Is that you?"

"Yeah, boss, it's me."

"Damn, where the fuck have you been?"

"Mexico, boss, and I haven't got time to tell you my story, but I picked up a couple of traveling companions, and I need to meet you at the General Aviation Terminal in Corpus Christi in four hours."

"OK, Ken, we'll get the Citation fueled, and we'll be in the air in 45 minutes."

"OK, boss, we'll be there in a black Crown Vic. I'm traveling with an angel and a new friend."

"OK, Ken, so where the hell have you been?"

"Puerte Grande prison, boss, in Guadalajara."

"How did that happen?"

"You're not going to believe it, but it's the Fuccerinos and Conveyance Mutual who put me there, compliments of Joe Stalin."

"See you in Corpus Christi, dude. We'll talk there."

Chapter 31

It was about 3 o'clock when Ken caught sight of the Citation on final approach into Corpus Christi. He was standing at the terminal window, and Este was at his side. She had slipped her arm through his, and she had gently nudged her cheek into his arm.

He turned to see the most beautiful creature he had ever met staring back into his eyes. They had lunch at the terminal and not a word was said, nor was it asked, about what had brought her to his rescue. All he knew was that she was at least 20 years his junior, but he was never letting her go. Willie was upbeat, wondering what his new life was going to be like. That would come later.

The Citation pulled into the gate, stopped, and the door opened. Out popped Jack, Dragman, and Tiffany. They met at the gate and hugged.

Ken introduced everyone all around, and he said, "Let's go home, man. We've got a lot to talk about."

"I couldn't agree more, Kenny."

They walked out to the plane, climbed aboard, and took a seat. Este was quiet and only smiled.

Looking at Este, Jack asked Ken, "Who the hell is that?"

"She's my angel, Jack, and without her I'd be either dead or still in that hellhole."

"She's beautiful, dude," Shook whispered.

"Yeah, angels usually are beautiful, aren't they, boss?"

"How did that happen, Ken?"

"Well, let's just put it this way: the Fuccerinos and their friends put me in prison as Paco Sanchez, who is a semifamous drug dealer, who is actually dead. I know this is hard to believe, but this is the kind of shit that happens all the time in Mexico. That was their mistake. It should have been some anonymous streetlevel thug who nobody knew or cared about. Instead they used the identity of someone who was perceived as being powerful. I was instantly respected and feared.

I'll bet it was that fucking Calvin Fuccerino's idea. He's one twisted little fuck who, I'm sure, was very pleased with himself when he pulled it off. He's just one of those overthetop thinkers who wanted to make a big joke about it. I imagine he convinced some Cancún gangsters that I really was Paco Sanchez, and that worked, since hardly anyone had ever seen the real Paco's face. If they had, they would have been killed. So they actually bribed the guards; and, oh, by the way, I had to bring 500 kilos of coke over the border in a garbage truck to make my escape. More on that later, dude."

"So, who is she, Kenny?"

"Well, Jack, I'm actually not too sure, but frankly I don't care. She's with me, and I really care about her. I'm not asking any questions, but just so you know, if not for her I wouldn't be here."

"How about a drink, dude?"

"Thought you'd never ask. Let's get out of here."

The Citation ran out to the end of the runway, turned, and waited. Clearance was given, and the engines came up. The craft quickly accelerated and lifted into the afternoon due east over the Gulf. They leveled off at 35,000 feet and cruised east.

Este head tucked herself quietly in with Ken, who continued to be debriefed.

"I watched them pull the Quattro into the warehouse and made it inside. I managed to get out and decided to go to dinner before I came back. They caught me in the parking lot of the Tiger Lounge. It was Calvin Fuccerino. The next thing I remember, I woke up in prison. That's where I met Willie. So, what do you think, boss?"

"Kenny, you're about to meet Detective Ralph Willis of the Broward Sheriff's office. He's on the case. Something tells me we need direct law enforcement involvement here."

The flight across the Gulf was smooth and quiet. Florida's coast just south of Tampa is where they crossed, just about at Sarasota. They flew south over the lake and lined up on PBIA direct from the west and landed effortlessly.

"We found your truck, Kenny, at the Fort Lauderdale airport. Dragman brought it up to your place and parked it in the garage after it was processed."

"Just take me home, boss. I've got to relax." He motioned to Este, "Incidentally, she's coming with me."

"What about Willie?"

"I'll take him to Joe Caruso's. He lives in my complex. I'll get Caruso to put him to work."

"Don't let him get a look at Este, dude."

"She's way ahead of guys like Crutch, Jack. I'm not concerned."

"OK, Kenny, see you tomorrow at the office at about 10?"

"Make it 11, boss.

"Eleven, it is. Oh, by the way, bring Este. We'll introduce her to Erika. She needs an assistant. Something tells me they are going to be BFFs. She needs clothes, and Erika can fix her right up. They are about the same size. Maybe Erika could bring some clothes to my place in the morning?"

"Sounds like a plan."

Dragman drove them a ways up I95 to PGA Boulevard, east to alternate A1A and south to Catalina Lakes, dropped off Willie at Crutch's and made some small talk, and then on to Ken's place on Capistrano Drive.

The rest of the night was memorable.

Chapter 32

It was nine o'clock in the morning, and Detective Willis walked through the door with Sgt. Datchko.

"Hi, Tiffany. I got an appointment with Mr. Shook."

"Yes, you do, Detective. I'll show you in. Can I get anyone a cup of coffee?"

"No, thanks, Tiffany, I'm already running on three cups."

Shook and Dragman met them in the waiting room and greeted them. "Hey, Bubba, good to see you. Come on back, have I got a story for you."

The inner sanctum at S&M is the modern version of a man cave, except on steroids: lots of wood, lots of leather, a fullservice bar and kitchen, two bedrooms, flat screens everywhere, a conference room for 12, and a video room with recliners. Shook took his naps there. There was really no reason ever to leave the place. Shook stayed there sometimes for days at a time.

They settled in in the conference room and Shook began, "There's someone I'd like you to meet."

"I'm all ears, Mr. Shook. You know we have some history between us. I worked with you on a homicide 25 years ago up here in Palm Beach that involved the Chicago mob."

"Yeah, remember that case. They were trying to kill me but gave up and fed their own guy to a bull gator out in the Glades."

"Oh yeah, that's one I'll never forget."

"So you don't need to call me Mr. Shook, Detective, call me Jack, Johnny, Johnny Ray, JR or Bubba, I don't care."

"No problem, Bubba. You can call me Ralphie or R.W."

"Yesterday, we flew to Corpus Christi to pick up Ken Wheeler. He's been in a Mexican prison for months and only escaped with the help of two people who, at first, thought he was this wellknown but mysterious cartel character. They knew who he really was and decided to use him for their own purposes to get themselves out of Mexico alive, apparently with a lot of money. Ken will be in this morning in about an hour, along with his traveling companions."

"Mexican prison?"

"Yes, Puente Grande, no less. Some operatives at Conveyance Mutual kidnapped Ken when he discovered the existence and location of the car that Harrison Davis was driving when he collided headon with the vehicle that my client was a passenger in. That collision rendered my client a paraplegic and killed the driver and front passenger back in July of last year. These guys forcibly drugged him and shipped him to the Mexican authorities under the name of this Paco Sanchez."

"That's fantastic, Bubba, tell me more, but I've got a quick question."

"Ask me, Ralphie."

"Why did they do all that? Why not just kill him and be done with it?"

"Two reasons, Ralphie: First, they are a bunch of twisted fucks. Second, they wanted to teach him a lesson, because he used to work for them and knew about some of the shit they use to pull."

"Are you serious?"

"Yes, I am, my man. For certain cases, they adopted a scorched earth mentality and used their 'unit' to get things done."

"The unit?"

"Yes, the unit. Kind of like the plumbers at Watergate, their dirty tricks crowd, you know."

"No shit?"

"No shit, baby."

"So how do we catch them, Bubba?"

"Well, I'm leaving that to you, but Wheeler can help identify his abductors."

"So, how was he able to do this Bubba?"

"Well, it's the only explanation that makes sense at this point. No one else had any reason to do this, Detective Willis"

"You're not talking about Calvin Fuccerino, are you?"

"None other, Ralphie."

"I've been after that slick little sociopath for years. We caught his brother a few years back involved in some chop shop scam, but he walked on probation."

"Well, R.W., I represent this young man who was in the backseat of the car. Greg Crutchfield represents the two dead boys. We got intel that Davis was drunk. We also suspect that a trooper is somehow involved, and we have an Audi Quattro that has a tampered black box."

"No shit?"

"No shit, Ralphie, and there's more, a lot more."

"Tell me, man."

"It seems Davis is in the middle of a nasty divorce, and his wife is pissed as hell because he's got film of her giving head to her personal trainer."

"Damn, I knew this was going to be good, but I didn't know it was also going to be fun, Bubba."

"Yeah, she's represented by Mike Kahn, another buddy of mine who is ready to provide info on Davis, but he is not really your criminal target. He's just being used by the unit."

"Where does all this lead, Bubba?"

"Well, you're going to have to flip someone and right now the leading candidate is Calvin Fuccerino and his brother, Melvin. If you get to them, they can take you to the top; right now, you've got Calvin by the balls."

"OK, Bubba, I'm with you on that, but I'm still a little fuzzy on how they pulled off the Paco Sanchez shit."

"Well, Paco was a cartel member who was almost never seen and remained a mystery most of his life. This made it really difficult to catch him."

"But what about fingerprints, dude?"

"Well, we believe his prints were lifted off the dead Paco by surgical removal and storage. They were then literally glued onto Ken's fingers when he was printed at the prison. This would have required a bribe or two, which is common in Mexico."

"Yeah, but what about his mug shot?"

"Well, Wheeler and Paco are about the same size, and they are actually similar in appearance. Keep in mind, pictures of Paco are exceedingly rare."

"I've heard about this fingerprint transplant, boss, but I've never seen it," chimed in Datchko.

"Well, apparently this is quite the going thing in Mexico. They have plastic surgeons who have perfected the procedure to lift only the top three or four layers of skin, preserve them between two micro slides, and then glue them over the receiving fingertips."

"There's more to this story, right, Bubba?"

"Yeah, there is."

"OK, what's the bad news?"

"Well, I don't think it's so bad. It's actually pretty cool. You can use this little bit of information as you wish. I only ask that it remain confidential."

"OK, Bubba, lay it on me."

"Well, right now, as we speak, a semi with Wisconsin plates is driving to Miami loaded with refrigerated cheese and 500 kilos of 100 percent pure Mexican cocaine."

"No shit, Bubba?"

"No shit, R.W."

"Yeah, Wheeler and his two companions had to bring it across the border at McAllen, Texas, to gain their freedom."

"No shit?"

"No shit."

"For obvious reasons, this information remains confidential. Use it for whatever purpose you want, but it cannot get back to Wheeler or his two friends."

"Speaking of that, who the hell are they?"

"Well, his prison mate is a disbarred lawyer from Cleveland named William James. He moved to Cancún about 10 years ago and got mixed up with that cartel. He was busted and sent to prison."

"OK, and the other?"

"Well, the other is a young Mexican woman named Este Ramirez—a beautiful woman, incredibly smart, and, at one time, one of Paco Sanchez's girlfriends. She was the moving force behind getting 'Paco' out and decided to go through with it, even though she knew Paco was dead, because she wanted out of Mexico to start a new life here."

"Did she get out with any money?"

"Well, I haven't asked and frankly don't care. I hope you don't ask, because it doesn't matter. Who cares? She made her break. She did what she was told to do, and she pulled it off. She's probably free and clear of those people."

"OK, Bubba."

"Just wait until you meet her. This woman is a 10 out of 10, and Wheeler is in love. I'm asking you as consideration for what we've given you to let it go. Incidentally, R.W., I think we're going to need new identities for these two, especially the woman."

"OK, Bubba, I'm intrigued, but where does this all lead?"

"Well, let me tell you more. We think we got a corrupt trooper. We're working on that. We have a young female rookie trooper who is pissed off and wants to tell us what she saw and what she knows. We got a lawyer who is running for State Senate, who got to a bartender at the club where Davis was drinking the night of the crash and bribed him using a Conveyance Mutual bagman named Donohue. I'm particularly interested in that asshole."

"Who's that, Bubba?"

"Ed Baldwin, dude."

"Oh shit. So, what's the beef with him?"

"Well, he's dishonest. Years ago, he almost scammed me into a jam by claiming he never authorized dispersal on a case we had partially settled that ended up in a $6-million verdict. He's a treacherous bastard who is just bad to the bone. He's bought and sold by big sugar, big insurance, and big medicine. We got a towing company who doesn't want to tell us where they took the Quattro. When we know where it went, we got a tampered black box."

"OK, where does all this take us, Bubba?"

"There's more. We got a Doc who is treating this young man, who, all of a sudden, has the Conveyance Fraud Unit up his ass, and he can't get any of his bills paid. His name is Stan Cooper."

"So where does all this lead, Bubba?"

"It leads directly to Mary Jo Stalinowsky, claims superintendent, for Conveyance Mutual Insurance Company, southeast Florida Division."

"That's quite a story, Bubba."

"Yeah, I know, and these people are not stupid, so they will be slick as shit. You've got to be careful and build your case carefully."

"I'm thinking I need to go see Calvin with Wheeler in tow."

"Calvin is your key, R.W. If you can get him to flip, you can get a lot of the other people. After all, you got him by the short hairs right now."

"OK, we'll need to debrief your people and statementize them."

Just then, Shook's intercom went off.

"Mr. Shook?"

"Yes, Tiffany."

"Everyone's here, Mr. Shook."

"OK, Tiffany, bring all of them in.

"Just remember, R.W., the enemy will not go down without a fight."

The double doors opened, and Este and Erika walked in. They were looking fine. Willie followed with Wheeler and Dragman.

And so it began.

Chapter 33

It was one of those cool but crisp south Florida mornings when R.W. and Datchko had assembled their arrest team in the parking lot of the Denny's out on Broward Boulevard. Armed with his arrest and search warrants, Datchko was prepared to take Calvin down. For good measure, the search warrant obtained allowed them to take control and seize the surveillance hard drive in the warehouse. R.W. wanted to make the point with great gusto and decided to take Ken Wheeler with him to amp up the shock value he needed when he confronted Calvin. Once the team had a perimeter established and executed the search warrant, they would attempt to interview anyone they found on the premises.

When word came that Calvin had just arrived at the warehouse, the operation quickly got under way. They drove into the warehouse parking lot and exited quickly through the main gate.

Calvin was just inside the main door when he saw them coming. He didn't run; he froze. His eyes were as big as saucers. He stared transfixed at Wheeler, who flashed a grin that wouldn't subside.

"Calvin Fuccerino, you're under arrest for the Aggravated Kidnapping of Ken Wheeler with a weapon. That is a first-degree felony punishable by 30 years in the State Department of Corrections. You're also charged with tampering with evidence. At this point, I need to advise you of your constitutional rights: you have the right to remain silent . . ."

"Save it, detective. I know my rights, and I'm invoking them at this time. I have nothing to say. I want my lawyer, and I want him now."

"OK, Calvin, have it your way, but I am reading them anyway dipshit. You can be a defendant or you can be a witness. It's your call. We know all about your work with Conveyance, and, if you want to spend your life in prison for them, so be it. You feel me, Calvin?"

"I feel you, asshole. I still want my lawyer."

Wheeler could not contain himself any longer. "Hey, Calvin, Paco Sanchez says hello."

"Fuck you, Wheeler. I have nothing to say to you either."

"Calvin, we've got a warrant for Melvin, too, and he's already in custody. We got him at his place 10 minutes ago."

Sitting on his desk in the office, the deputies found Calvin's cell phone, which was blowing up nonstop. One of the deputies picked up the cell phone, waving it at R.W. "What do I do with this, chief?"

"Give it to me now." R.W. flipped open the phone and said, "Hello."

A voice on the line spoke. "Calvin, this is Howard. The cops are on the way. Get the fuck out of there."

Without missing a beat, Detective Willis responded, "What are you talking about, Howard?"

This was met with silence and a "click."

Willis turned to Wheeler and said, "Who is Howard?"

"That would be Howard Donohue, Stalinowsky's butt boy."

"Very interesting." Waving the phone, he continued, "I think I'll get a warrant for this thing, too."

Calvin sat in silence during the ride downtown. They walked into the detective bureau, and, since Calvin was in custody, he was placed in an interview room, which was fully monitored by video.

"We've got to give him a phone call, R.W.," Datchko reminded him, but then offered, "Why not offer him coffee and his cell phone, so he can make the call, and then leave the room and watch who he does call?"

"What if he destroys the damn thing, Joe?"

"Good point. He's not that stupid. It was just a thought. Besides we've already got Howard on the line. Let's keep it clean. Some smart lawyer will claim we used the phone to subvert Miranda."

Calvin was provided a landline phone, which was brought in and plugged in by the detective.

"Make your call, Calvin," he said as he left the room.

Calvin immediately dialed a local lawyer named Dinkmeyer, who asked to be put on the phone with the detective and was obliged.

"My client is not speaking to you, detective. He has invoked his Fifth Amendment rights. No further contact with my client is authorized without my express authorization and presence."

"Well, thank you for that, Mr. Dinkmeyer. I've got the message. Now, I've got one for you. After you get here and talk to your client, you will learn that we want to know if your client wants to be a witness or just another hapless idiot on his way to the Department of Corrections (DOC). We already know a lot about him and his brother's activities with Conveyance Mutual. You feel me, Mr. Dinkmeyer?"

"Yeah, I feel you, detective. I'll see you in a few hours. By the way, what is his brother charged with, detective?"

"Conspiracy, of course. His lawyer is on the way as well."

"See you then, detective."

Meanwhile, Calvin sat stoically. The interview room was windowless and lined with cork paneling. There was one light centered on the ceiling in the middle of the 10-by-10 box, and an obvious camera stared down from the corner. He knew he was being watched. His mind was racing.

Suddenly, the door unlocked, and Willis walked in. "Anything you need, Calvin? Cigarette, coffee?"

"I'll take both, detective. Coffee, black with lots of sugar, and any filtered cigarettes, not menthol.

"No problem, Calvin. You understand this is not personal? I'm just doing my job."

"Yeah, I understand, but you sure got a shitty job."

Willis laughed at Calvin's attempt at humor and departed. A few minutes later he returned. "Here you go, dude."

"Thanks, detective. I appreciate it.

Willis departed and spoke to Datchko. "I think he wants to talk. He knows we got him by the balls. Let's see what happens."

It was 11 o'clock in the morning when Dinkmeyer was escorted into the "D" Bureau. He was introduced to Willis.

"What's my client charged with, detective?"

"Right now, a first-degree felony of kidnapping with a firearm, a second-degree felony of tampering with evidence, and insurance fraud."

"What's with the tampering?"

"We know about the Quattro and how it was moved and disabled. We think it's clear insurance fraud. We know your client wiped the surveillance tapes of his security system, but we now have the hard drive."

"Insurance fraud?"

"Oh, yeah, reverse insurance fraud. You know, the kind committed by insurance companies."

Dinkmeyer feigned his understanding and offered no disputing response.

"Go talk to your client, sir. We want his cooperation."

"I want him moved into one of the clean holding cells where you cannot monitor our conversation, detective."

"But of course, Mr. Dinkmeyer. Consider it done."

Dinkmeyer was ushered into Attorney Interview Room No. 3, and Calvin was brought in and chained to the metal table in the center of the room. Dinkmeyer had been searched and complained about the thoroughness of the frisk, which included his genitalia.

"Just doing my job, sir," was the deputy's response.

The door closed, and Dinkmeyer spoke first. "Calvin, I know who you work for and who is going to pay for your inconvenience, and we are expecting your cooperation."

"Listen, Dinkmeyer, don't give me that shit. I'm looking at spending the rest of my life in the DOC, because I handled the Wheeler thing just the way she wanted it. Look what it got me."

"Relax, Calvin, we got a ways to go on this, and we feel your pain. But you never should have allowed Wheeler to see you in the back parking lot."

"I don't think he did see me, Dinkmeyer."

"Well, he's saying that he did, and it's not looking too good for you now, Calvin. So you need to play ball, man."

"Play ball?"

"Yeah, play ball with us, not them."

"Let me change the subject, Dinkmeyer, what's going on with my brother? I'm concerned about him."

"He's charged with conspiracy right now, but that could change."

"Change?"

"Yeah, they may try to intimidate him into cooperation. We got that covered. We got him a lawyer."

"OK. Well, you better make him feel better real quick, or he'll talk. He's not the strong one, you know. He is also on probation."

"We've got it covered, Calvin."

"OK, Dinkmeyer, I'll play along, but what about bail?"

"Well, right now, it's none, but you have a first appearance scheduled for tomorrow."

"Why tomorrow?"

"Because you got arrested today, and they don't have to take you to first appearance to see a judge until tomorrow at 1:30 p.m."

"So what's the chance of a bond? I mean, I have a right to bond, don't I?"

"Yeah, Calvin, you do, except that this charge has you actually trying to prevent a witness from testifying, and it's a charge of kidnapping. They will argue that, under the circumstances, you are not entitled to bond."

"Well, will I get a bond or not? And who is going to post it?"

"Frankly, I think we should make an effort, but it will possibly be denied. The jail duty judge is well known to us, and you're not going to get one. We'll need to set a fullblown bond hearing down the road in a few weeks after we get a look at their discovery response."

"Shit, I hate jail, dammit. What about Melvin?"

"Well, his chances are a little better, but probably no bond either."

"I need to talk to Melvin."

"Yeah. Well, they're probably going to get a no-contact order and keep you separated in jail, so just be ready."

"Dammit, Dinkmeyer, I'm not feeling too reassured right now."

"Look, Calvin, you've got to just hold tight. Anything I can do for you in the meantime?"

"Yeah, get to my wife and keep her calm."

"No problem, Calvin."

On his way out, Dinkmeyer encountered Willis.

"What's it going to be, Dinkmeyer?"

"My client chooses to remain silent, detective."

"OK, have it your way, but we're going to do this thing with or without his cooperation. It's up to him."

"If we change our minds, we'll let you know."

Willis sat back and shook his head.

Datchko was sitting next to him and said, "Who the hell is 'we'?"

"Yeah, Joe, it did sound like there was some kind of committee of 'we,' didn't it?"

"No doubt, R.W."

"Who do we have inside the jail who can be Calvin's new BFF, Joe?

"Let's work on that."

Chapter 34

From the street, the Broward County Jail looks like another downtown Fort Lauderdale highrise complex, but, when you look close and realize the windows are either nonexistent or very small, then you wonder what kind of view that tenant purchased. Then, you start to realize the magnitude of the place when you realize this is a jail.

Very conveniently, just across the street to the south is the courthouse, which in itself is imposing, now that they had finally finished it. Much like the Palm Beach County Jail, Broward is so large that if it were a prison, it would rank in the top 50 in size in the United States.

It had been three weeks since Calvin and Melvin were picked up, but they had only been to court once. Calvin was denied bail because, according to the duty judge who handled the first appearance, "there are no circumstances, sir, where I can grant you bail and not endanger the witnesses or the community."

Both were handled by video. Melvin's bail was set at $1 million, but no one had seen it fit to post his bond, and there was a nobond for his violation of probation (VOP).

His wife, Doris, was so traumatized by the charges that she just couldn't bring herself to put her house on the line and empty their savings account to spring him, and, even then, he wouldn't be released because of the VOP. This is not to mention the fact that she had been visited by Melvin's attorney to assure her that he would be OK to leave him inside, especially since his safety was a serious issue.

And, so, Melvin sat, pissed off but quiet about what he knew, unable to see or talk to his brother. Calvin had been separated from him and secretly housed several miles north in Palm Beach as a courtesy to the Sheriff and for Calvin's safety.

Donohue had called Mary Jo the day of the arrest, and she went ballistic. She got him off the phone, met with him at the Jupiter inlet bar, and gave him his marching orders never to talk to her again.

"Howard, get down to Cancún and alert Diablo Rojo of the situation. Tell him that we need him to handle it."

Howard was in Cancún within 24 hours, and the gears were set in motion.

Manuel Gutierrez, the only redheaded Mexican that Howard had ever met, was quietly determined to stop this leak and was not happy about the escape of Wheeler the week before. His operatives were already in south Florida to hunt him down and the whereabouts of Este and Willie were also in question.

Gutierrez, or "El Diablo Rojo" (i.e., "the Red Devil"), was aptly named after the Humboldt squid that patrolled the West Coast of the Baja, which could change colors and attack fishermen and divers who foolishly got into the waters when they were around. At six-feet tall and 100 pounds, a Humboldt was a menace and vicious beyond belief. It was a perfect match for Gutierrez. He enjoyed the name and matched the squid's reputation for lethality.

It was in the cafeteria that Melvin encountered the Red Devil's hit man. He was hit from behind and stabbed multiple times while surrounded by at least eight Mexican illegals who were being held under Immigration and Customs Enforcement (ICE) holds. It was not clear who had stabbed him. The video was poor. It looked like a scuffle, and everyone scattered. Then, there was Melvin on the floor bleeding to death.

The guards got to him quickly, and he was at Broward General within 20 minutes. Although Melvin was cut to pieces, the surgeons had stopped the bleeding and, with 12 units of blood, had saved his life. Willis was at the hospital within two hours and waited until Melvin came out of surgery. His lawyer was called. Willis wanted to talk to Melvin, but his lawyer refused.

Willis was on the road to Palm Beach to meet with Terry Glocker, Calvin's new jail roommate, to have a sit down.

The meeting with Glocker was quick and to the point. "Terry, we need you to deliver a message to Calvin. They tried to kill his brother, Melvin, and we're betting he's next. We don't think his lawyer is going to tell him about the attempt on his brother's life. So, if he wants to talk, with or without his lawyer, we're ready. But we know Dinkmeyer is not working for him; he's working for someone else. Do you think you can do that, Terry?"

"What's in it for me, man?"

"You do this for us, and you'll be out of here in 72 hours on your Own Recognizance. Do we have a deal?"

"Yes, we do, detective." Terry left and went back upstairs to the 18th floor where he and Calvin shared a cell. Good to his word, Terry delivered the message promptly.

"Melvin was in bad shape, man," Terry explained.

Calvin was in shock and turned to the door and shouted, "damn it guard, I need to talk to Det. Willis, now!"

Willis and Datchko were downstairs when they received word that Calvin was ready to meet. Calvin was brought down and brought into a room with a phone already on the table. Willis spoke first.

"Calvin, here's the phone. Call Dinkmeyer. I'm betting he'll claim he knows nothing. You need to handle this. It's completely up to you."

Willis and Datchko left the room, and Calvin got Dinkmeyer on the phone.

"Calvin, why are you calling me on the phone? This line may not be secure. I told you we only talk in person."

"Fuck you, Dinkmeyer, I want to know some things. First, how is my brother doing?"

"He's fine, Calvin, but you've got to get off the phone, and you've got to do it now. If you want to talk, I can be there tomorrow morning at 10 o'clock, OK?"

"Be here, Dinkmeyer. We definitely need to talk."

Calvin hung up the phone and summoned his guard. "Tell Willis and Datchko I'll see them tomorrow at noon."

Willis and Datchko were on I95 south within 10 minutes and discussing the situation.

"So, do you think Calvin is going to want to talk, R.W.?"

"I know he does, Datch. When he looks Dinkmeyer in the eye and hears lies about his brother, the deal will be hatched. He's being lied to, and he's too smart to go down the road his brother went."

"He's going to need a lawyer."

"Yeah, well, we can't interfere in that, but I'll bet he has a new one within 24 hours of our chat."

"Come on, man, get on it. Rushhour traffic is starting to build, and I want to get to the jail by 7 tonight."

"You'll make it, dude. Relax."

Chapter 35

Over on Flagler Drive, Dennis was sitting in the bar at the Schooner Club, waiting for his date, Erika. He used to work there years ago and still knew some of the waiters and the bartender. It was about 5:15 p.m. when she came through the door. She looked great, of course, and walked to the far eastern corner of the bar where he was sitting and took the high top directly behind at the window.

It was a beautiful night, and Dennis had already downed one Wild Turkey with a splash. Erika ordered a white Zinfandel.

"Still drinking wine, I see."

"Yes, Dennis. I like it, and, if I like something, I stay with it."

Their drinks were delivered immediately, and Erika smiled and began. "OK, Dennis, you called. What's on your mind?"

"Well, two things: First, you told me to call you. Second, I enjoy your company."

"OK, Dennis, I think you know I've always enjoyed your company as well."

"Yeah, I've always felt there's been something between us. I don't know where this can lead, except to tell you that I think the time has come, Erika."

"OK, Dennis . . ."

"But there's something else, and I want you to keep it under wraps."

"What is it, Dennis?"

"I can't stand working at Oeste Palma anymore. I just can't deal with the abuse, and I'm going to leave. But I need to land somewhere."

"Well, Dennis, I'm sure we can help you there. Mr. Shook has influence everywhere in Palm Beach and even Melbourne Beach."

"OK, I was hoping you would say that, because I've got something to lay on Shook that will rock his world."

"Really? Let me have it. Dennis, you have our word that you will be protected."

Dennis pulled an envelope out of his jacket pocket and pushed it across the table.

"What's this, Dennis?" Erika asked, nudging the envelope.

"It's Harrison Davis's bar tab the night he killed those kids. He was shit-faced. Something told me to print it out, and I made a copy the next day. These charges were purged from his monthly bill, and the club manager said some strange things to me that pissed me off about protecting client confidences."

"So, how much had he had to drink?"

"He knocked down nine Silver Bullets and was flying high."

"Silver Bullets?"

"Yeah, straight Absolut Vodka martinis. I had tried several times to cut him off, but no go. He was in his typical obnoxious mood, abusing the shit out of me. He even insisted on a gocup when he did leave. And I'm telling you, he could barely stand upright going out the door."

Erika picked up on it immediately. "What did the gocup look like?"

"Clear plastic with our logo on it."

"OK, Dennis, thank you for that."

'There's more, baby."

"More?"

"Yes, a lot more."

"Lay it on me."

"So this other prick, Ed Baldwin, corners me about a month ago and tells me that he appreciates my discretion on the Davis matter and that, within the hour, a delivery would be made to me that was a token of 'their appreciation.'"

"No kidding, Dennis?"

"No kidding, Erika. So, within an hour, that prick that you were with at the Baldwin thing, Howard Donohue, was in the bar and handed me an envelope containing five grand in cash."

"I was never *with* Donohue, Dennis."

"I know, I know, but I was a little surprised to see you at the Baldwin shin-dig with that prick."

"Yeah, I was there, but I needed a date, Dennis, to get in. I'm not exactly trusted, you know."

"So what's the history there?"

"It all goes back to the days when I worked for Farmington Mutual, and we all knew each other through the 'Claimsmen.' Yeah, me, Ken Wheeler, Donohue, Dragman, we were all once members when we all worked for the carriers."

"I remember those bashes, Erika. I've never seen such drinking in my life."

"Yeah, it was the entire insurance defense bar and all the adjusters, claims managers, and superintendents."

"Hell, I remember Stalinowsky used to come to those. And look where she is now, Erika."

"Yes, those were the days. I didn't enjoy them too much because I was always getting hit on, especially when I was drinking heavily."

"Well, that's the story, baby, and I'm sticking to it."

"Well, thank you for that, Dennis. Now, let's get some dinner. I hear the stone crab claws are unbelievable. It's on us."

"Damn, dinner with a beautiful woman, and I don't even have to pay. What could be better than this?"

Chapter 36

It was 10:30 Thursday morning. Erika had just debriefed Shook, and he and Dragman were preparing to take the deposition of Trooper Odalys RosoMartinez.

Baldwin had tried three times to cancel, and Shook had obtained a discovery order requiring its completion. It was the same old crap from Baldwin. He couldn't be there because of scheduling conflicts. Judge Murphy had heard this same old story many times before and granted the motion, pointing out that his firm, including the Broward and Dade offices, had 50 lawyers and that, surely, someone could attend this routine discovery deposition.

Within three days after the order, rumors began to surface on the street that Judge Murphy would face opposition for his seat and that Baldwin had handpicked the reported candidate.

"Don't you love this asshole, Dragman? He is so predictable. He has become so arrogant that he actually believes this type of intimidation is acceptable."

"I don't know, boss. This kind of crap never quits."

"So, according to Erika, Trooper RosoMartinez is going to drop the rock on Trooper Thomas?"

"We'll see about that. We know Davis was drunk, and we know where he came from. According to Erika, the trooper is going to tell the truth."

"Well, if she does, boss, then it's off to Willis to let him in on this. I mean, do you really think the Broward Sheriff's office will do something about Thomas?"

"No, Dragman, they won't be directly involved. It will go to the Florida Department of Law Enforcement (FDLE) and will be handled by the agent in charge, Wayne Ivey."

"I've got a question, boss."

"Yeah, Dragman?"

"How can an insurance company be involved in insurance fraud? It's my understanding that those laws were designed to protect the insurance industry."

"Well, Dragman, I'm glad you asked. It's a littleknown fact that—when the general insurance fraud act was set up under Chapter 626—somehow, someway, some minority legislation out of Dade County added four little words in the statute to cover that."

"No shit?"

"No shit, Dragman."

"So, what were they?"

"Well, it provides that any person who knowingly, and with intent to defraud, presents or causes to be presented any claim offered to or by an insurer any fraudulent statement claim of evidence is guilty of insurance fraud."

"No shit?"

"No shit, Dragman."

"Damn, I like it. Imagine an insurance company involved in insurance fraud. So, what is the penalty?"

"It's a third-degree felony, each count, Dragman."

"Wow, let's go get a deposition from the trooper."

Meanwhile, Trooper Roso-Martinez entered the room and all conversation stopped. The first thing you noticed about her when you met her was her size. She stood just over five-feet tall but looked professional and crisply dressed in her uniform. She was, of course, a goodlooking young woman who was well spoken, had a south Florida Hispanic accent, and was obviously well educated. In fact, she attended and graduated from Miami Dade Community College and transferred to Florida State when she received her Bachelor of Science from the school of Criminology and Corrections. She went directly to the FHP Academy and graduated third in her class.

She was just recently promoted to corporal and works almost exclusively Broward and Dade County as a road patrol trooper. She previously worked up north in Brevard, but requested a transfer last year, which was granted.

Shook took all this information with him in hopes to skip some of the small talk. With the preliminaries behind him, Shook steered the conversation directly toward the accident involving Marvin.

"And so, Trooper, were you dispatched to the scene of this collision west of I-95 on New Haven Avenue last year, Friday, July 8, 2001?"

"Yes, I was, sir."

"Did you prepare any report as a result of your involvement?"

"No, sir, I did not."

"Why not, Trooper?"

"Well, the trooper in charge was Sgt. Billy Thomas, and he took over the investigation. He directed me to handle traffic control and speak to the eyewitness, who was an elderly woman. So, Thomas prepared the report."

"Upon your arrival, who was on scene?"

"Well, Deputy Wilson was actually first on scene, me next, and then Trooper Thomas arrived and took over. It was obviously a headon collision between an old Sentra and a newer model Audi. The front seat occupants of the Sentra were deceased. The rear passenger was alive but severely injured."

"What about the Audi?"

"There was one occupant, the driver, whom I determined to be Harrison Davis. He was still in the car. The airbag had deployed, and I was able to speak to him."

"Did you notice any odor of alcohol when speaking to Davis?"

"Yes, I did, which I reported to Thomas. I also noticed a clear plastic cup with a Oeste Palma logo in the front seat passenger floorboard that smelled of alcohol, which I also reported to Thomas."

"After your report to Thomas, what did he say or direct you to do?"

"Do you want his exact words?"

"Yes, we do, Trooper."

"Well, he said to check on the eyewitness and to look after the rear passenger of the Sentra and to see if I could cover the two dead brothas in the front seat."

"I see. Did you comply?"

"Yes, I did."

"Did anyone else arrive on the scene before it was cleared?"

"Aside from the paramedics?"

"Yes, aside from them."

"Yes, an insurance adjuster, a Mr. Howard Donohue, was on the scene; and Mr. Davis's wife arrived, spoke to Thomas, and apparently took her husband home."

"So, Trooper, did you speak to Thomas about this removal of one of the drivers involving a traffic homicide?"

"Yes, I did. I asked Thomas where Davis was going and why he wasn't being held for a blood test when we had two deceased persons in the other car. Thomas told me to leave it to him. It was obvious what had happened. The Sentra was totally at fault, according to him. I needed to do what I was told, because he was my superior."

The deposition lasted another 20 minutes, and the lawyer from Baldwin's office asked no questions. The deposition was terminated. Trooper RosoMartinez departed, and Shook ordered the deposition be transcribed.

Shook returned to his office and called Detective Willis.

"R.W., we need to meet up. Got some great intel for you."

"I'll be up there later this afternoon, Jack. I'm meeting with Calvin Fuccerino later."

"Well, I just took Trooper RosoMartinez's deposition, and you've got to come see me as soon as you can."

"OK, Jack, I'll be up later. I'll call you."

Shook and Dragman kicked back and discussed the day's events. "This thing is starting to come together, Dragman."

"Yeah, boss, but how far is this thing going to go, and where is it going to lead?"

"Well, Baldwin is bribing witnesses, and the bagman is Donohue. Thomas is looking like he's involved. This thing is about to collapse. I think it's going straight to the top, Dragman."

"She's too smart to get nicked on this, boss. I can't believe any of this is going to get tied to her."

"Well, this time I beg to differ. She's too mean to let anyone get anything over on her—that's her weakness. They should have just eliminated Wheeler, but she wanted to torture the poor bastard by putting him in a Mexican prison and accuse him of working for drug dealers. It was too elaborate a plan. It could have worked if Wheeler hadn't escaped. He was in the Mexican gulags, and no one was going to believe him. By the way, how is Wheeler doing?"

"He's in Nassau with Este. We've got him on ice for a while."

"Sounds like he's finally happy, dude."

"Yeah, but who knows what that woman is capable of?"

"She's capable of anything, man. She's proved that."

Chapter 37

Calvin was brought down to one of the interview rooms at about 10:30 a.m. He hadn't slept all night, and he was cranky as hell, operating on about four cups of coffee. He was chained to the metal table in the middle of the room. He sat quietly for a few minutes alone, looking out the small sliver of a window that overlooked the golf course next to the jail.

Within 10 minutes, Dinkmeyer was brought up and came into the room. Calvin said nothing for a while, and then finally spoke.

"So, Dinkmeyer, what's going on with my case?"

"Just got the discovery response, Calvin, and I brought it with me. They got Wheeler and nothing else directly tying you to the kidnapping. They do have your cell phone, which they haven't finished with, and they haven't finished downloading your surveillance computer. They also reference a towing company that brought the vehicle up from Palm Beach. Aside from that, we know very little else."

"What about my brother, man?"

"What about him?"

"Well, what's going on with him?"

I don't know, Calvin. I'll need to check with his lawyer."

"You mean to tell me you got nothing to report on my brother?"

"No, Calvin, I do not."

Calvin sat back for a moment, looked at Dinkmeyer, and sighed. "That's enough for you and me, Dinkmeyer. You're fired. Get the fuck out of here and make it quick."

"What are you talking about, Calvin? You can't do that, you'll screw everything up."

"I know damn well that you know about the attempt on Melvin's life, so you're a fucking liar. Get the fuck out, and get out now."

Calvin began yelling for the guard, who appeared within seconds. Dinkmeyer got up and said nothing. Calvin looked at the guard and refused to speak until Dinkmeyer was gone.

"You need to get Detective Willis up here as soon as possible. I need to make a call."

Calvin was taken down two floors to the phone banks and called Willis.

"Detective?"

"Yeah, Calvin."

"I just fired Dinkmeyer. I'm ready to talk, in case you're still interested."

"I'll be up this afternoon, Calvin."

"Good, don't take forever, man."

Willis hung up the phone and smiled.

Dinkmeyer waited until he got to the parking lot to call Stalinowsky to report the development with Calvin.

I knew there was going to be trouble with that Calvin, she thought as she hung up the phone. *I'm going to have to up the ante on that asshole.* She immediately got Donohue on the phone.

"Howard?"

"Yes, boss?"

"Dinkmeyer just got fired, and those idiots out of the Yucatán fucked up the job on Wheeler. Sever all ties with Calvin, and do it now. It all has to stop with him. He's got to be the wild hare who took all of this on himself, and we can't know what the hell he did or why. Stonewall this thing, Howard, and I mean now!"

"It's done, boss."

"What's the deal with this tow company that we used to move the vehicle?"

"You mean Jack's Towing?"

"Yes, you moron, who else would I be talking about?"

"He's been paid off, so let it go."

"Well, he better stay paid off, Howard. I don't want any more surprises, OK?"

"Got it, boss."

Mary Jo hung up the phone and sat back, looking out her window over Palm Beach Lakes Boulevard.

"I don't like this," she muttered to herself.

Meanwhile, about 70 miles south, Willis and Datchko had just gotten into the Dodge Charger sedan with tinted windows and began heading out Broward Boulevard to go north. The ride up I95 was easy this time of day.

I live on this road, yet I don't ever see it, he thought as they drove North.

Calvin had just finished lunch, which consisted of bologna sandwiches and some kind of meat soup. *The food in here sucks*, he thought. *I want a decent meal. I need to get the fuck out of here.* Just then, Calvin was called to the interview room and chained, again, to the metal table.

"Anything I can get you, Calvin?"

"Yeah, detective, get me the fuck out of here."

"OK, Calvin, we'll check you out, but we're taking you to Fort Lauderdale. We got a lot to talk about."

"Let's go, Detective."

Calvin sat back and looked Willis straight in the eye. "Look, man, I know I'm not going to walk on this, but what am I looking at if I give you what you want?"

"Well, Calvin, you're 42, and we'll see to it that you get no more than 10 years, and you will have do at least 85 percent of your sentence in Florida. That means you will be out before you're 50. You might even be out before that, and we can make sure it is minimum security. We know a lot about you and Conveyance Mutual, but you need to fill in the blanks. It's damn lucky for you that you didn't kill Wheeler. If you had, no holds would have been barred. The only condition is that you have to tell the truth. You can't lie to us."

"What about my brother?"

"He's going to recover. We know he was not directly involved, so he's looking at straight probation after some jail time."

"I want him out, so my family will be protected, detective."

"I understand that, Calvin, and I think we can make that happen. You'll be taken down to Broward. I'll meet you there late this afternoon. I've got to go talk to a lawyer."

"Lawyer?"

"Yeah, Jack Shook, why?"

"It figures, what's that about?"

"Like I said, Calvin, you've got to tell us all you've got. If you leave anything out, you're going to get fucked."

"I want to see my brother."

"We can arrange that."

"OK, I'll see you in a few hours."

The drive over the middle bridge to Palm Beach was always thoughtprovoking for Willis. There are two Palm Beaches separated by the Intracoastal Waterway. When you cross one bridge, you enter an enclave for the rich. Shook never liked it in Palm Beach but agreed to have the office there so that Meisel could serve his wealthy divorce clients. The rent wasn't bad; it was nonexistent. They had bought the building ten years ago, and they bought it right.

Shook was waiting for Willis and Datchko, and they were ushered in without waiting.

"What have you got, Jack?"

"I think we have a dirty trooper, R.W. Howard Donohue was on the scene of our collision, and this trooper ignored evidence of impairment and allowed Harrison Davis to be removed from the scene without a blood or urine test. Furthermore, he had two dead bodies and a seriously injured survivor—my client."

"Hmmm, what's his name?"

"Billy Thomas."

"I know him, Jack. He's been around for a long time."

"Yeah, he has, R.W., and he's all jammed up. He's got three exwives, and they got all he had. He lives in an old townhouse up in Palm Bay and doesn't appear to have much, just the kind of guy who might be vulnerable to a bribe or two."

"Yeah, Jack, I'm afraid so."

"So, what about Calvin?"

"He's fired Dinkmeyer and says he's ready to talk. He's being brought down to the 'D' Bureau as we speak. He's seriously pissed about what happened to his brother, and Dinkmeyer is lying to him about it. I think he understands that he no longer has any friends and that he's in great danger himself."

"Well, let me in on it when you get it. We've got something else, R.W."

"What's that?"

"Well, we got a bartender at Oeste Country Club who gave us Davis' bar tab that he saved from last year on July 8, and it shows serious alcohol consumption by Davis."

"Really?"

"Yeah, and there's more."

"Lay it on me, man."

"Well, he claims to have been bribed by Ed Baldwin and his bagman, Conveyance's field adjuster, Howard Donohue."

"No shit?"

"No shit, R.W."

"All we need now is for Calvin to fill in a few blanks, and we will have the whole picture."

"And then what, R.W.?"

"Then, we go to the grand jury."

Chapter 38

W illis and Datchko were about to statementize Calvin by videotape. Calvin had been brought in and requested a Five Guys burger with a large fry. Calvin loved these burgers and was very appreciative. The food at Palm Beach County Jail was better than Broward's lockup, but just barely.

Willis cornered Datchko and prepared their strategy. "Before any statement is taken, we got to Hollywood this Miranda thing, Joe."

"Couldn't agree more, R.W."

"Where is he, anyway?"

"He's in Interview Room 2, and he's cooling his heels. He's got coffee and cigarettes, R.W."

"OK, well, let me handle it. Let me have that written waiver."

The video showed Calvin looking relaxed and deep in thought when Willis walked in.

"Hey, Calvin, how's it going?"

"OK, R.W., but I've been better."

"I understand. Calvin, we've got some formalities to go over before we talk to you."

"Yeah, I understand, detective."

"OK, well, I just want to make it clear that this meeting has been called by you and that you fired your lawyer, Dinkmeyer."

"That's right, detective. That's exactly right. I fired that fat, lying bastard because he wasn't doing shit, and he lied to me. And when that happened, I called you."

"So let me read you your Miranda, OK?"

"OK, go ahead."

"I've also got a written waiver card here, OK?"

"OK."

Willis read the Miranda rights and concluded, "Do you understand?"

"Yes, I do, detective.

"Do you want to waive your right to remain silent and your right to an attorney?"

"Yes, I do, detective."

"Here, sign this, but read it first."

Calvin signed the waiver, and the interview began. It was even better than Willis could have expected. Yes, he was a member of a "unit" that worked for Conveyance Mutual. He and Melvin put Wheeler in the trunk of their car and delivered him to Stalinowsky's contact at the Miami-Opa Locka airport. They drugged him and put him on the plane to Cancún, where he was delivered to Manuel Gutierrez, a.k.a. El Diablo Rojo. He asked her why she was handling Wheeler in this way, and she told him this was their first business exchange with Rojo—to build trust. Calvin knew most of the plan with Wheeler, because it was Stalinowsky and Donohue that had the contacts in Cancún.

The shocker was the money, 50 grand in cash. It all came from Rojo and was sent to Donohue to launder. It was not traceable back to Conveyance Mutual. The money had been used to set up multiple businesses in Florida, all owned by associates of El Diablo Rojo. He only knew of a few in Fort Lauderdale, and one of them was the strip cub where Wheeler was abducted.

Donohue handled all the money, and Calvin suspected that it was all locked up in one of Donohue's bedrooms in his townhouse in Melbourne. He had been there once, and Donohue had retreated to the bedroom, which was locked behind a metal door, and emerged with a bundle of cash while he was there on another job for Stalinowsky.

Baldwin was involved, but only on the money pot. She didn't trust him and actually disliked him intensely. She enjoyed ordering him around and laughed at the idea that he would actually be elected to the Senate. Donohue had told him that much of the money actually being used in Baldwin's campaign came from Mexico, and Donohue was in charge of the "slush" fund. The money was converted to campaign contribution checks, which were delivered to Baldwin.

After the statement was concluded, Calvin and Willis talked about their understanding and the fact he needed to get himself a lawyer. Arrangements were made to take him to Broward General to see his brother.

A call was made to Shook who sat quietly and listened until Willis was finished recounting the details. "R.W., that's one hell of a story. Do you think we can make it stick on Stalinowsky and Baldwin?"

"We're sure as hell going to try, man."

"When are you going to the grand jury?"

"Next week, Jack. Make sure your people are available to be subpoenaed, and get that Wheeler dude and his girlfriend back from Nassau. I also need the bartender."

Shook hung up the phone and sat back for a moment. He had a lunch date with Yovanda and needed to talk to her about this "mystery man" she had told him about.

"Dragman, can you get me a driver's license photo of Donohue within the next hour?"

"No problem, boss. I got a contact at the DMV."

"Good, I don't want to bother Willis on this. I've got a hunch, and I need to run it down."

Within an hour, he had the color DMV photo of Donohue, and he headed out the door to meet Yovanda at Tito's for lunch. She had beaten him there and was in back looking bored until he walked up. Her face lit up when he made eye contact.

"Hey, baby, I'm sorry I'm a little late."

"That's OK, just don't make a habit of it, Jack."

"I've got something to show you. I need to know if you recognize someone, honey."

"OK, Jack, let me see it."

Shook pulled the printed photo from his pocket and pushed it across the table.

She immediately reacted. "That's him. That's the guy that wanted me to get to you. Am I in danger?"

"No, baby. As long as you're with me, you're perfectly safe. Let's have lunch and talk about something else. This place has the best strawberry pie on the planet."

Lunch was light, and the wind was perfect.

The rest of the afternoon was memorable.

Chapter 39

Manuel Diego Gutierrez Sanchez was born May 5, 1968, in Veracruz, Mexico. He was a child of privilege. His father, Juan Carlos Gutierrez, was born in Puerto Rico and educated at the University of Puerto Rico in San Juan. He'd received his medical degree and was completing his residency in orthopedics at Jackson Memorial in Miami when he met a young Mexican nurse named Miriam Sanchez. Her family was from Veracruz, and her father also was a medical doctor. After a brief courtship, Juan and Miriam married. Upon the completion of Juan's residency, they moved to Veracruz where he began his practice in orthopedics.

Manuel was born within three years of their marriage and was a good student but rebellious, constantly getting into trouble with the law. His father constantly bailed him out and enabled him. He was a big child, by Mexican standards, and grew to six feet, three inches tall and weighed 230 pounds in high school, where he starred in athletics of all kinds, particularly soccer, known as *futball* in Mexico.

He eventually dropped out of school and became estranged from his father and formed a notorious organized street gang, which grew to about 50 members. This group was organized and powerful beyond all others in the area; only gangs in the Mexico City and Cancún areas rivaled it. These criminal "families" modeled themselves after the Italian Cosa Nostra in the United States.

Manuel was a handsome kid who was lightskinned and was a redhead by age 25. He weighed in at 250 pounds and spent his days watching reruns of "The Godfather," "Wise Guys," and the "American History of John Dillinger." He was once described by one of his competitors as "250 pounds of 'I can do whatever the fuck I want to do.'" The same competitor labeled him "El Diablo Rojo," and the name stuck. Manuel approved of his "street name" and made no effort to dissuade its use.

Manuel's Veracruz cartel controlled all narcotics and prostitution from Veracruz to Campeche. He chose not to challenge the Corev Cartel and remained allied with its leader, José Morales. The spirit of cooperation endured over the years, which included doing "contract" work for each other on an asneeded basis.

Morales, it seems, had developed a relationship with a group of criminals out of South Florida who knew Calvin and Melvin Fuccerino. Most of the work was drug trafficking, but occasionally they trafficked in Mexican "dancers" who worked at adult entertainment venues in South Florida and New Orleans.

Morales had agreed to assist Fuccerino in relocating a certain gentleman who was causing trouble by passing him off to Gutierrez to be incarcerated in Mexico City as Paco Sanchez, one of Morales's former competitors who was rumored to be dead but was actually very much alive, hiding out in the mountains in the Sonora province of Mexico. Paco was one of these mysterious characters that had never been taken into custody, and his actual physical appearance was not known.

The fee for Morales' service was modest—$100,000 in cash, a reasonable fee under the circumstances.

All of this would have provided the real Sanchez with a new identity, and he could have come out of hiding, since the "real" Paco Sanchez was in prison. The problem that developed involved a woman named Este, who was one of Morales's exgirlfriends and who pressured Morales to let her relocate to Texas to be with her family. The price for her freedom was to run a load of Mexican cocaine into Texas and to break Paco Sanchez out of prison. This grand scheme was actually hatched by Gutierrez to scam the Mexican Federales.

Now that they had *a* Paco Sanchez incarcerated, and the Federales knew what he looked like, whether he should escape, get killed, or disappeared did not matter. They would be looking for the wrong man. Meanwhile, the real Paco Sanchez would now be free to work or blend back in under his new name, Juan Diego Rodriguez, to work for Gutierrez.

Gutierrez joint-ventured the 500 kilos of coke with Morales, and Este was to deliver the Coke and take Wheeler, a.k.a. Paco Sanchez, out of the country. Everything went south when the load wasn't delivered to Fort Lauderdale, and Morales and Gutierrez were out their investment totaling about $1.5 million, the street value of their coke.

Wheeler, it seems, was supposed to be killed just before his crossing into Texas at McAllen, but Este had intervened and misled the people she met at the border by convincing them that Wheeler was not Paco and that Paco would be delivered the next day. She just couldn't be a part of the scheme, especially after meeting Wheeler.

This change of heart occurred during the night as she drove across the Mexican wilderness with Wheeler asleep in the backseat and could place her in great danger. Este had been smart, however. She never really had any family in Texas but actually lived in Alamogordo, New Mexico, and she had kept this information from Morales and Gutierrez.

Unbeknownst to Este, Morales and Gutierrez had their own cargo insurance. They had put the Fuccerinos on the hook for the last load of cocaine. When the money wasn't paid, El Diablo Rojo moved into action. After all, he could reach anyone, anytime, anywhere. And so it was only fitting that he engaged with one of his contacts to procure the services of a willing inmate in the Broward County jail to "tune" Melvin up a bit to send the appropriate message.

Phase I of the mission was accomplished without difficulty. The fee was paid, and the inmate assailant was arrested but taken care of. A defense was provided, including a lawyer. The only problem was that the money for the last was not coming as fast as it should have.

Phase II of the plan was to have a lawyer to send a message to Shook, who was to pass it on to Willis, about payment or return of the load. Fred Case, Esquire, worked out of Broward County and promptly made an appointment with Shook.

Shook was in his office when the lawyer arrived, and Tiffany ushered him into Shook's office.

"Mr. Shook?"

"Yes."

"I'm Fred Case. Thank you for seeing me."

"No problem, Fred. What is this about?"

"Well, Mr. Shook, I was hired by an unknown person and given a fee to deliver a message."

"OK, you have me intrigued, Mr. Case. What's the message?"

"That you are to deliver a certain semi with Wisconsin plates, with its trailer, to the parking lot of the Desert Inn at Yeehaw Junction by five o'clock this Friday, and all further collection efforts will cease if the truck is driven away unmolested and not followed by law enforcement."

"That's very interesting, Mr. Case. Is there anything else you can tell me?"

"There is nothing more I can tell you, because I know nothing else. I presume that you know which truck I'm talking about. Aside from what I just told you, I know nothing else. Since this is Tuesday, I'm sure that you will have adequate time to complete this request for service. I now must bid you farewell, my friend. You have a good day."

Case stood up and extended his hand. Shook took it, and they parted ways.

Shook sat back and reflected upon what had just occurred. He picked up the phone and called Willis.

"Ralph?"

"Yes, Jack? What can I do for you?"

"We have a development. I was just visited by a South Florida lawyer named Fred Case. Do you know him?

"Yes, I do."

"So, what can you tell me about him?"

"Well, he's reputable, as far as I can tell—does a lot of criminal work in Dade and Broward Counties. Why?"

"Well, he was just here and delivered a message that he had an anonymous client who had retained him to deliver the message that all collection efforts would cease if we delivered the semi with its trailer that you have in custody to the parking lot of the Desert Inn at Yeehaw Junction by five o'clock this Friday."

"Hmm, that's very interesting, Jack."

"So, what do you think?"

"I think it's doable, but the FDLE will have to bless this maneuver. I can call Ivey. I'll bet he'll put some type of GPS device on the truck."

"Well, the message was unmolested."

"Yeah, I hear you, Jack, but you know how cops are."

"Well, are you going to do this or not?"

"I would say yes, Jack, but only because not to do so would endanger further lives. They just want their money or their load. They're willing to accept the load."

Three days later, the truck with trailer was delivered to the parking lot as directed. It sat for two hours and was driven off on Route 441 to Holopaw. From there, it was driven east on SR 192 to Melbourne where it was left in the parking lot of the Waffle House at the I95 exit. It was searched within hours of its arrival, but it was empty. The load was gone.

Shook was at home when Willis called.

"Jack?"

"Yeah, Ralph."

"The deal with the Red Devil is done."

"Good. Let's see if he keeps his word."

Chapter 40

The two Assistant State Attorneys in charge of the grand jury in Broward County were Thomas J. Brown and Brynn Brito.

Brown was a tall handsome guy who wore tailored suits and spoke with an upstate New York accent. Always impeccably dressed, he sported Wayfarer sunglasses and a day's growth of beard. He wore a Submariner Rolex and, during his off hours, enjoyed wearing anything New York Yankees. He likened himself to the new James Bond type, always appropriately dressed for any occasion.

Brynn had had a life before law school as a teacher and was educated in Florida. She was also well spoken and effective with a nice way about herself and made friends of strangers instantly. Because of this, she was particularly adept at picking jurors. It also helped that she was exceedingly goodlooking. Solid citizens with a brain, especially women, were in her wheelhouse when she selected a jury.

The grand jury was another matter. They were selected out of the jury pool once every three months in Broward, met three days a week, and served for three months. This grand jury had served a month and had referred several indictments or "true bills," mostly first-degree murder cases.

The next case up was the Wheeler abduction, and all those involved were the targets. The witnesses for the State, Ken Wheeler, Calvin Fuccerino, and Detective Willis were on tap for the day. None of the targets of the grand jury had been notified until the last minute. None of the targets were subpoenaed. This was done to ensure that none of them were immunized.

The invitation to appear before the Broward County Grand Jury was sent by return-receipt mail to Mary Joe Stalinowsky, Howard Donohue, Trooper Thomas, and attorney and State Senate candidate, Ed Baldwin. Willis and the State Attorney had purposely chosen not to go after Harrison Davis. That would come later, if necessary.

Calvin was called as a witness but not under subpoena. He was testifying at his peril but with the disclosed understanding that he would receive sentencing concessions that capped his sentence at eight years.

Tom and Brynn chose to call Calvin first to see how he did. Willis, as the main investigating detective, was permitted to sit in the Grand Jury Room and listen to his testimony and assist the two prosecutors in presenting the case.

Stalinowsky, Baldwin, and Donohue lawyered up. They ignored Thomas, who found a lawyer that presented his client to the Broward State Attorney for a Statement Under Oath but could not agree to any concessions, because none were offered. He could testify, if he wanted to, but he testified at his peril. He chose to do neither and waited for the axe to fall and a knock on the door.

He had about 200k in cash and made his move to disappear. Now that he had sold everything, he planned to drive out west where one of his friends belonged to an Aryan Nation enclave. After that, he planned to go completely "off the grid" in Alaska. He made contact and started his preparations immediately. He was an outdoorsman and could hunt and fish and felt comfortable that he could survive there. He vanished within three days.

Meanwhile, the New York home office of Conveyance Mutual Benefit was aghast at the news that Stalinowsky was the target of a grand jury probe. She was fired immediately and promptly escorted by Security off the premises of the Palm Beach office and was barred from any office. Her car and keys were taken. The company abandoned her.

She chose to barricade herself in her house out in Wellington to contemplate her future, which was bleak. She purposely made no contact with anyone else who was a witness or a contact. Instead, she dealt with her Mexican contact who was able to get her a Mexican passport for the nominal sum of 10 grand. She converted everything she could to cash and prepared for her next life as a fugitive.

Within the week, she chartered a private flight to Nassau. From there, she flew to Ireland, and then on to the Isle of Man where there was no extradition treaty with the United States. Once there, she purchased a Polish passport to return to her father's country of birth, which also does not extradite its citizens to the United States.

The passport was put in her name correctly, and she set out to establish dual citizenship. The flight to Kraków was uneventful. She was surprised to learn it was very inexpensive to live in Poland and was preparing to return to her roots. She was on an Aer Lingus flight to Dublin within three days and had over $2 million in cash and securities with her. The connecting flight was equally uneventful. Her cover story and new background seemed plausible enough: the wealthy widow of a Mexican textile manufacturer.

When Stalinowsky did not return her lawyer's calls, he drove out to her place. It was locked and abandoned. She was a "gone girl" in every sense of the term. She had no children. Her father had passed away, and her mother had Alzheimer's. She had no siblings, no one to contact, no one that would care. She did, though, have an exhusband who hated her. He had no idea where she was but was not surprised at the allegations and that she had fled. He knew she was capable of anything. They had vacationed in Poland once, and she loved the country, but he wasn't asked about it, and it didn't occur to him to mention it to her lawyer.

Baldwin was another matter. He was entrenched. He had a wife, children, siblings, partners, and he was a member of the bar, running for public office. No way was he going to disappear. His lawyer learned as much of the State's case as possible, and they prepared to brace for impact and fight this thing to its end. After all, it was all a lie and politically motivated.

Donohue was not so stupid. He knew that he was going to jail and then to prison and was having none of that. He had amassed 250k, all in cash, and was on his way out of town with his new ID. Next stop, Micronesia, Bora Bora, to be exact. He shaved his head, put his contact lenses away, and began wearing his glasses full time.

Back in Fort Lauderdale, the day was complete. Calvin had related his sordid tale to the Grand Jury in excruciating detail in the morning, and Willis testified for two and a half hours in the afternoon. The jury was instructed and summoned the State Attorneys at 4:30 p.m.

The true bill was as follows:

(1) Kidnapping: Calvin, Stalinowsky, and Donohue

(2) Conspiracy to kidnap: Calvin, Melvin, Stalinowsky, Baldwin, and Donohue

(3) Bribery: Stalinowsky, Baldwin, Donohue, and Thomas

(4) Conspiracy to commit bribery: Stalinowsky, Baldwin, Donohue, and Thomas

(5) Aggravated battery: Calvin and Stalinowsky

(6) Obstruction of justice: Baldwin, Stalinowsky, Thomas, and Donohue

(7) Insurance fraud: Baldwin, Stalinowsky, Thomas, and Donohue

(8) Conspiracy to commit insurance fraud: Baldwin, Stalinowsky, Thomas, and Donohue

Calvin and Melvin had cut their deals. They bonded out and prepared for their lives for the next decade. Calvin would be imprisoned for five to six years, and Melvin would be out on probation, running the business, taking care of family. They both were State's witnesses, and both had bodyguards, as did their families. Rojo and Morales had their load back and had made alternative arrangements for liquidation.

Thomas, Donohue, and Stalinowsky could not be located. No one had any information as to their location. They were fugitives, and unlawful flight to avoid prosecution (UFAP) warrants were issued and sent to the Federal Marshals office in Miami.

Deputy U.S. Marshal Kory Pyles was put on the case and spent some time with Willis and Datchko going over the possibilities of finding the malefactors who were now "lamming it." He was directly in contact with FDLE agentincharge Wayne Ivey as it related to Trooper Thomas.

Back in Palm Beach, Shook, Dragman, and Wheeler were in the office discussing the developments. Wheeler came in late and sat for a few minutes, listening before he spoke up.

"You know, boss, I used to be a bondsman back in the old days before I went to work for Conveyance Mutual, and I never let my license lapse."

"No shit, Ken?"

"No shit, boss."

"So, what does that mean?"

"It means, if you want me to go find these people, I will. It would be my pleasure to find them and bring them back to Willis's doorstep with a bow tied around their necks."

"So, Ken, you think you can find them before the U.S. Marshal, the Broward Sheriff's Office, and Agent Wayne Ivey?"

"No doubt about it, boss. They have hundreds of cases. I will have just one."

"What do you need, Ken?"

"Well, first, boss, I want to take Este with me, and I want access to the jet."

"Anything else?"

"Just my salary and expenses reimbursed, of course."

"Of course. I tell you what, Kenny, my boy, you got a deal. Who are you going after first?"

"I don't know yet, boss. Give me a little time, and I'll get back to you on that."

"Stalinowsky has an ex, Ken. I suggest you go talk to him. Thomas has three exes. That should be a nobrainer. Donohue has an ex as well."

"Yeah, I see your point, boss. No one tells the truth like a pissed-off exwife."

"How about an exhusband?"

"Well, if I were the poor bastard married to Stalinowsky, I would be more than happy to help you find her."

"One would think so, boss. I'm on it like a piranha on a roast."

"What?"

"You heard me, boss."

"What happened to the cake and fat man?"

"That's history, boss."

Chapter 41

Billy was running north on I25 north of Denver listening to a country and western station out of Cheyenne. He had abandoned his cell phone. He had thrown it in the Intracoastal Waterway off the Pineda Causeway Bridge. He purchased a throwaway at Walmart in Pensacola for cash, and he made sure he was wearing a hat and sunglasses. He also had a quality fake goatee, which he picked up in a novelty shop in Tallahassee.

He had run west on I10 all the way to El Paso before turning north on I25 to make his way to southeastern Montana where he was going to meet up with his first exwife, Lorraine. She lived in a mobile home park in Hardin, Montana, just north of the Little Big Horn on I90. He felt relieved and, in a way, unchained by his last 30 years in Florida. He had always stayed in touch with her, and, since she wasn't married, Billy, before he went completely crazy, made a deal with her that he would ensure that she got her share of his State retirement to the exclusion of all other wives. This meant that her marital interest in his retirement was 50 percent of his salary upon retirement. Before he left, he sent all his retirement papers in and left a suicide note. If he were dead, she would get her survivor benefits.

The note was bloodied from a selfinflicted cut to his finger, and his truck was run off the road into the Southern Boulevard canal just west of 20 Mile Bend. The top rack of the truck was visible. He smashed the windshield from inside and embedded pieces of hair and blood all over the windshield. Years of digging cars out of canals with bodies occasionally missing, especially in the Glades, where they presumed the gators got to them, was his only plausible plan. This was the best he could do on such short notice. He had considered borrowing a dead body and leaving only a torso, but he just couldn't pull that one off. He did the best he could; it would just have to do.

Phase II of the plan was to drop off the grid. He planned on assuming a new identity and was convinced he could trust Lorraine, who would send him a portion of the retirement and survivor check she received. After all, if she turned him in, she would lose any check.

He had called her as he passed Denver, and she was happy to hear from him. She was recently divorced again, for the fourth time since the divorce from Billy, and was living alone in a double-wide at Horseshoe Acres just off the interstate.

Billy purchased a truck, a 2000 GMC, in New Orleans, sporting Louisiana tags. He bought it with cash and used his dead cousin's identity to take title. He was now Mike Brady. His cousin, Mike, had lived in Baton Rouge until his death two years before. Billy, his favorite cousin, had kept all his IDs: driver's license, Social Security card, etc. The truth be known, he had been planning his big getaway for years. Lurking in the back of his law-enforcement brain was the fear and realization that, someday, he may get caught, and he was not going to prison at age 60, no matter what. NFW.

He had gone over the edge 10 years before when he was forced to take bankruptcy after his third and final divorce, which left him with nothing except his retirement, which he shared with wife number one. Wife number two and number three were short-timers and didn't vest in his retirement. He found himself totally broke and in a deep financial hole at age 50.

He had met Donohue about five years before his last marital debacle, and Donohue smelled blood in the water. He was able to see Thomas' desperation, and he seized on it. He worked on him, slowly at first, but, within a year, he had Thomas on the payroll. Thomas was good for an "important" case about five times a year on average and the usual payoff was 10 grand.

He knew he had to keep the money secret from Lorraine and kept it in the metallic box he had bolted to the frame in back in the rear compartment. He knew he couldn't completely trust her and kept his flight money in his bag, which rounded off at 200 grand. He had consumed some along the way and would have had more, but he spent it on loose women, usually hookers in South Florida and on hunting and fishing trips. These he preferred in the South and the islands, primarily in the Bahamas.

Finally, after about 20 hours of nonstop driving, he pulled into the entrance of Horseshoe Acres and made his way back to Big Horn Avenue. He pulled into the driveway at about eight o'clock in the evening and saw her in the window with the lights on. She met him outside of the truck. She was very happy to see him. He grabbed his bag, his guns, a Glock nine millimeter, and a Winchester .30-30 hunting rifle with scope, and came inside.

He had forgotten that she was a smoker and the inside of the trailer smelled like stale cigarettes sitting in an ashtray. He quietly got past that after one cold beer and an immediate blowjob resulting in sex in the back bedroom.

After sex, she lit up, of course, and he decided to just ease her into his plan. He was going to have to tell her the truth, at least most of it, and then get on the road to meet his Aryan Nation buddies in Billings. He was counting on them to help him get off the grid in southern Alaska until everything blew over.

This would occur, according to the plan, within a year, and Lorraine would start getting her retirement and survivor's benefits. If she started getting them, he would know that his plan had worked and he was presumed dead.

The next two days were spent easing her into his plan. She seemed receptive. After all, she was always an outlaw, anyway. And it was a plausible plan. He lied to her about the facts, of course, and told her that he took a bribe only once out of desperation and that the State's case was based on lies and the testimony of the actual kidnapper, who had turned State's evidence for a deal.

Lorraine had never been too bright; she was suspicious by nature but chose to believe him, because she was into it for a good check, if it all worked out. She was, after all, a survivor. She did have some street sense, and living on her disability check was getting to be difficult. Billy had "primed the pump" by sending her money orders over the years—a thousand here, a thousand there—when she would call. He was good to her.

The day came when he had to run up the road to Billings to meet with his Aryan buddies. He left her $15,000 in cash with her believing he only had $5,000 to get to Alaska. It worked like a charm. It was a tearful goodbye, but he promised to come back at least twice a year until it all blew over, and then he would come back permanently. What a great story, and she believed it.

He left early, at about six o'clock in the morning, and was in Billings by nine o'clock. He drove west out of town 10 miles and took a dirt road south exactly four miles west of the old water tower. He drove another few miles south, up into the foothills, and made a left turn on Lincoln Rockwell Road that he followed up to the gate. A gunman who was expecting him met him there. He was a small, slightly built young man with a shaved head and a swastika tattoo between his eyes, just above the bridge of his nose.

"You Billy Thomas?" the gunman asked.

"That's me, partner. What's your name?"

"Cleetus James, but you can call me C.J."

"OK, C.J., you need to take me to the man, OK?"

"Yes, sir; I will, and it's damn good to meet you, Billy."

"Climb in, dude. I'll drive, and you tell me where to go."

C.J. climbed in the truck, and Billy studied him. He looked like the banjo picker in the movie "Deliverance" starring Burt Reynolds back in the '70s.

As they drove in, the next sign came into view: "You are now entering a White Power Zone."

That's a great sign, C.J."

"Yeah, I like it."

"Very descriptive."

About a mile down the road, which was a singlelane dirt path, they encountered a woodframed house and a barn. There were several other small outer cabins. As Billy pulled up the road, he noticed the Aryan Nation flag on the flagpole, flying alongside the American flag. Next to it was another flagpole with a German swastika flag and a Confederate flag.

Joe Bob Barfield came walking out of the house.

"You must be Billy Thomas."

"Yes, and you must be Joe Bob."

"Welcome, Billy. Come on in."

They embraced and walked up the steps to the porch and inside the house.

Inside was a sparsely furnished main room with pictures and photos everywhere of Rockwell and Adolf Hitler. Over in the corner was a dartboard with Martin Luther King's face covering the target. On one wall, there were bookshelves containing hundreds of books and DVDs. The house had power and water and flushing toilets. He wondered how they got the power out there from the main road until he noticed the wind turbine.

He spent the day talking with Joe Bob and the fellows. It appeared to Billy that there were about 50 people living out there. As he sat and talked with them, he regretted that he had ever come. These people were truly idiots more than just the gardenvariety racist that he was, but he was stuck with them, at least for a while. He needed to cut it short, though; his patience was wearing thin.

They had made arrangements for him to take a cabin about 10 miles northeast of Healy Lake off the Alcan Highway. It was about a 1,500-mile drive to get there. The cabin had no power but had a wind turbine that took care of that. It had well water and was used by the members as a summer getaway from time to time, but no one had been there for a year. He would have to find it and set himself up.

The deal with Joe Bob was simple: 10 grand in cash for the cabin for a year.

The Nation knew nothing about his criminal charges, only that he was a retired brother out of Florida who worked in law enforcement.

Joe Bob wondered why he had Louisiana tags.

"Bought it in New Orleans," Billy told him. "My old truck died out on I10."

Seemed plausible to Joe Bob. As long as he got his money, he couldn't give a shit. If this dumb bastard wanted to live like a hermit off the grid in the middle of nowhere where he could be eaten by wild animals, he didn't care.

"You know you're going to be stopped by some young Johnny Law because of your tag, Billy."

"Yeah, I know. I think I need to transfer it to Montana tags in Billings."

"Good idea, Billy."

That evening, Billy and Joe Bob were sitting on the porch, and Joe Bob spoke up. "Billy, you want to tell me what the fuck is really going on?"

"No problem, Joe Bob, I figured you'd asked if you wanted to know. Otherwise, no news is good news."

"I understand, Billy, but I actually do want to know."

"OK, my man, I'll tell you the truth. I'm running from the law. I was indicted in South Florida for bribery. It's mostly bullshit, but I'm not going to prison at my age. Check it on the internet. No one knows where I am or how I got here.

"The State's main witness is some greaseball Italian named Fuccerino who they caught kidnapping some dude and shipping him off to Mexico. I got caught up in the middle of it because of some spic female trooper who got pissed, because I refused to change my report on an accident caused by some black dude in a piece of shit Sentra. Look it up on the internet. You'll see I'm telling the truth."

"Already have, Billy, and what you just told me sounds like what is out there."

"Thank you, Joe Bob, I appreciate that."

"It always goes back to some brotha causing some kind of trouble."

"That's right, Joe Bob, and I'm not going to stick around and let them cast me down with the brotha sodomites."

"I hear you, dude. We have to help and cover you. No one will ever know."

"I know that, Joe Bob. That's why I'm here."

"God bless you, dude, and good luck."

That night, Billy couldn't sleep too well contemplating the next move.

Into Billings, change the tag. Head north and hit the Alcan Highway. That cabin better be standing, he thought. He left with the directions. *Maybe I should go back and pick up Lorraine? Nah, stick to the plan.*

Billy drove north after he picked up his tag and a new throwaway cell phone that he purchased for cash at Walmart. Everything was cashandcarry except the check he used to pay for the tag. His new Mike Brady identity and ID passed without question.

The next step was to get a credit card, but we'll wait on that, he thought. *Let's see if they buy the suicideanda-gatoratethebody story.*

One thing he was very happy to be rid of was Joe Bob and his idiot wannabe Nazis. He had miscalculated just how little patience he had for those misguided, miscreant racists. He felt less confident about them than Lorraine. He would call her tonight using the old phone. There was a risk if they ever got a hold of her cell records, but he had to trust someone.

Meanwhile, 3,000 miles southwest, Donohue began to feel better as he winged his way across the Pacific on his flight to Singapore and then on to Bangkok. Loose women everywhere. He had considered staying and going to the State Attorney and turning State's witness against Stalinowsky, but he just couldn't face going to prison. He had his stash and had spent two weeks in Thailand years ago while on vacation and planned on staying there before heading for the South Pacific. The place was overrun with women.

Time, he figured, would be on his side. After a few years, he might be able to return and avoid prison. As it turned out, he had enough time to purchase property. All he knew was that he wasn't mentally ready to go to prison.

His plan to buy a boat and sail to Polynesia with some receptive, young island girl seemed a lot more enticing. He figured he could last a couple of years before his money ran out.

Chapter 42

It was morning, and Shook was down on the beach sipping his Starbucks, contemplating his world. The grand jury had met, his enemies were indicted, and his new girlfriend was a keeper. She was intelligent and beautiful, which was a dangerous combination, and he may have to commit to this relationship. Every time he had done it in the past, it blew up. Maybe this one was different.

It was just before eight o'clock in the morning when his phone went off. It was Cooper.

"Jack?"

"Yeah, Coop, what's up?"

"I've got to talk to you about Marvin's case."

"Yeah, Coop, I've been getting your notes. All looks well, except he's a paraplegic."

"That's not what I wanted to talk to you about."

"OK, man, shoot."

"Well, Jack, every Conveyance Mutual case I have is in collection. They won't pay my bills. Every accident case that has a lawyer ends up with the Fraud Unit, and the patient is scheduled with an Examination Under Oath. It's not just the Mutual Company either, it's the Fire and Casualty

Company and even the Sunshine Benefit Company; they just aren't paying any of my submitted billings."

"How much money out are we talking about, Cooper?"

"Right now, I have 300 grand in collection status, all since I took Marvin's case."

"Coop, I can't tell you now, but I can in about three days, that all of that is about to come to it an end."

"Why? What are you talking about?"

"This is graveyard, Coop. You cannot say a word. Do I have your word?"

"Yes, of course, you do, Jack. You know that."

"OK, but I really mean it. Mary Jo Stalinowsky, Ed Baldwin, and Howard Donohue have been indicted for multiple felonies, including insurance fraud.

"No shit, Jack?"

"No shit, Coop. So, hold on. The Calvary is coming."

"Does this have anything to do with your man Wheeler escaping from that Mexican prison?"

"Oh yeah, Coop. It's what broke the whole fucked up thing wide open."

"No shit?"

"No shit, Coop."

"Damn, Jack."

"Yeah, I know. The whole fucking Conveyance Mutual Stalinowsky power-house is about to crack wide open."

"What's this shit with that asshole Baldwin?"

"He's right in the middle of it."

"Holy shit. His ass is grass. I can't imagine him going down without a fight."

"Oh, there is no question that he will pull out the stops. I'm sure it will get really weird before it's all over."

"You mean even weirder than it is now?"

"Oh yeah. The dumbass was bribing law enforcement."

"No shit?"

"No shit. So, how is Marvin doing?"

"Well, we stabilized the fracture surgically. He is painfree, but he's para-lyzed from the waist down. He doesn't care for the adult diaper and doesn't like having to catheterize himself; but, aside from that, he is in remarkably good spirits."

"What's next for him?"

"Well, depending on how this case of his goes and the money he may re-cover, I'm thinking stem cells are in his future. He is young and a perfect candidate stem cell treatment."

"I agree, Coop. Keep me informed. God bless you for the great work you've done for him."

"No problem, Jack. Just get me paid, man. I could use the money. My staff likes to get a paycheck, and the rent has to be paid—not to mention my exwife."

"I'm with you on that, dude. Just stay tuned. Besides, just send it all to Greg Crutchfield. They will get you paid for sure"

Shook hung up the phone and began his walk back to his office. The morning was perfect. *Just another day in paradise,* he thought.

His day was set with office conferences and depositions. *Another 12hour day coming up. This is a far cry from the days where he actually prosecuted these whitecollar criminals. You would have thought that would have been all over and tucked in the past. But, no, I had to tangle with an insurance company with a claims superintendent who was running amok and a crooked lawyer.*

You grew accustomed to the incessant delay tactics and the paid liars masquerading as doctors who testify for the insurance company who will pay their bill, so they can make their Porsche payments, but that shit was nothing compared to what was coming next.

All of these thoughts raced through his mind as he hit the elevator in the lobby. *If they come for me, it will be messy. I better start carrying the Glock again.*

"Where the fuck is it?" he muttered. "Oh, it's under the mattress at home— at least it better be."

Tiffany had just walked in and cornered him as he came through the back door.

"What do I have today, Tiffany?"

"Mike Kahn is going to be here shortly to talk to you about this Harrison Davis divorce."

"Oh yeah, well, as soon as he gets here, get him in, OK?"

"Yes, sir, boss."

"So how's that boyfriend of yours doing, Tiffany?"

"It's going. We had a big blowout last night, and I'm pissed at him right now."

"Ain't love grand?"

"Yeah, about 50 grand, boss."

"Just don't marry the bastard until you know it will work out, OK? Enough of this 'I'm in love shit,' you don't need another financial and emotional catastrophe."

"Well, OK, boss. I love you, but what about you? You've been seeing this one now for six months, which is an eternity for you. What's up with that?"

"We'll see, Tiffany."

"Yeah, and what's up with Wheeler? He's in love. She's living with him. What's going on there?"

"I think that one is going to work out. She's a real person who saved his ass. I think there's a future there."

"I agree, boss."

"Don't call me boss, please."

"OK, boss. Mr. Kahn is here. Shall I call him in?"

"Please."

Shook got up to meet him at the door. "Hey, Mikey, how's the world of gratuitous blow jobs and generalized debauchery these days?"

"I love talking to you, Jack. You are such a piece of work. How is the ambulance chasing business? How's the trip-and-fall lawyering doing?"

"Not bad, Mikey. It pays the bills. So what's new with your client, Gretchen Davis?"

"Well, she's pissed, of course. She's ready to drop the rock on her husband. He's a drunk, and the bartenders up at the club have been covering for him for years, the head bartender, especially."

"You mean Dennis?"

"That's the one, Jack."

"Well, I'm going to give you some intel, and you cannot tell anyone, especially your client. Do I have your word?"

"Of course, you do, man. Lay it on me."

"OK, Dennis is our witness, and he's going to drop the rock on Davis. He doesn't like him. Davis has abused him for years. We have a 'real' bar tab for the evening. Davis was shitfaced on seven Silver Bullets."

"Silver Bullets?"

"Yeah, vodka martinis, straight up."

"It figures."

"Yeah, it does."

"So, if he goes public on that shit, he will lose his job, right?"

"That's right, Mike. There's a confidentiality agreement."

"It figures, so what can you do?"

"Well, I can defeat the agreement because of my criminal obstruction trump card."

"Yeah, I see that. Requiring employees to obstruct justice isn't too cool."

"Right, Mikey."

"But what about Dennis? I'm sure he makes at least 100 grand up there."

"We got him another job, head bartender of Club Coline."

"OK, when is that going to happen?"

"Soon. Very soon, my friend."

"So, Jack, what else on that?"

"Well, the club has liability under the Dram Shop Act, serving a perpetual known drunk who goes out and kills people on the road and leaving those who survive paralyzed."

"Ohhh, I like it, Jack. Oeste must have a huge liability policy."

"Massive, my friend. Ten mill underlying, 50 mill excess."

"You have my attention, Jack. So, what else do you have up your sleeve?"

"Would you believe blatant bribery to protect their members?"

"Bribery?"

"Yeah, bribery."

"No shit?"

"No shit. Yeah, Davis is just a party to this lawsuit. We're after bigger fish. When we get finished, I may consider retirement."

Chapter 43

S hook was in his office late that day. Kahn was gone. Willis was down south riding the Grand Jury when his cell phone rang. It was Jake Sheridan with the Sheriff's Office, who was with Wheeler.

"Jack?"

"Yeah, man, what's up?"

"Just thought you'd like to know that we found Thomas' truck in the canal just west of the 20 Mile Bridge."

"No shit?"

"And Wheeler's here, he wants to talk to you."

"Put him on, please, Jake."

Wheeler got on the phone. "Jack?"

"Yeah, Ken, what the fuck? Why are you calling me about Thomas' truck?"

"Well, it's in the water, perfectly submerged. There's a cracked windshield with blood and hair stuck on it."

"OK, Ken, so what?"

"Well, there's no sign of Thomas. This place is filled with bull gators, as you know."

"OK, so what?"

"Well, they're thinking the gators got him."

"No shit."

"No shit, boss. They got forensics here now processing the truck, and guess what!"

"What?"

"You're not going to believe this, but they found a suicide note at his house."

"Hmm, so if the blood and hair shows his DNA, they're going to close it out as a suicide?"

"That's right, boss. You know Sheridan; he's not going to spend a lot of time on this case."

"The path of least resistance."

"Yeah, boss. They're gonna to close this out."

"I smell a rat, Ken."

"Yeah, me too, boss, but what can I do? They're not going to listen to me. You know it's the comradeinarms syndrome."

"Yeah, another Blue Knight, but this one's a khaki and white trooper."

"That's right, boss."

"So where's his exwife?"

"Which one, boss?"

"The one that's vested in his retirement, stupid. That's where the money's going. You follow the money, and you'll find her and Thomas, if he's still alive.

"Listen, we've got to play this handout. We both know he's alive, right? The best way to find him is to let him believe that his little hoax has worked. So play along with the cops. It's a win-win situation. If we obstruct his plan, it will drive him underground. By the way, wasn't Thomas an outdoorsman? Wasn't he a hunter?"

"Yeah, boss, and a fisherman."

"Well, that means he's going off the grid. He will be in the islands with a new ID. He'll be living on a boat someplace or something like that."

"No one knows where the ex is, and she's not going to surface until she finds out he's dead. They've been split up now for at least 20 years."

"Well, find out where she is. He had friends, didn't he?"

"Well, actually he didn't. He was a loner. No one knows much."

"Well, keep digging. I guarantee there is a way you can find him."

"Got it, boss."

Shook hung up the phone, sat back and considered what he had just been told. *Damn*, he thought. *What next?* He immediately called Wheeler back.

"Ken, when you get finished there, go by Stalinowsky's place and sit on that for a while. She lives there in Wellington, and you're right down the road."

"OK, boss, but why?"

"Well, something tells me she's not going to stick around. If she knows what's going on, she will be gone."

"Got it, Jack. I'll call you back."

It took 10 minutes for Wheeler to drive over to Stalinowsky's little western mansion. No lights or sign of her, and two newspapers were lying in the driveway. It was after seven, and she should be home, but no lights and no sign of Mary Jo.

Wheeler sat for an hour on the street just to make sure, and then he called Shook back.

"No sign of Little Joe, Jack."

"Didn't think she would be there, Ken. Get Sheridan over here to do a wellness check."

Wheeler got Sheridan there within an hour. The knock on the door produced nothing. The garage was empty. They debated on how to get in. Instead of breaking in, they decided to call a locksmith. Once inside, a search of the house found nothing. She was gone. Not much in the closet. Jewelry gone. Luggage gone, except one that was left open on the bed. She was history.

Wheeler was on the phone with Shook immediately. "She's gone, boss."

"OK, find her. But where is Donohue? Check on Donohue, Ken."

Within 45 minutes, Wheeler was back on the phone. "No Donohue, boss, but I drove by Baldwin's, and it appears that everyone is there. He already bonded out and surrendered his passport."

"OK, Ken, it's unlikely Baldwin would run. He's got a wife and kids, not to mention partners and a business. Now that the indictments have come down, if anyone flees, warrants will issue, and we'll turn them into UFAPs. Go home and get to bed. We'll find these people."

"Well, boss, maybe Willis will find them."

"Look, Ken, you know how that works. They just wait until someone stops them. They don't actively look. We'll have to find them."

"Yeah, I guess that's right. So whom do you want me to find first?"

"Thomas, of course. He's obviously not dead, and he will flip. Since he's a law enforcement agent, Wayne Ivey will handle that. Mary Jo will surface on her own. Donohue is stupid, so he will end up in jail somewhere. It's pretty well known that Donohue has a drug problem and dallies with hookers."

"Yeah, boss, but mostly just weed. The hookers, who cares?"

"Well, Kenny, there are some parts of the world that, if you do weed and they catch you, you will be fucked. You will be thrown down with the sodomites for decades. Just remember, Donohue is a greedy dumbass, and he's a druggie, so he will fuck up. It's a nasty combination. Thomas, on the other hand, is not stupid. He is just desperate. Out of the three, Thomas is the most dangerous. He is desperate, and he's a cop. He will kill you if he doesn't have a choice, so be careful."

"What about 'Little Joe?'"

"She's clever, and she will be found. She may go public. She might be in Venezuela."

"Venezuela, boss?"

"Yeah, or, better yet, someplace that has no extradition treaty with the U.S. She's not stupid; she's just a sociopath. She's smart, but she'll be found with no way to get back."

"No way legal that is, boss."

"Well, we're keeping this legal, Wheelman. Now go find Thomas. I'll handle Baldwin with Willis."

Shook hung up the phone and decided it was time to go home. Eighteen hours of work was enough for one day. He was deep in thought. *Everyone leaves a footprint somewhere*, he reflected. *Everyone leaves ripples on the pond.*

So, what about Baldwin? he thought. *He crossed his Rubicon eons ago. Baldwin is a machine. Me, I do it with finesse. Some men are robots. Some just stumble along, and others function with purpose. Baldwin functions with an absolute corrupt purpose. Baldwin was obvious and arrogant. I function intuitively. I knew the day I met him he was corrupt. Being intuitive has its limits, though, unless you can act on what you see and what you feel. Me, I am relentless. That is why they hate me.*

I really dislike Little Joe and Baldwin. It's hard to believe they would be taken down so easily. They are worse than 90 percent of all those sociopaths in prison. Most people just stay out of their way and step aside. They choose not to fight with them. Not me, but, after this fight is over, I've got to do something else.

What can I do? I can't just retire. That would end it for me. Enough of that. We've got work to do, people to see, places to go.

Chapter 44

It was Friday the 13th, Baldwin's lucky day. The indictment was in, and the warrant was issued. Willis was at his office at two o'clock. Baldwin knew he was coming and had left with his lawyer, Mike Rothstein, and was in the lobby of the Sheriff's Office on Gun Club Road. Baldwin's cell went off, and he answered it. It was his secretary.

"They're here, Mr. Baldwin. What should I tell them?"

"Tell them I'm at the jail on Gun Club with my lawyer and my bondsman."

Baldwin hung up the phone and looked over to Rothstein. "They're on the way, Mike. I bet they're pissed. No perp walk and no cameras. It's a beautiful thing. I wonder what the bond will be?"

"It will be in the seven figures, Ed."

"I wonder if there will be any bond?"

"There will be, Ed. You're not charged with murder, but you're not going anywhere. It might be wise to go to first appearance tomorrow and get it reduced, Ed."

"No way am I spending one minute longer than I have to, Mike. Whatever it is, I'm paying it and walking out of there, and I'm walking out the back door."

"Gotcha, Ed. How do you know about the back door at the Palm Beach County jail?"

"I just know, Mike."

Willis was there within 30 minutes. They met in the lobby. The cameras were coming, so they all went back through security, and the dance began.

"We've got to go, Ed. It's about an hour down to Broward."

"Wait a minute, detective. My client is surrendering. He's not going to Broward. The warrant says 'to any and all sheriffs,' right?"

"Well, yes, Mr. Rothstein, but . . ."

But nothing. We're here, and we've surrendered. Process him, and we'll pay the bond. By the way, how much is it?"

"Two million dollars and a passport surrender."

"Got the passport right here, and you can have the 200 bucks in his wallet. Are you going to take his Rolex?"

"You've planned this very well, Mr. Rothstein."

"I didn't plan any of this, detective. I'm just doing my job."

Rothstein began reviewing the warrant: wanted for insurance fraud, organized scheme to defraud, grand theft, conspiracy, obstruction of justice, public corruption. *Just a walk in the park*, thought Rothstein, *not as bad as it could have been. At least he's not facing any murder charges.*

Baldwin sat quietly, knowing that his license to practice law was over and that his partners would buy him out of his practice. The campaign was over. His manager would issue a terse announcement that it was being suspended.

His wife would be humiliated, but she would not say a word. She would stay at the house for a few weeks before venturing out. He would go to the condo in Marathon and go into lockdown for a while, grow a beard, go fishing. *Leave it all to Rothstein. He'll tell me what to do next*, he thought.

The mug shot would be on the front page of the Palm Beach Post tomorrow and on the six o'clock news tonight.

He began to feel depressed. *Maybe I should take the contender south, just about a hundred miles and just vanish*, he thought. *That would deprive them of their fun. Nah, I still want to live. Whatever the future holds, I am now officially just another citizen accused of a crime by the overreaching government.*

It took about three hours to process Baldwin. The bondsman paid his bond after his wife cosigned and everything they owned was on the line. His fee would be taken care of. He was taken out the back, but one camera crew was ready.

He walked quietly with Rothstein and didn't say a word until he was in the black suburban.

Rothstein issued a statement. "Mr. Baldwin has been booked in and has paid his bond. He will be pleading not guilty to the charges and will be cooperative. He has nothing but the utmost respect for the criminal justice system and looks forward to justice being done, which will result in his acquittal. Thank you. We'll see you in court."

Rothstein took no questions and climbed in the back seat, and they drove off.

"Where are we going, Mike?"

"Let's go to my office and talk, Ed."

Later that day, Shook watched the six o'clock news in his office with Dragman and Tiffany. Willis had called but went back to Fort Lauderdale.

"One down and three to go, boss."

"Yeah, I wonder where everyone else is. At least Baldwin didn't run."

"He couldn't, Dragman. He's too entrenched. But, right now, every judge and lawyer in town is happy to see this news. The arrogant bastard finally got nailed."

Chapter 45

M eanwhile, Howard was deep in thought.

Fourteen hours in an airplane gets to you, even in a 747. Two movies, three meals, and a lot of booze. After about eight hours you've had enough, and you just want to get there. Finally, you land and you walk from the plane and you feel the heat and the humidity. The Southeast Asia atmosphere nearly knocks you over. Maybe it's all the dry air you've been breathing for the last 14 hours.

Walking through the terminal in Bangkok, you first hear all the noise. There are crowds of people everywhere, and you understand nothing.

Gotta clear customs and then catch a cab downtown to the Imperial Hotel, he thought. *Easy to clear. They love American tourists but wonder why you are traveling alone. No matter, you're cleared.*

Traffic in Bangkok is a joke and not for the faint of heart. Forget about defensive driving; it's all about the race to open space. He who gets there first wins, and the other guy backs off.

The cabdriver's ID is posted in the back with his photo. It's in English, French, and Thai. This guy's name is Hung Ho. *Great name,* Howard thought. The driver's English wasn't bad.

"'Scuse me, suh, you want good time in Bangkok?"

"No, thank you, driver. Just take me to the Imperial. I'm good."

"But I show you good time, sir, any time. Take my card and call me."

"Thank you. I appreciate that." Howard took his card, and Ho nodded and smiled.

The drive downtown was frenetic. *Too many people and not enough space.*

Finally, he arrived. He paid with cash, no problem, and checked in. A deluxe room paid up front with cash for a week worked out to about $40 a day. What a bargain.

His baggage was taken upstairs just as the jet lag was setting in, and all he wanted to do was sleep. When you travel with the sun to the west, the day seems to be endless. Go to sleep or drop dead.

Six hours later, he was awakened by a knock at the door. He got up and went to the peephole. It was a woman. He didn't want his room cleaned, and the "do not disturb" sign was on the handle.

He opened the door, and there stood a good-looking, small, impeccably dressed woman in her little black, spandex cocktail dress, and said, "Hung told me you want me to show you good time."

He thought for a moment and let her in. She was young and attractive. She looked slutty, which attracted him immediately. She moved quickly, pushed him back on the bed and began her work. She did it all. Howard just lied there quietly and enjoyed the moment.

Damn, I love this place, he thought.

Meanwhile, 10 time zones away, Billy Thomas was winding his way up the Alcan Highway listening to country and western music. He had bought a black 5X Stetson back in Billings and some fairly conservative Tony Lamas that were soft, even though they were brand new. He resisted the temptation to buy a sixpack for the road. *Need to stay straight.*

He spent the night at the Days Inn in Spokane and was making good time. The truck was an '00' GMC that sucked up gas, which seemed to be excessively expensive out here, but there was nothing to do but pay it.

He was deep in thought, wondering why he wasn't trying to hide in plain sight rather than off the grid but recalled that that was Phase II after at least a year.

He crossed at Vancouver and was basically just waved through. It was so easy he could hardly believe it. Tom Brady heading north to Alaska, to go off the grid, at least for a year or so.

The next leg of his trip was by sea—ferry, actually—and it was going to be arduous, at least three days from White Rock up past Vancouver Island to Bella Bella and onto Juneau, and then up the Haines cutoff to the junction and up the Alcan Highway. He spent the night in some place named Burwash Landing, and then went up the road again to Healy Lake. He got there at midday and calculated that it would take him another hour to find the cabin. He decided to wait until the next day and that it was best to spend the afternoon stocking up provisions for his stay. He even bought firewood. He loaded it all and locked it in his truck and spent his last night in civilization. Good thing the truck had a topper with a lock on it. He covered it all with a tarp and backed the truck up to the front door of his room at the Great Western Motel.

"What a laugh," he thought. *This place is anything but great. It's a far cry from Palm Beach to Healy Lake, but so be it. It's all part of the plan.*

The next morning, he was up at daylight and on the road with a cup of coffee and a toasted bagel. The dirt roads were plainly marked and where the map said they would be. He drove in and, within an hour, found the cabin. It was small and on a lake, about a half mile off the dirt road he came in on, but it was right where it was supposed to be.

Need to text or call my boy Joe Bob and let him know I made it, he thought.

It was relatively small but had a garage. The inside was just a large single room with a kitchen, a bathroom, a shower, and a woodburning stove. He turned on the water outside and let it run for a while. The quality was good. It was actually relatively clean inside the cabin, and there was a television—but what would he be able to get here?

He got to the wind turbine located about 200 yards up the hill and unlocked it. It began to turn, and he figured it would take about eight hours to get any electricity.

As he was walking back, he saw a black bear. It was close and moving away. *No mamas with cubs, please,* he thought.

He unloaded the truck and iced everything down. He had plenty of bottled water. He started a fire in the wood-burning stove. He opened the flue and got some heat. He flipped on the light and noticed a flicker. That meant the turbine was working. *Just a matter of time.*

He decided to take a walk down to the lake. It was about a quarter mile away. There was a canoe in the garage. He took his Glock with him with an extra clip, and he holstered it on the outside pants.

The lake was pristine, and he realized that he needed to score a rod and reel. *Maybe tomorrow, I'll go back to town.* He walked back and spent the day cleaning.

At four o'clock in the evening, he turned on the refrigerator, and it worked. He had lights. He turned on the TV, and it worked. He had two stations out of Fairbanks, 170 miles away. There was a hot-water heater, which worked.

Holy shit, he thought, *This isn't going to be so bad.*

It got dark early, and the noises set in. He heard the wolves in the distance and the rustle of the bear that was outside.

He sat watching the evening news while frying two pork chops on the wood-burning stove. He could smell the chops and realized that the bear could smell them, too.

At about nine o'clock at night, he decided to read and fell asleep. The place was locked up tight, but he woke up at three o'clock in the morning, hearing noises outside.

Maybe this wasn't such a good idea after all, he thought. *I'm going to need a dog and a woman, dammit. Dog first, woman second.*

He sat in his cabin and reflected evermore. *How did I get here, and where am I really going? History really matters*, he thought. *You don't know where you're going without knowing where you've been. I wonder if they're going to buy the missing dead body scenario or whether they think I just took the midnight train to Georgia.*

He looked around the cabin and shouted to the vast surrounding wilderness. *I already don't like this, and I just got here.*

Of course, there was no one to hear him.

He quietly walked back into the cabin and started a fire. Warming his hands, he muttered, "Damn, it's cold already. Where the fuck am I going to get WiFi out here," but then he realized that he was truly going off the grid. "I'm going to have to spend some time at the Great Western just to keep in touch."

Meanwhile, Mary Jo was up and surveying her surroundings. Not off the grid for her. She found herself checking her email, and, sure enough, Julio had checked in with her. She wondered when they were going to meet in Barcelona and cruise the Mediterranean together. She missed him so.

He probably misses my money, too, she thought. But he was worth it. Of all the men she had in the last 10 years before and after the divorce, he was the one she needed most. It was her weakness. She had needs. She was lonely and needed his companionship—and the sex, of course. *Well, mostly the sex,* she admitted to herself.

I'll email him back later this afternoon, she thought. *Don't want to look too eager.*

She was doing her best to enjoy her surroundings and had picked up a Berlitz course on Polish. She found it difficult, even though her parents and grandparents had spoken it in her presence as a small child. She had a leg up, however, because she had fortunately traveled in Poland a number of times and had kept somewhat current. It was a Western Slavonic language. There were no *q*'s or *v*'s that connected to the English alphabet, and there were multiple pronunciations on every other letter. It was a bit strange but at least understandable. She was just glad that the alphabet wasn't Cyrillic.

She was able to read road signs, menus, billboards, and advertising and could understand about half of what was being said around her. It was easier to read than speak, and she tried her best not to resort to English. Fortunately, it seems, the whole world speaks English, at least in the major urban areas, and most signs and directions are in Polish and English.

It will take me a month, she thought. *With total immersion, my Slavic accent will be up and running. I made my break, let's see if they try to come get me. This will be my travel period.*

The first few days were spent banking and moving $2 million through Switzerland and into Warsaw, rather easily. She was welcomed with many smiles and promises of great service. She needed to make sure that her money would last a while—at least five years. That wasn't going to be a problem, but, after that, she began to worry. She was fully aware that extradition from Poland to the United States, though permitted was virtually always contested, and she felt very confident that she would not be discovered.

Chapter 46

Shook and Dragman were in early for a Saturday. They were both insomniacs and had texted each other at about 4 a.m.

So there they sat in Shook's office in the "vault," drinking coffee and musing about the week's developments. The vault was the 16-by-20 foot windowless room off Shook's office that contained a reclining leather loveseat, a refrigerator, a widescreen, computer, and printer. This is where he napped during the day, usually at about 3 p.m., and where he would go for complete solitude. When you closed the door, it was pitch black and silent.

It was also used frequently for the occasional reunion of old friends, including his girlfriend. It was virtually soundproof and locked from the inside. It also contained a wellstocked liquor cabinet and a small table with two chairs.

He and Dragman were sitting together sharing their thoughts.

"I thought the perp walk by Baldwin was covered rather well by Channel 13, boss. What'd you think?"

"They had it all set up and planned ahead, which made it not as memorable, Dragman."

"Baldwin had that shiteating grin on his face, but I know the bastard was in serious pain, boss."

"Yeah, just imagine: your campaign for State Senate crashes and burns, your partners suspend you from the firm, your friends and followers are appalled. This has been one hell of a collapse."

"He doesn't have any friends, boss."

"Yeah, you're right about that, but I do feel sorry for his wife and kids. They're actually decent people. I don't know too much about the kids, but his wife is a decent person. She must be in total shock."

"I don't feel sorry for her, boss. To me, she's just a rich bitch who will have some minor embarrassment down at the club where all her superficial friends will lie to her and tell her how much they support her in her hour of need."

"Yeah, I guess you're right, but I'll never get used to the obligatory comments by his lawyer, saying he 'maintains his innocence and looks forward to his day in court, where he expects to be completely vindicated.'"

"The $2 million bond and the collection of his passport was to be expected, but going home to face his wife must have been the worst part."

"Yeah, well, enough of that. We've got a lot of work to do. The first things I need to do are amend Marvin's complaint and bring in Oeste Palma International Golf Club and allege Dram Shop violations. That will bring in another $10 million in coverage, at least.

"We've got Dennis, the bartender, on the line and Davis's actual bar tab to counteract the one the club suppressed and falsified. We've got the soon-tobe exwife fellatio expert who wants to bury her husband just for good measure. We got the young trooper and the corrupt, old redneck trooper, Billy Thomas, who has obviously tried to stage his unfortunate demise. And, finally, we've got auto carriers with bad faith and complicity in tampering with evidence and actively involved in criminal activity, including kidnapping, abduction, and drug trafficking. There's almost too much."

"There's never too much, boss."

"Yeah, I guess so, Dragman. Let's figure out where we go from here. First of all, we have UFAP warrants on Billy Thomas, Howard, and Mary Jo, so let's find them. Any thoughts?"

"Well, I made arrangements with Detective Willis to help get back into Howard's computer."

"And Thomas and Mary Jo have disappeared, of course. So, I'm thinking we'll have to find some clue on where they are."

"Well, boss, I've got some thoughts."

"OK, Dragman, lay them on me."

"Well, Howard is a degenerate. I guarantee you he is somewhere where he can be shacked up with young women and probably children."

"Yeah, I had heard that, but I never paid any attention. I figured it was just bullshit."

"Well, it's really not bullshit. He's somewhere where he can indulge in all that bullshit. I'm thinking Mexico, Central America, or maybe the Far East, like Thailand."

"OK, I follow, Dragman. Let's see what the computer generates. What about Thomas?"

"Well, he's not dead. I can guarantee you that, boss."

"OK, so where is he?"

"I've known him for a long time, and he's a hunter and a fisherman. So, he's off the grid somewhere in the Islands, maybe the Bahamas, Micronesia— could be Mexico, maybe Canada, I don't know. We'll see what develops."

"Put a call in to FDLE and talk to Wayne Ivey about that. Thomas is law enforcement, and they will actively run him down."

"What about Mary Jo?"

"Well, her computer is missing, but her big vice was her young boy toys that she collected along the way. Surely, we can get some leads on that."

"Well, boss, the last big event that I can remember was Baldwin's big bash up at the club, and she showed up with some young Hispanic dude named Julio. It shouldn't be too hard to run him down. We find him, and I'll bet we can find Mary Jo."

"OK, Dragman, sounds like a plan."

"Didn't Thomas have a couple of exwives?"

"Yeah; four, to be exact."

"Well, let's find out which one is trying to collect his survivor benefits now that he's dead."

"Yeah, boss, exwives are always fertile ground for dirt. I'll look into that, too. Speaking of exwives, what's the story on your ex?"

"Nothing new, Dragman. She's still out there and got a new boyfriend. My son is 21 now, and he's in school. Seems to be doing well."

"I always liked her, boss."

"Yeah, me too, but it was too intense. Someone was going to end up dead or in jail. I came to my senses just in time."

"Yeah, you did, boss. You also stopped with the motorcycles?"

"Yeah, Dragman. I can still remember laying one down at the southern end of Australian Avenue and the curve when that stupid bastard came into my lane like I wasn't even there. It cost me a bum knee and two surgeries."

"You're lucky that's all it cost you."

"Yeah, nearly hit two little old ladies coming the other way. I can still remember the shock on their faces when I picked up my bike and hobbled to the curb."

Later that day, Dragman came into Shook's office. "Got some leads, boss."

"What you got, man?"

"Well, Thomas's cell phone pinged in Louisiana and he's got an ex in Montana. I'm running that down."

"So, he's heading west?"

"Yeah, and get this. Willis got some call from some Aryan Nation bigots inquiring about any possible reward for Thomas' return and whereabouts."

"You mean information leading to his arrest?"

"Yeah, you got it."

"So, it's the fucking Nazis?"

"Yeah, it's the Nazis."

"Unbelievable, Dragman. What about Howard?"

"I've got him too, boss. He's in Bangkok."

"Bangkok?"

"Yeah, he made virtually no effort to disguise his actions. He's in Thailand. Got the flight information and everything. I let Willis know, and he's making some inquiries. Hell, I even know what hotel he's in."

"No shit?"

"No shit, boss.

"OK, what's the plan?"

"Well, I've got an old Vietnam buddy of mine who's in law enforcement in Bangkok."

"Unbelievable, Dragman. Who would have thought? Who is it?"

"It's Phat Dat Ho, boss."

"What?"

"It's Phat Dat Ho, boss."

"Yeah, that's what I thought you said. Are you shitting me?"

"I shit you not, boss. I've known Phat Dat since my days in 'Nam. I was in the military police station at Nha Trang when I met Phat Dat. He was also military police, but was a South Vietnamese regular. He managed to get out in April of '75 when Saigon collapsed. He made his way to LA and stayed there for 10 years before he got his big break in Bangkok. He went back to school at the International Law Enforcement Academy there and got on with the Royal Thai Police.

"It's just a matter of time before we find Howard. I've got to call Phat Dat tonight and catch him at his office. If the degenerate is hanging with whores, he'll be OK, but, if he's got drugs with him, he's going to be fucked. Americans with drugs are treated harshly, and I'll bet Howard's got plenty of that."

"What about Mary Jo?"

"Well, boss, I'm still running that down. I'll get back to you on that."

"OK, I think I'll go home. I've had enough for one day. Got the complaint filed. I want to think of something else for a while, Dragman."

Chapter 47

It was about three o'clock in the morning, Bangkok time when they came through the door. There was no knock of the door, just crash and boom. Howard was quickly surrounded by Asian stormtroopers who were pointing automatic weapons at him and yelling at him in their native tongue. Howard was in shock and terrified.

They had him out of bed on the floor in a flash and manacled his hands and feet behind his back. They didn't seem to care that he was nude.

The two young women that he was sleeping with screamed at first but stopped suddenly. They dressed and were summarily dismissed.

The search of the room yielded a Glock, 20 grams of coke, and two ounces of weed. Howard was totally fucked.

Phat Dat Ho was particularly pleased that this takedown had gone so well. It was beyond his wildest imagination based on the information provided by Willis and Dragman. The takedown on the UFAP warrant was clean. His intel from his old friend in the States was spot on, and there was no question about the ID. Howard would now have to face local drug trafficking charges before making it back home to face the American Justice System.

Phat Dat would wait until the evening to call Dragman. It was a 12hour time difference. Hell, travel to the other side of the world and think you're safe? No chance, baby. The world is small and the world is round. It's easy to reach out and touch someone, if you know how.

Howard was taken downstairs and thrown into a prisoner transport truck and taken to Ho's office. He was brought upstairs to his office and chained to a chair in front of Ho's desk. He asked for a cigarette, and they laughed at him.

Ho made him wait 30 minutes surrounded by armed guards before he came into the room.

"Mr. Donohue?"

Howard gave no immediate response but finally spoke. "I want to see someone from the American Consulate, and I want a lawyer."

Commander Ho was amused at first and then just scoffed at Howard's impertinence. He immediately reacted to Howard's lack of respect and rudeness but maintained his professionalism.

"Mr. Donohue, you are in custody on an international unlawful flight to avoid prosecution warrant for bribery, insurance fraud, conspiracy to commit kidnapping, attempted murder, and drug trafficking. You also face local charges of drug trafficking and illegal weapons possession. You do not have a right to a lawyer, much less see one, and no Consulate representative will visit you until I make the arrangements. And that won't be until after I complete my interview. Do I make myself perfectly clear?"

Howard knew he was in trouble but didn't appreciate the gravity of his plight until hearing from Commander Ho. Whatever fantasies he harbored about being released had just evaporated completely. Hell, he had been there only five days, and, suddenly, he felt completely defeated.

"Mr. Donohue, did you hear me?" Ho spoke perfect English.

Howard was completely intimidated. "Yes, sir, I heard you."

"Good, Mr. Donohue. You will start by telling me where you got the drugs."

Howard didn't answer. Instead, he just sat back and considered his situation until finally he spoke. "Sir, I want a lawyer before I give you any statement."

"Mr. Donohue, I told you, no lawyer. You're not in the States any longer. Answer my question."

"I'd rather not, sir."

"So you are refusing to provide that information?"

"Yes, sir, I am," Howard replied.

Howard did not know that his refusal to respond to that question just elevated his local charges to at least a 20-year prison term under Thai law. Commander Ho considered telling Donohue about this little quirk in the law, but decided against it. Rather, he dismissed him to his cell.

Howard was taken into the subterranean jail beneath the Royal Thai Police Station and thrown into a cell with two other miscreants who spoke no English. There were no beds, no bathroom facilities, just an open cage. Howard was traumatized to his core. He could not speak.

Later that evening, Ho called Detective Willis who conferenced in Dragman. Ho was told Dragman was on the line and spoke first. "Douglas, what's this Dragman stuff?"

"It's a long story, Phat. It's been a long time."

"Yes, Doug, it has. Thirtyfive years, but I'm glad to be working with you again."

Willis spoke up. "Commander, as you know, we would like to be able to bring Mr. Donohue back to prosecute him."

"That will be no problem, detective, as soon local charges are concluded. He's likely going to receive a lengthy prison term, but we will make him available for interview and return, as long as we get him back."

"Thank you for that, commander. I'll need to consult with my superiors to decide on a course of action."

Dragman spoke up. "Mr. Donohue is a witness in a civil action here in Florida, and we may want to take his deposition."

"Douglas, our cooperation will be my pleasure."

After the call, Willis and Dragman remained on the line.

"Well, that's one down and two to go, detective," Dragman said.

"So, you think Billy Thomas is alive?"

"I know so, detective. You can count on it."

Meanwhile, Donohue is not coming home anytime soon, Dragman."

"At least we know where he is."

"Yes, we do."

"So what's with the Nazis, detective?"

"They want a reward for giving up Thomas."

"Are you going to kick up some money?"

"We're working on it, Doug."

"How much do they want?"

"They said 50 grand, Doug."

"I assume that's not going to happen, Ralph."

"Well, right now I've got 5 grand, and I think I can kick it up to 10. If they don't come across, then I will start threatening them."

"So, where are they, Ralph?"

"Montana, Doug, Montana."

"Isn't his third ex out there somewhere?"

"Yes, she is, and she needs to be interviewed. She's actually his first ex."

"Do you mind if I attend?"

"No problem, Doug. I'll set it up."

"It occurs to me that, if you inform the Nazis about the exwife, they may drop their price to some manageable figure like seven pieces of silver, Ralph."

"Well, whatever they get, it will be too much; but it's going to happen quickly."

"I'm ready to go anytime, detective. Just give me a few hours notice."

"Well, Dragman, I'm not in charge of Thomas now. FDLE Agent Wayne Ivey is, and he'll be running Thomas down. He's been fully briefed, and he has your number."

"Thanks, R.W., I'll do that."

"So, is this agent actually going to run him down or just wait until he's arrested somewhere?"

"I've known Ivey for years. He's relentless. He'll have them back here before you and I know he's gone. Yeah, he's your kind of guy, my friend. Looks like Arnold Schwarzenegger."

Chapter 48

The flight into Billings was uneventful. Dragman, Willis, and Ivey were scheduled to meet with the local Sheriff at one o'clock. You gain time flying west. The day seemed much longer, two hours longer to be exact.

The drive down to Thomas' ex's took a couple of hours. When they pulled in it was 5 p.m. local time. Lorraine was there and shocked when she came to the door. Inside the doublewide, the smell of smoke knocked everyone over. Dragman could not understand why people continue to smoke after all they know about smoking, not to mention the cost: $6 a pack. *Only the truly idiotic drug addicts continue to smoke*, thought Dragman.

Ivy and Willis took over.

"Ma'am, we know Billy Thomas was here, and we have another source that will tell us where he is now. He's not dead, and he's on the run. He's charged with insurance fraud, bribery, and obstruction of justice. If you don't give him up, we'll charge you with being an accessory after the fact and obstruction of justice."

Lorraine was stunned but knew she had no bargaining power. *Damn that Billy Thomas. He's screwed me again*, she thought.

She quickly sized up the situation and decided to give him up. "He was here about two weeks ago. He left here and headed north. He told me Alaska. I don't know exactly—all I know is Alaska. That's the truth."

"OK, Ms. Thomas, we're willing to believe you. Has he been in contact since?"

"Yes, detective. He's called me twice on his cell phone. Do you want the number?"

"Yes, ma'am, we do," Ivey replied.

Lorraine retrieved the cell phone and handed it to Ivey.

"Ma'am, we need your phone. We'll return it to you eventually but we will have another delivered to you in a few hours. Did he say when he would call again?"

"He called me last night, and he calls me weekly at 6."

"OK, ma'am, we'll take it from here. Do not call him and tell him we were here. If you do, you will be charged. Do you understand?"

"Yes, I do," she replied.

They left with her phone, and she waited for her replacement.

Damn that Billy Thomas. He thinks he's so damn smart, she thought. *So much for his latest scam.*

The drive up to the Aryan Nation compound would have to wait until the morning. No way they wanted to arrive in the middle of the night and, perhaps, be challenged by any triggerhappy AR15s.

They settled into the hotel in Billings, pleased with their accommodations. Willis called Joe Bob Barfield and told him they would be there at their place at 10 o'clock. Then, they walked down to the corner restaurant the hotel had recommended and enjoyed a great steak dinner.

Up the next morning, the group enjoyed a great breakfast at this same restaurant, and then headed to the local Sheriff's office. The Sheriff there had assigned one of his deputies to accompany them. So, with the local deputy in tow, they weaved their way to the Aryan Nation compound.

They met Cleetus at the gate and followed him up the road to the compound. Barfield was sitting on the porch when they arrived. He stood when they arrived and watched them as they walked up the steps to greet him.

"Come on inside, officers," he greeted.

Willis, Ivey, Dragman, and the deputy walked inside. He offered them coffee, but they declined.

"Mr. Barfield," Ivey began, "we know where Thomas is, generally, and we can find him specifically because of the information we have, but we don't need to go to the trouble if you would just tell us precisely where he is."

Barfield sized up the situation quickly and realized he also had some potential criminal liability if he didn't cooperate.

"Did you bring me some money, detective?"

"Yes, I did, Mr. Barfield. Five grand in cash. Here it is."

Willis held back the additional five grand. Dragman was impressed but understood what it meant to be a public employee.

Barfield took the money without counting it. "He's in a cabin about 10 miles out of Healy Lake, about 50 miles south of the intersection of the Richardson Highway and the Alcan Highway. I'll give you directions from the road and Healy Lake. The closest airport is Fairbanks, and it's about 250 miles south from the airport."

"Suffice it to say, Mr. Barfield, you cannot tell him we're coming. If you do . . ."

"Yeah, yeah, yeah. I know. I'll be charged," was Barfield's reply.

"Thank you, Mr. Barfield. We'll be on our way."

Driving out of the compound, Dragman was taking in the sights: the flags, the signs, the skinheads. *Morons*, he thought. Then, out loud, he said, "I hate Nazis." He laughed.

To Willis he said, "Didn't John Belushi have that line in the Blues Brothers?"

"Yeah, but he got to run them off the bridge with the Bluesmobile. I gave the bastards reward money, Dragman."

"Let's get to the airport. We've got a fugitive to catch. So, Ralph, tell me: are we on a mission from God or what?"

They all laughed.

The flight to Fairbanks took four hours, and there was turbulence, making for a bumpy ride. They arrived late the next day.

There, they met two Alaskan troopers who were to take them down to Healy Lake. It was a six-hour drive, and, even though everyone in Alaska is a pilot and planes pretty much outnumber cars, they decided to just drive down.

They left in the morning, early, and got there at one o'clock the next day. They met four other troopers there. They all huddled and devised their takedown plan. There were nine of them and only one of Thomas. It did not appear to be a problem.

They slowly drove out and stopped a quarter mile out and walked in slowly. They came in from three sides with only the lake on the escape side. They got within a hundred yards and stopped. Everyone set up according to plan.

Billy was inside making himself a grilled cheese sandwich on his wood-burning stove. He had caught some fish the day before and had filleted it out for dinner.

Standing there, tending his grilled cheese sandwich, Billy suddenly sensed a stillness in the air. Listening intently, he realized that everything had gone completely quiet. No birds, no wind. A spooky feeling came over him. He walked softly to the window and peered out from the side for about 15 seconds. Out of the corner of his eye, he thought he saw some brush move; and then he saw the top of a hat.

He grabbed his AR15, loaded it, and then grabbed his Mossberg pump and loaded it. He went back to the window. Now, the hat had moved, but he could still see it. He opted for the shotgun and opened fire at the hat. Immediately, he was getting return fire, and then all hell broke loose for about 60 seconds. He had no idea who was shooting, but it was on. He grabbed his Glock and reloaded his Mossberg.

Back at the window, he was shooting at any direction where there was gunfire. He emptied the Mossberg and opened fire with the AR15. Then, suddenly, he was hit—and then hit again. It was over. Billy's lights went out, and he was gone.

Now that the gunfire had stopped, Willis hailed the cabin repeatedly but got no response. He signaled to the others, and they cautiously surrounded the cabin. Still drawing no additional fire and hearing no movement, they broke the door down and found Thomas crumpled on the floor near the window, his AR15 still in his hand. Willis ran over to him and kicked the AR15 away. But there was no danger. Thomas was dead—two bullets had caught him square in the chest. He was probably dead before he hit the floor.

The flight back to Florida was sobering and long. Dragman reflected upon what he had just witnessed. A former law enforcement officer himself, he understood the significance of Thomas' last moments on earth.

He went out in a blaze of gunfire, he thought. He respected Thomas for his choice of exit from this earth. *It never changes when the shooting starts.* For Dragman, everything went into slow motion, and adrenaline took over. It took him about two hours to calm down. He always wondered what his blood pressure was when the shooting started.

OK, that's two down and one to go, he thought. *Where the hell is Mary Jo?*

Chapter 49

It was easy getting to Julio, Mary Jo's lover. He was already on probation for miscellaneous miscreant shit. His rap sheet was pathetic: multiple petty thefts, drug arrests for paraphernalia and dangerous drugs, and DWIs, of course. His latest was a theft out at Walmart. Of course, he had chosen the most surveyed place on the planet.

Dragman also led him to believe that there was money in it for him; he just had to play ball. He was basically a degenerate druggie that preyed on anyone, especially older wealthy women like Mary Jo. I mean, if you're going to be a thief, at least be a good thief. Go big or go home was one of Dragman's famous lines.

This dipshit never got that message. He just stole everything, anytime, anywhere, from anybody. He also had an arrest for indecent exposure, but no conviction.

Dragman wondered if Mary Jo knew about all this. Shook had said, "Yes, hell yes," but that it wasn't important to her. The only things important to her were his looks and the size of his penis.

Turns out, Mary Jo is basically a degenerate herself, Dragman thought.

So, they had a joint meeting with Julio Velasquez. Shook, Willis, and his PO set everything up. He admitted being in touch with her and that he was flying to Barcelona to catch her on the boat for their cruise.

All this would be coming up in two weeks. Preparations were made for a sting, and Julio played along. He was to meet her in the lobby at the Alma in Barcelona on Thursday afternoon at three o'clock in the afternoon, local time.

The flight was on Iberia Airlines, and, fortunately, the dirtbag did have a current Puerto Rican passport with no outstanding warrants to stop or delay him on his trip. Dragman also made sure there were no other bumps along the way and even made sure he was not on any nofly lists. Julio was clean and green and ready to go. He also didn't seem to have any reluctance, especially when they offered to terminate his probation early and waive all the costs of supervision and court. That was set up for the month after his return to ensure his cooperation. The flight from Miami was very nice, even in economy.

When speaking with Mary Jo, Julio had insisted on paying for his own flight, and she had liked that development. Actually, she was thinking maybe there was more to Julio than just the obvious. She was taking a big risk, of course. The extradition treaty with Spain contained virtually no restrictions with "maximum assistance in the rendition of fugitives," and she was not charged with any capital offenses anyway.

Willis was confident all was in place. Contact with the local authorities was in place. Willis planned to go alone, because she knew Dragman and Shook and didn't want to tip her off.

The flight landed at noon local time in Barcelona. After they cleared Customs, they had lunch together and planned to take to taxi to the hotel. Now Julio started getting a little nervous and didn't want to be present when Mary Jo was taken down. At first, it was decided that Julio would be allowed to wait in the cab, but Willis vetoed that. The Spanish Civil Guard had a great reputation and was locally known as the "Benemérita."

At 2:45 p.m. local time, Julio pulled up in the cab, gathered his bags, and walked into the lobby alone. He was wired.

Willis came in in plainclothes, as did Capt. Wilfredo Benitez, acting undercover.

There was no Mary Jo. The plan at this point was for Julio to sit and wait. Suddenly, his cell phone rang. It was Mary Jo. "Hey, baby," she opened. "Any chance anyone followed you?"

"No chance, M.J." M.J. was what she liked to be called by Julio.

"OK, well, let's just wait 15 minutes, and I'll meet you in the lounge," she said.

"I'll be there, baby."

"I just want to be sure there's nobody following you, baby, OK?"

"Whatever you say, baby. I'll see you in 15 minutes."

He wondered where the hell she was and whether she was watching him. He played along. There was no way he could back out now. He was committed.

Fifteen minutes later, he walked into the lounge. Still no Mary Jo. *OK, I'll just sit for a while*, he thought.

Five minutes later, in walked Mary Jo looking all cougar in a red spandex short dress and a big floppy hat, no bra and no underwear, completely commando, looking fine and completely fuckable to anyone who was watching.

She walked up to Julio who stood. She wrapped her arms around him. "God, I've missed you."

That was the last thing she got to say before Capt. Benitez, with Willis at his side, stepped up to them. "Ms. Stalinowsky, you are under arrest. You will come with me, please."

Mary Jo said nothing and just shook her head at Julio.

"Sorry, baby. They had me by the balls. I had no choice."

That was the last thing Mary Jo heard as Capt. Benitez and Willis led her out the door to the waiting Civil Guard transport vehicle.

She was on her way back.

Upon arrival at the Cuerpo Nacional de Policia Barcelona Headquarters, she requested a lawyer and an American Consulate representative. She got both, as well as a trip to the rendering Magistrate where she refused extradition. She was not released and was held without bail.

Mary Jo had money, of course, and she was able to have the finest lawyer in Spain who began his defense to the extradition process.

Willis left, assured that she would remain in custody but possibly on some form of house arrest in Barcelona pending the court fight over her rendition to the States.

Meanwhile, on the other side of the world, Shook, Dragman, and the court reporter, Shirley King, along with three insurance defense lawyers were in Bangkok preparing to take Howard Donohue's deposition.

Howard had worked out an agreement through the lawyers that he would give the deposition with the understanding that it only be used civilly. Nothing he said could be used in any criminal proceedings against him.

Ed Baldwin's lawyer, Daniel Rothstein, was notified and was instrumental in putting the agreement together. He was not a participant in the deposition, and it was not duly noticed in the criminal case involving his client.

Unlike Mary Jo, Howard wanted to return to the States as soon as possible. He just wanted out of that Bangkok hellhole jail and was trying to cut a deal—any deal.

They brought Howard into the conference room, and he sat down, looked at Shook and Dragman, and tried to be upbeat. He looked 10 years older and had lost at least 30 pounds. His skin was ashen, and his eyes were devoid of any life. He looked and sounded like the walking dead.

The deposition could not have gone any better. He admitted the payoffs to Billy Thomas and that he answered to Stalinowsky and acted at her direction. He admitted knowing about the attempted concealment of Harrison Davis's Audi and that the black box had been downloaded and tampered with. Mary Jo had the original data from the onboard computer, which showed Davis' speed at 40 mph over the limit, 85 mph at the point of collision. He admitted everything.

He also detailed in full the fact that Baldwin was also fully aware of all of his activities and that he would do anything demanded by Stalinowsky, because the firm's fees were paid in full without question, and they got all of Conveyance Mutual's business in Palm Beach County. He volunteered that he was truly sorry for all that he had done and had only hoped that he could somehow repair the damage he had done at the direction of Mary Jo Stalinowsky.

On the flight back, the insurance defense lawyers informed Shook that they would attempt to exclude all of this testimony, because Stalinowsky was involved in criminal activity which was never approved by the company.

That's so typical, thought Shook. Now, the war was on to gather the evidence to prove this special unit existed and that other employees knew of its existence—and, further, to prove the company's willingness to turn a blind eye to the special unit as long as its performance was favorable. This meant claims denial activity.

I'll bet the Fuccerino brothers got checks for their work and the payments were excessive. Lack of corporate oversight, as long as they liked the final product. That final product was a claim denial or a defense verdict for the company, Shook mused. *This ought to be fun after all.*

Chapter 50

S ome cases just break right. Some cases break wrong. Marvin's case started out wrong but came back strong. This was unusual, since, most of the time, the way they started was the way they finished.

Marvin's case just got better and better nonstop. Usually, you had to struggle to withstand the onslaught you faced when the insurance company directed all of its assets and advantages against you and your client.

So, here I am, thought Shook. *The first day of trial, about to pick a jury, and it has all broken right. My claim for the bad faith handling of Marvin's claim has been allowed by the court.* The judge, whom he had known for years, granted the amendments and commented that he had never seen a case as outrageous as this one.

I seem to recall that there was a "tort of outrage," which, in modern days, is the "intentional infliction of emotional distress." I decided to add it, and it was accepted.

Bringing in the club was of great benefit, because they were able to put in all of the evidence relating to the cover up information evidence. Therefore, Davis' speed, his alcohol consumption, the cover up and the black box tampering, all came into evidence The court did not allow the abduction of Wheeler and all of the criminality that occurred to be mentioned, reasoning that it was so inflammatory that the defendants wouldn't be able to get anything close to a fair trial.

The court came close to directing a verdict on liability for all of the ridiculous behavior by Stalinowsky and Donohue and reserved ruling. So, they were ready to go, and the defendants just stood up and admitted liability and causation and announced to the court that they were ready to try the case on damages alone. This was typical of insurance defense lawyers. They would work you into the ground, deny everything, make you prove everything, and then, at the very end, admit liability and lead the jury to believe that they admitted responsibility all along.

Judge Murphy came in and heard the stipulation, which the defense lawyers dictated for the record. He announced that he was leaving and told them to make one last effort to settle the case. He stepped off the bench, and the lawyers huddled.

They wanted Shook's number. He told them he was still at $50 million, and they said they were still at $10 million.

Suddenly, they were at $15 million. Shook still wouldn't budge but huddled with Marvin and his mother. Marvin was a paraplegic, and the life care study alone was valued at $10 million. However, there was movement in his lower extremities, and it was possible for him to walk again. Shook got their authority to accept $25 million and went to work.

Shook went to $45 million, and they went immediately to $25 million. When he went down to $40 million, they went up to $30 million.

Shook dug in his heels and told them he just couldn't budge. They whined and made a few calls but agreed to $40 million.

Shook's legal team summoned Judge Murphy, who was elated that he didn't have to preside over a two-month long trial on damages only with all of the exhibits coming, including the daylong "Day in the Life" film of Marvin coping with the reality of paralysis.

The clients were happy. They got a fair recovery, and they got their money right away. Marvin would have to meet with my forensic CPA and economist and put together a plan to live as comfortably as possible on those funds alone, and a team was put in place to care for Marvin.

This was far more preferable than waiting for the money and the appeal that, most assuredly, would have come if they'd gone to Verdict. There was always the uncertainty of what a jury might do. They could have decided that Marvin's damages were $10 million or less, which was a lot of money—and they would have had to accept it, even with an appeal by the defendants.

In the end, Marvin ended up with about $25 million. Shook's fees and cost reimbursement came in at a cool $15 million. *Not a bad day's work, and it only took a year and a half to get it*, he thought.

The end result was especially favorable for Marvin, because he had just begun stem-cell therapy with Dr. Stan Cooper. He was such a strong young man with a great attitude. He looked forward to the rest of his life with hope and optimism. He was an inspiration. In time, maybe he will get up and walk out the door with Dr. Cooper's help.

The stem-cell treatment was a new development that the defense was not aware of. They wouldn't have accepted it, anyway. They would have argued that it was experimental and probably that it should have been excluded from evidence as not being a wellrecognized therapy—the old junk science argument.

Meanwhile, down in Palm Beach, Baldwin's criminal case had concluded, and the jury was back with a verdict.

Guilty as charged on all counts.

The judge sentenced Baldwin to a total of 25 years in the same state prison system that he had his buddies work to privatize and turn into more of a hellhole than it already had been.

Dragman was downstairs for the verdict and watched Baldwin as he said nothing and was led through that little door on the left leading into oblivion, never to be seen again.

Meanwhile, Mary Jo had lost her appeal, contesting her extradition in the Spanish courts, and was cooling her heels in the Broward County jail. Her day was coming.

Howard Donohue was still in a Thai prison and had been sentenced to 20 years for drug possession. His lawyer was trying to cut a deal to get him back.

Dragman walked in looking very content, "Well boss, justice was served. Davis is no longer married to Gretchen, but she cleaned him out."

"Yeah, but he killed those two boys Dragman, and justice is coming soon. My buddy, Greg Crutchfield is on the case and Davis was just indicted on two counts of Manslaughter. Not bad since he already settled with the carrier on the civil case for a cool 20 mil. Good work for him, working closely with the State Attorney up there in Brevard County."

"So Boss, all is well with the world, right?"

"Yeah."

Meanwhile, the press was all over the day's developments. All Shook wanted to do was go home, pack up his 26 Grady White, clear the inlet at dawn, and be at West End by nine tomorrow with Yovanda. He met Dragman downstairs and told everyone that they were closing down for a month and the bonus meeting would be in his office in 30 days.

Dragman walked in and spoke up first. "Boss, I think I may retire now. After all, I am 75, and I just don't think I can do this anymore."

"Me either, Dragman, but I'm probably going to change my mind next month."

"I'm sure Wheeler's going to quit. He's had enough. He and Este are on their way out.

"Tiffany's been talking about doing something else, but she is so loyal that she'll do what I ask, Dragman.

"Meet me at the Schooner Club in 15 minutes, and we'll talk about it."

"See you there, boss."

Shook took a few steps, stopped, and turned back, but Dragman was already gone.

THE END